by William Wister Haines

SLIM

HIGH TENSION

COMMAND DECISION

THE HON. ROCKY SLADE

THE WINTER WAR

Target

WILLIAM WISTER HAINES

Target

An Atlantic Monthly Press Book

LITTLE, BROWN AND COMPANY • BOSTON • TORONTO

LIBRARY OF CONGRESS CATALOG CARD NO. 64-21482

FIRST EDITION

This book is set in 11 point Linotype Janson. It was set from tape produced by a new computer process developed by Itek Corporation, Lexington, Mass. The type was cast by Wolfset, Inc. and plated by Plastic Printing Plate Corp. The book is printed on Monadnock New Hi-Bulk paper. Presswork and binding are by the Plimpton Press.

ATLANTIC-LITTLE, BROWN BOOKS
ARE PUBLISHED BY
LITTLE, BROWN AND COMPANY
IN ASSOCIATION WITH
THE ATLANTIC MONTHLY PRESS

Published simultaneously in Canada
by Little, Brown & Company (Canada) Limited

PRINTED IN THE UNITED STATES OF AMERICA

For Jack and Gertrude

Target

1

ONCE toward the end of their early, uncritical phase, shortly before D Day, Lois had burst out at him:

"Major Brett, you take this war too seriously."

Even as a captain in the WAC she retained a private female scorn of subordination, and when she was irked she enjoyed needling him about his superior rank. That evening it was not pique. He had been able to keep their date. As soon as she had discovered that he made his junior officers in the Hole take one afternoon a week off she had insisted that he take one too.

The next slack day he had phoned her office across town and then invented a pretext to go out to the American headquarters in Bushey Park. She proceeded independently by train to Hampton Court.

When he had validated his pretext by a talk with his boss, Hal Brett walked across the park to find her tossing PX peanuts to the mallards in the Thames. The season, latitude and British double daylight saving time had given them a long green and gold gloaming.

Lois had stipulated that they would not say a word about the war. They had strolled aimlessly through the park and around one of the big loops of the river. The skies had reminded them of Constable. The suburban vistas were not so rustic, but the old brick houses and walls through tender, budding copses were serene.

They made up stories about the housewives reclaiming laundry from the lines, youngsters playing cricket and the fifty-year-olds giving up their evening to another drill of the Home Guards that would never be needed now. She told him the elms were like those in her Connecticut. At one tranquil reach of the river he had confided that there wasn't that much water in all of his southern California.

They had intended to dine at the Mitre. Dusk found them a long walk from it and Lois had made an impetuous counterproposal. They would go to a closer hotel, have dinner and the country sunrise as well, and catch an early train to London in the morning.

"Spontaneous things are always best," she urged.

He had acceded until a reflex raised the question of contact. He'd told the duty desk he'd be in his billet by ten. Even a correction by phone would leave him too far from Whitehall for an emergency. Lois had swallowed her disappointment quietly. They had caught the train from Teddington to Waterloo, had fish and chips at the Blue Boar off the Strand, and then gone to his room in Air Force's floor of the ultra-modern hotel known to the service as the Riding Academy.

While she splashed in the tub he had checked with his office. There were no scramblers on Academy phones and no need for them. His section was drilled in a simple conversational code that covered essentials. From here the jeep could get him to his desk in ten minutes. That night things were quiet. He had gone to the door of the bathroom to console her for the interruption of their idyll with assurance that they would probably not be disturbed again. That was when she had exclaimed:

"Major Brett, you take this war too seriously."

Lois could overwork at being facetious. Then, when you least expected it, her observations could pierce. This one had. Pomposity and self-importance were the occupational hazards of staff duty. And yet if you spent your working hours in a bombproof dungeon with even the slightest shred of responsibility for saying when and where other men should fight, you lost your levity.

Among themselves Hal and his colleagues policed severely any tendency toward soul-searching: "You're lucky. You've got a good safe job in Intelligence." Lois had unlocked so much of him that he was becoming conscious of personal as well as official security. Sometimes in the night when she awoke to find him staring at the ceiling and asked: "What's wrong, dear?" he had wanted to blurt out that everything was wrong. It was not lucky to be safe in holocaust, to know that other men would bleed for your inadequacy, your mistakes.

He had never been able to blurt it out. Perhaps there were things you couldn't say to anyone, perhaps only people to whom you could not say the closest things. That night he had stifled explanation for a long look at her dark hair against the gleaming porcelain of the tub. Then he had lifted her out of it, laughing and splashing and soaking wet.

"So I'm too serious. Take my mind off it, Captain Medford."

2

Ever since a flying bomb had blown the upper storeys off the building over the Hole, the Target Committee had held its meetings in the commandeered board room of a company in Piccadilly. There on a gray December afternoon in 1944 Hal had convened a special meeting.

Hal represented the American Section in Allied Air Intelligence and today he had summoned his colleagues to bad news. An exhaustive time and place analysis of combat crew sightings had confirmed beyond doubt the addition to the 11th German Fighter Wing of a brand new Group of Messerschmitt 262 jet fighters. Warning had already gone to the operational commands. The committee had to consider facts more ominous than the existence of the thirty new fighters. Unchecked production would multiply these rapidly. The analysis offered no clue to the source of their manufacture.

The committee could not find targets. Its duty was to evaluate the significance of those known and to assign priorities for British and American heavy bomber attacks. Sometimes their knowledge of ramified industrial relationships could be suggestive. Today painstaking deliberation had only underlined the question mark at the top of the current list. They were all too old at this for breast-beating or panic. At the end of a fruitless session little Mr. Bewley, presiding that day for the Ministry of Economic Warfare, had lifted the toupee off his shining skull:

"Afraid I've nothing left to tear out, chaps. But don't take it too seriously. We've still got plenty of hospitals and orphanages to prang."

Incongruously, the bald head against the dark wainscoting of the room had evoked for Hal the memory of Lois's black hair and white shoulders above the rim of the bathtub the night she had told him he took the war too seriously.

On his way back to the Hole he loitered through St. James's Park, prolonging respite from the ill-ventilated dungeon to savor the crisp winter air under the low overcast, the silence in the midst of metropolitan clangor, the tranquillity of bare branches reflected in placid pools. There was no use hurrying back to the Hole because the information was not there.

More than a hundred meetings of the committee had concentrated primarily on reducing the original German Air Force to ineffectuality. Beyond their troubled deliberations the effort had required a large part of the British air offensive and the preponderance of the American one. It had already cost upwards of six thousand bombers and their sixty thousand crew men.

The prize of this protracted struggle had been the aerial supremacy that had covered the successful landings in Normandy. It had promised also to expedite the Allied advance by opening the skies of Germany to unopposed bombing of indispensable war industry, and, for a time, it had done so.

The portents of the air war, however, had been as clear to victims as to victors. Systematic destruction of their conventional aircraft manufacture had spelled the lesson plain for the Germans. Their only hopes of resurrection were in the qualitative superiority of their revolutionary new jets and in the secrecy that shrouded their production.

Obscured by the fresher drama of the land battles that summer, the air war had taken on a deadlier urgency. Jet production had been put at the top of the Allied list. In a relentless game of hide-and-go-seek every suspected source of it in Germany and in France had been devastated. In some places the ashes and rubble had been bombed again. The effort had given German production a hard check and Allied air supremacy a precarious continuance. Now the phoenix was rising again from some undiscoverable nest.

Quickening his pace, Hal left the park. From a tobacconist's in Victoria Street he called his boss at American Main headquarters over the open phone. Joe Collet's equable voice took on wariness at Hal's request to come right out.

"Something new at meeting?"

"No. That's it."

"You want to fight about Topic A again?"

"Not if you'll let me have my way."

Joe wouldn't rise. There was a perceptible silence.

"Come on out. If you're free I'll buy you dinner."

It was like Joe to put it that way. He knew that Hal was free every night now. A second phone call routed Sergeant Prine out of the snug cubicle off the canteen in the Hole where drivers and dispatch riders maintained a nonstop poker game. In three minutes the jeep drew up at the curb.

"Big flap, Major?" asked Prine, turning into King's Road. Even American drivers became Anglicized in the Hole.

"I don't know."

"They send for *you*, we could be out there all night."

Prine's girl came off shift in a Clapham fuse factory at eight and late hours always aggrieved him.

"Rather be over in the Bulge, Sergeant?"

"Not me, sir! I know when I'm lucky. But don't forget, them guys aren't driving through blackout with our air raids and buzz bombs, either."

He was suddenly ashamed of bullying Prine. It was probably pure envy.

"You can go straight back. I'll take the train in."

"Thanks, Major! Thanks a million! You know, I always tell the other guys . . ."

"Knock it off, Prine. I have to think."

He didn't have to think. He had to convince Joe of conjectures for which there was no evidence. He drew his short coat tight against the chill of early dusk and relaxed, daydreaming of the first time he had taken this drive past the bomb gaps and grimy facades of Kensington and Hammersmith to meet Joe.

That had been a summer day in 1942, bright with the exhilaration of his arrival in a theater of war, portentous with orders to report to the new American headquarters. A blue Thames had sparkled between flowery banks as he crossed and recrossed it through the lush foliage of Kew and Richmond. Blobs of cumulus dappled shadows on emerald leaves and lawns.

The incompleted buildings in Bushey Park had smelled of fresh cement blocks and wet plaster. Staff officers in uniforms as new as his own had groped through scaffolding and jumped mortar tubs, asking each other where the various sections were. Joe Collet, then a major, had arisen from behind a G.I. plywood field desk to return the self-conscious salute with a handshake and wave Hal to the only other chair in the little cell.

He sat forward while Major Collet perused his orders with deliberation. The papers were authentic. Hal's anxiety was about himself. The thin tense face, the receding hairline, the gaunt figure in the ill-fitting uniform were not the stuff of warriors. No matter what the papers said, he was an impostor, a civilian who had fooled the Army. Now its own mysterious machinations had brought him to the place where good intentions were not enough. He was going to be unmasked.

"What would you like to do, Lieutenant?"

"What I'm told, sir."

"If I could give you a choice?"

"Assignment to an operational squadron, sir."

"Why?"

This man understood and could use the ugliest word in the language. The only certainty that had crystallized through Hal's previous bewilderments with military life was the universal prejudice against higher headquarters. The heart of one was not the place for a new lieutenant to express it.

"To help the men doing the fighting if I can, sir."

The echoing puerility of the words and attitude turned him crimson too late. Major Collet answered soberly.

"That's all any of us do."

It was the first time a major had spoken to him as to an equal. Joe never wore his First World War wings and ribbons on his working jacket. For the twenty-odd years since he had earned them he had been a stock-broker. His plumpness and pallor were the going insignia of the retread. Despite the latent force under that urbanity Hal had been astounded, much later, to learn who Joe Collet had been.

"We all have romantic ideas of war" – Joe was patient – "but there are only two kinds of soldiers: combatants and services of supply. The Air Corps won't train you for combat at thirty-one. We supply Intelligence. I want to use your experience in London."

"I have no experience of Intelligence, sir."

Joe had taken from a drawer the thin, cardboard-covered file that Hal was still too green to recognize as his own.

"Neither has the rest of the Air Corps. The regulars all want to fly or command. Intelligence is scholarship. You're a teacher, you have French and German and the man who wrote that exam of yours can learn anything.

I'm going to apprentice you to the British to study the German Air Force."

"As you say, sir." At least he wasn't kicked out yet.

"Tell the billeting officer I said to get you a room in London. Then report to Squadron Leader Halford in the Air Ministry in Whitehall. You'll be working for me, in there. It will be confining but you can make it a useful job." Suddenly the smile over that dismissing handshake had glinted frost. "The Air Ministry is full of attractive WAAFs. I'm not sending you down there to screw them."

It had tempered his relief at having a tangible job. A duller man than Collet should have seen at once that he was not the kind over whom women made fools of themselves. Hal was used to winding up as the cherished friend in whom they first confided the news of their engagements to others. He was halfway back to London before it occurred to him that perhaps Major Collet had perceived exactly that.

Justifying Joe's gamble on his other qualifications took longer. The evidence that he had was negative. Hindsight knew now that he would not have lasted three days if his boss had been dissatisfied.

The headquarters he entered through the leafless winter melancholy of Bushey Park had the deceptive quiet of a backwater now. The highest American brass had followed the invading troops into France for proximity to Shaef. An indispensable nucleus tended the store here. The heavy bombers and the fighters that escorted them were still based in Britain. They still fought the German Air Force to get at German targets. Magnified Intelligence services still worked around the clock to help them.

The traffic in information ran two ways now and, as nearly as mattered, Joe and Hal, with expanded sections, were the focal points of exchange. From a hundred American subcommands flowed the combat crew, reconnaissance and bomb damage reports. The gleanings of a thousand diplomatic, technical, commercial, military and espionage tentacles still flowed back from central processing in the dungeons of Whitehall. Today Joe arose from behind a mahogany desk in a vast, carpeted office. The handshake was warmer, the gray eyes still quizzical, the voice direct as ever.

"You want to go to Strasbourg-Litard?"

"That's why I came out."

"Without any new evidence?"

"Not a shred and we won't get it this way."

"I'll listen." Joe looked at his watch. "I've booked us for jugged hare and brussels sprouts at the Mitre at six."

It was going exactly as Hal had foreseen.

"Damn it, Joe! You can break that Rule."

"Not for a hunch. We haven't one solid fragment to connect Litard with jet components at all."

"If it isn't we've killed a lot of Frenchmen for nothing."

It was wrong; you didn't have to hit Joe below the belt. He stiffened and his voice took on edge.

"We all knew that when we did it."

Hal took a deep breath and tried to speak persuasively.

"We didn't kill everyone in the factory. Somebody down there must know something."

It was a record stuck in a groove. They were going around the old sounds again because there were no new sounds. Joe cued in with weary patience.

"Strasbourg is a city of two hundred thousand, half of 'em as German as Goering. You could spend the rest of the war looking for your needle in that haystack—even if they didn't kidnap you and work you over till you spilled all our beans."

"Our own troops are holding Strasbourg."

"By the width of the Rhine," Joe reminded him. "Technically the French divisions hold it anyway. We let them go in first for face. Ours are just backing them up in case of trouble. We should hear from our people soon, too."

"Infantry G-2 doesn't even know what to ask!"

"You wrote the queries we sent them," said Joe dryly.

"Oh, they'll try. Doing this takes special training."

"So does what you do here," said Joe. "It's not just risking you. It's risking what you know."

He looked at his watch again and then reached into his desk and put a bottle of whiskey and two glasses on top of it.

He poured generously and shoved a glass toward Hal. "Drink up. The Mitre may be out of booze."

"We can't even talk about this in a pub!"

"That's why," said Joe calmly. "You've been down in that Hole too long. You need a night off, Hotspur."

Joe might be right. He usually was. The subordination that sometimes handcuffed you absolved you, too, if you wanted to be absolved. There was rarely any certainty in this business and yet failure always stung.

"Joe, are we getting stale, now that we're winning?"

Joe took a long look at the thick carpeting and the glass on his desk. Hal saw the lines in his face deepen.

"Maybe. We still work on evidence."

3

He slept badly, tossing and turning with it until the sirens awoke him at four minutes after two. He sat up disbelieving their lugubrious wail, disapproving. The German Bomber Command could not afford raids on London now. With every allowance for the Führer's tantrums, or sheer Teutonic malignance, this was stupid waste. Reviving consciousness rebuked him; it was only waste on the known evidence. There always could be something new.

He pulled the blackout curtains, opened his window straight out to minimize glass hazard and put flashlight, pencil and pad on the chair. Hal never went to shelter in raids. The paradox that had assigned him to aerial warfare in the dungeons of Whitehall extended to his billet. The steel and stone structure of the Riding Academy was a safe bet for anything short of a direct hit: obliteration, or nothing worse than flying glass. In the rooms around him luckier officers would be making their girls get under the beds now. Lois had enjoyed air raids.

"They make me part of it," she had exulted.

She had arrived in London a few weeks before D Day with the rank of simulated captain in one of the quasi-military agencies that had proliferated with the expanding war. This one had specialized in buying the fantasies and deception plans that awaited innocence in every neutral bar from Stockholm to Cadiz. These usually alarmed ignorance in high places, and it cost good time to confute them. After her agency disseminated the tidings that fifteen hundred new German bombers were awaiting the Allied invasion fleet, Joe had growled to Hal,

"Go tell that Captain Medford the facts of life."

The personnel of that agency were not even cleared for admission to the Hole. Hal had gone around to their opulent offices in Grosvenor Street reluctantly. He disliked chewing people out. His reluctance had become dismay at the sight of Captain Lois Medford.

She was pretty, even in uniform, and confidently aware of it. She had bold black hair and eyes. The perfect teeth and dark, creamy skin testified to a sunny life. The buttons on her privately tailored blouse strained over a peerless bosom. The alert appraisal that went first to the leaves on his shoulders told him before she spoke that she had little time for uninvited majors.

Anxious to be done with it, Hal had explained bluntly that the agency's report was nonsense and should be retracted. Before he had finished the first sentence her face was aflame; her indignant respirations made him wonder if the buttons would hold. It seemed as unlikely as the fifteen hundred bombers.

Curtly, Captain Medford retorted that his visit was an insult. The Major was obviously a victim of the military mind. He was exactly the kind of man who had caused Pearl Harbor. It was to counteract precisely such dangerous arrogance that her agency had been formed.

"It still wouldn't hurt you to have someone in here study the German Bomber Command," he replied.

Her volatile anger had congealed in icy triumph. She informed him that her agency made indefatigable use of every possible source. She was representing it that night at a discussion on that very subject by an authority so hush hush she could not even disclose his name. Hal wished her good listening and retreated, a little disappointed about the buttons.

At his office Hal found a message that Colonel Collet would pick him up at seven forty to take him to a lecture he wanted Hal to hear. The audience turned out to be the senior staff of one of the Army Groups, biting its nails off with inactivity in the preinvasion lull. The ranking General admonished his captives that lectures on every phase of the war were a part of tactical training. He was gratified to be able to present Colonel Collet as the foremost American authority on the German Air Force. Hal was settling comfortably in his seat as Joe concluded his graceful acknowledgments with a dry smile.

". . . and so I've brought a man who knows more about it than I do. Come up here and get to work, Hal."

At the little rostrum before the big map he had paused to regain his self-possession. Looking down at the resigned faces between the stars and eagles he saw Captain Medford seated behind the higher brass with a Colonel of Field Artillery. Not sure whether he was avenging himself on Joe or hamming it up for her, Hal had given the defenseless staff the full treatment.

Beginning with the original four Luftflotten he had proceeded from elementary history through five years of the war's changes in the German Air Force's organization, composition, disposition, production and wastage, right down to that morning's estimates of front line strength, serviceability, reserves and capability. After two full hours of it they kept him twenty minutes more for sharp questions.

At the end of the little line offering congratulations under the General's eyes were Lois and her Colonel. Before that glowering gallant she had been at once meek and exigent.

"If you'll forgive me I'd like to discuss your suggestion. Perhaps over dinner tomorrow night?"

The woman he met at the Dorchester bar the next evening had come to ingratiate. Her easy sophistication scarcely bothered to mask purposes transparently primitive. Even on the make Lois was selective. Life had given her a strong sense of her own importance and it had given her brains and energy to sustain it. More than sex was required to get a female into an Army Group staff briefing, and Lois had had what it took.

Over black market horse steak at Mario's she had deprecated herself as a camp follower from Connecticut, "simply dying to do something in the war." Before he could laugh at the naïveté of the words he found himself reflecting that an identical aspiration had brought him here. She had gone on to disarm him with a twinkling, impenitent apology.

"You were so right. In our shop they're all phonies and married at that."

She had never really understood anything about the war until Hal's lecture. He had brought it on himself and this was fair warning. She was going to learn the real inside of things and she was going to learn it from him.

Over their third dinner she told him that for the first time in her life she had a Real Purpose. All the rest of it had been no more than a dreary prelude to This. It was right for a girl to have an affair in wartime. The only real satisfaction for any female was Doing Something for a man who was truly useful. It challenged everything she had. Lois knew some of the absolutely top people in Etousa. She would make it her business to see that he met them. Before she was through they were going to appreciate Hal.

He had vetoed those ambitions unequivocally. He already knew all the people he needed to know to do his work. He could not discuss most of that, even with her. What little time he had to spare from it would be for play.

"All I've ever done in my life is play." She had smiled.

She was expert at it, even for a while to the detail of playing at being submissive. Through the late spring and early summer of that year she had brightened this barren room with the severely functional furniture, steam heat and tile bath that might have been the setting for a burlesque on modern war. In the narrow bed and under it, through silence, flying bombs and air raids they had clung together with laughter, terror and rapture.

The pressure had returned insidiously, indirectly. Lois had cajoled him into augmenting his minimal PX wardrobe with a tailored job by Shepard. She had shown him where to wear it, made him take her to the greyhound races, to the Haymarket and the Old Vic, to Quaglino's. She had unearthed and quoted to him the *Army Field Manual* that included dancing in its list of wholesome, off-duty recreations.

"The mind is a muscle, too. You have to rest it."

She had been right about that, as about many things. He had worked better on less sleep. It had been exhilarating to look forward to more than stag poker at the end of another twelve hours of reading the gen in the Hole. She could be utterly compliant about nonessentials. Her deeper probing continued.

"You could teach in a better school, in the East," she had said once. "Daddy knows a lot of trustees."

He was aware that there were better schools than the little college that employed him in southern California. He was also aware that they were not talking about education. This was an opening gambit, an overture from her world of power and prosperity. It was a world serenely confident of buying what it wanted.

Hal's father had been a salesman and shoestring speculator in real estate who had managed to ruin himself in the midst of western expansion. He had had boundless optimism and an unerring instinct for oil wells full of dust, orange groves in the frost belt and subdivisions where no one wanted to live. In consequence Hal had pumped gas, patched tires and ground valves for most of his tuitions. Physical work had been a welcome relief from a home environment of mirage and mortgage.

Curiously, the exactions and reality of the garage had stimulated his increasing absorption with American literature. In a mechanized civilization there was a dearth of competent writing about the relations of man and machine, perhaps because the imaginative mechanics were having too much fun to write. At graduation time the English Department had been delighted to accept his application for an instructorship.

The deeper purpose his routine work supported was one of the many things he had never told Lois. She would have asked if he had sold any of his stories. So far he had not. Now she was probing a future that sooner or later they would have to face.

"Teaching isn't geographical," he said.

"If you're going to the top, it's not out there."

"Don't be so sure. The ignorance in California is unlimited."

"You're always turning things around! You can't change the world, dear. You have to take it as it is."

"Maybe, but you can choose the parts you take."

She had exulted when the aftermath of D Day brought him a letter of commendation for a signed estimate of enemy fighter resistance. She would not believe that the act of signing it was an accident of his job. She was indignant when he pointed out that his whole section had worked on it.

"But *you* signed it. You took the rap. You can be so strong and yet . . . you could get yourself into Shaef if you were more aggressive."

She would have been furious to know that Joe had gone to the three star level twice to resist orders transferring him to Shaef. He explained dryly that Shaef had competent men. You didn't have to be aggressive to read the gen carefully.

"I love your pigheadedness," she said. "I really do. But I could get both of us assigned there. Honestly I could, Hal."

One night after the breakout at St. Lô had ended the long anxiety with rosy delusions, their talk had turned again to peacetime life. Abruptly it had stopped. She had sat up, and through the darkness he could tell that she was frowning.

"I'm not sure I could ever marry a teacher."

He had never asked her to marry him. It might have been the conditioned reflex of financial stringency, of the price he had elected to pay for his other purposes. It might have been that he had already weighed her against them. Now he had to face it.

"You'd never be satisfied with it," he said gently.

She had sat very still through a ticking silence and then suddenly laughed and reached for him.

"We don't have to decide that now."

A few days later she had met Colonel Wilts in the Charles Street Red Cross Club. The next night she had broken a date with Hal. The next week she told him that LeRoy Wilts was really a tragic figure. In spite of his brilliant record on the staff of Shaef his marriage had been a youthful mistake and he was probably going to get a divorce after the war. The rest of it had been mercifully brief. Hal had covered his pain without protest when she told him of her new orders.

"We have to be absolutely honest with each other, Hal. I am interested in LeRoy, of course. But I've seen London and I want to be up at Forward, near the real war."

Longer hours of work filled the solitary evenings and postponed return to his desolate room. There was no shortage of girls in wartime London. He would find another when he was ready. You never got something for nothing, and he was very sure he had not wanted a lifetime with Lois. Even so, there had been moments when they were closer than flesh.

Sometimes air raids could still reduce disobedient nerves to shivering terror. Tonight, perhaps because this was a further respite from the enigma of Strasbourg-Litard, Hal found himself calmly objective. Before he had finished his first cigarette he could hear the progressive, rising rumble of the lower ack-ack belt marking an approach from the south. His window gave on that prospect. As the din of closer batteries rose and the searchlight pencilings swept toward him he could time the green blossoming of the first two marker flares.

Forty-three seconds apart was smart work, and the spacing looked as proficient. The first one was a trifle east of Croydon, the other somewhere between Hammersmith and Wandsworth. After three minutes he knew he would not see the third flare. It was far behind the mass of his hotel, as it should be, to the north. It put him and several hundred thousand others roughly in the center of the triangle.

The clanging reverberations of the 4-incher in Hyde Park drowned the barking of the Bofors, and through the blast he began to hear the faint, mosquitolike whining. There were veterans of the first blitz who could identify BMW, Jumo, or Daimler-Benz engines on vibration alone. It was one of the details in which the hardest work would never catch up to British experience. Hal could not distinguish the drone of the attackers from that of the night fighters chasing them through the ack-ack.

Three times his blackout curtains stirred languidly with the faint shock wave of distant bombs. Half the guns in London were in full cry. The more remote bursts, masked by buildings, were hard to tell from the heavier guns until the sky reflected the growing flicker of new fires.

The main force of the raid was passing northeastward, and so far he had seen nothing in the sky except shell burst and searchlights. Now, perhaps on a signal, the batteries stopped. The brief vacuum of silence refilled with the chatter of light machine guns and the heavier splutter of 20-millimeter cannon far above.

A searchlight waved and stabbed and pounced on a mothlike speck four miles high. Its silvery surfaces became pink and then deepened to red, pluming through wild evasion patterns until it escaped the lethal clutch of the light in a crimson dive through the darkness. The comet's tail brightened, the chatter of machine guns stopped and a multicolored explosion showered bright expiring fragments.

Behind Hal, the receding detonations of the ack-ack marched the fleeing invaders toward the safety of the sea. In five minutes the long monotone of the All Clear sounded its requiem for a fruitless effort and the lives it had cost. Hal sat very still, tasting the soot and dust of the bombs and the acridity of the lingering gun smoke.

Professional judgment should be gratified. A bomb on London was a bomb spared the weary Allied riflemen on the Rhine. The staunch people around him had accepted nearly sixty months of air attack with grim satisfaction in essentially those terms. Tonight professional judgment seemed as futile as all the paper work in a war of fire and steel. Theoretically paper work influenced the war. Men had to make it do so. He should have found a way to make Joe Collet let him go to Strasbourg-Litard.

4

At the concrete pillbox before the street level door to the Hole, Leading Aircraftsman Watkins saluted with a sly burlesque of formality he would not have risked upon British officers. He had once confided to Hal he found the Yanks easygoing like.

"You're early this morning, Major Brett."

"Someone has to win the war," said Hal.

Watkins chuckled appreciatively. Frustration was part of the kinship of the Hole that the guards shared. Dexterously Watkins juggled the tommy gun and Hal's pass with one hand while he accepted the daily ritual of the American cigarette with the other. He had examined Hal's blurred official photograph several hundred times. He still compared it with his face before returning it.

"You to the spit, sir. I'll just smoke this with my tiffin and thank you very kindly."

Three flights down Hal repeated the identification process with Dustin who rewarded his cigarette with the knowing wink of a man closer to the mysteries than Watkins.

"Tidy bash we gave the blighters last night, sir."

Hal winked back in complicity. The fact of the air raid was known, so far, only to the other eight million inhabitants of greater London and to the Germans. It was still a breach of security for denizens of the Hole to discuss it outside that steel door.

He took a last breath of the relatively good air in the stairwell and then heard the door clang behind him as he stepped into the blue haze. Inside you couldn't tell night from day. There was always the same choking opacity of tobacco smoke and human sweat, the same hum of inadequate ventilators stirring it along the rows of blue and brown shirts bent over the tables of the outer bullpen.

The colors of the shirts were the only thing that had changed in thirty months. They had all been R.A.F. blue the first time the guard walked Hal to the inner cubicle. Squadron Leader Halford had unfolded his astonishing angularity, flashing white teeth below a six-inch mustache and quarter-inch spectacle lenses.

"Welcome to fame and glory, Leftenant, or do you call it Lute?"

"As you like, sir. My name is Hal Brett."

"Quite. Are you good at puzzles?"

"No, sir."

"Ah. We rather dread the genius type. Do have a pew."

Hal had taken the steel folding chair and tried to keep his eyes off the half-inch stack of legal-sized foolscap with "Top Secret" and "Most Secret" stamps bristling in bold red.

"Before you meet the bods, have you questions?"

"What does A.I.2 D.F. do, sir?"

"We try," said Squadron Leader Halford, "to answer the questions people ask us about the German Air Force."

"May I ask what people, sir?"

"Relevant ones, you know. Sometimes Prime Minister people, sometimes Pilot Officer people. I'm afraid your Flying Fortress people will be asking us a lot of questions soon, so I'm starting you off on Single Engine Fighters."

"Thank you, sir. Where do I begin?"

"I'm afraid you'll have to read the gen." Halford had waved toward the bullpen. Through the eternal smoke Hal saw a gallery of library stacks the size of a tennis court crowding a nine-foot ceiling. Blue-shirted officers, male and female, circulated through them, climbing ladders or stooping to boxed files.

"A year should do it. Provided you keep up with the new as you go along. Good job you're used to libraries. I'm afraid I must ask you a question, Brett."

"Please do, sir."

"You realize that once in, you're here for the duration?"

That had been his first intimation of the Rule. Joe Collet hadn't mentioned it. Hal had gulped the blue haze with claustrophobic remembrance of the steel door.

"I hadn't, sir. My orders were to report to you."

"Up to a point they can be changed. After that I'm afraid you can't just go frolicking off to the front lines or home with a head full of our gen."

"I'm not really a soldier," said Hal. "I just got in after Pearl Harbor. They gave me tests and here I am."

"Quite." Halford consulted a long full sheet apart from the secret material. "Gen on you looks a good risk. But I should like to know how you got through the eye examination."

"I gave the medical corpsman at March Field a bottle of whiskey for a transcript of the chart."

"Good show," said Halford. "I had to give our blighter two bottles. Come meet the bods."

The bods had been a bewildering succession of Terences and Pamelas, Joans and Reggies, Daphnes and Cyrils, diffident at first, helpful as friendship grew over the long tables, over mashed and sausage roll in the canteen, over half and half at the Wheatsheaf across a grimy alley.

The gen, for probation week, had been an unclassified encyclopedia's lucid exposition of the four Luftflotten on which Hermann Goering had predicated world conquest. The air fleets broke down, through an infinity of subcommands and changes, to the foundations of Air Intelligence: the German pilot and the German plane.

Only in retrospect did Hal realize the exact moment when his probation had ended with a final, inaudible clang of the steel door. He had been comparing rates of climb of Focke-Wulf 190 Es with light machine guns, 20-millimeter cannon and loaded bomb racks when Halford tapped his elbow.

"Figgers blur: helps to break 'em and browse a bit."

His first guided browse had been as seemingly casual as the rest of it. He had read quotations on the prices of ferromanganesian steel in Stockholm and the three-page statement of a captured German pilot who enjoyed brandy. He had examined a digest of radar blips and looked at stereopticon views of aerial reconnaissance photos. He had fingered a bloodstained German field order, delivered by the French Underground, and perused a transparent deception plan purchased in a bar in Geneva. He had memorized the serial number of a Messerschmitt 109 dredged out of the Dnieper and been shown the translation of a Polish slave laborer's note removed from an unexploded bomb in Hyde Park.

"Bits and pieces," Halford had summarized. "But they add up. If the gen promised us a hundred Ju. 88s bombing London tomorrow night, we should laugh now. But if it suggested another Gruppe of 190s retraining at Flying Fortress altitudes, I'm afraid we shouldn't laugh."

It had been precognition, like Hal's presence in the Hole, of the big change. German bomber production was being diverted to the manufacture of fighter planes. Operational Single Engine Groups were denuding the Russian and Mediterranean fronts in response to a threat implicit in the waiting, empty file boxes labeled: Combat Crew Reports, American.

Hal's had been the first brown shirt at the working level in the Hole, instrument and precursor of the Fortresses, Liberators, Lightnings, Thunderbolts and Mustangs that were coming. A decade too young for the First World War, he had read of it with a sense of being misplaced in time. As the clouds darkened again, he had read Douhet, Seversky and the propaganda of the Army Air Corps. He had perjured his way through the eye examination with a romantic hope of recapturing his youth in the wild blue yonder, only to meet again the barrier of the calendar. He was too old for flying training. That afternoon's look at the gen had sentenced him to the study of how other men fought.

This morning a brown uniform came to attention behind the American section duty desk. The Strasbourg-Litard gen was on its top and young Henderson was struggling with exuberance.

"That was a 262 they got last night!"

"You should have called me for a jet, Henderson."

"You'd just left the Academy, sir, when our first tech report came. The pilot's dead and the pieces were blown all over town. One is a fragment of what they think is main exhaust, and Xray has already lifted the imprint: Strasbourg-Litard!"

"Can they lift the date?"

"It's too badly fused, sir. Civil Defense is alerted for Most Urgent Search for other scraps and I've pulled the Litard gen in case you want to review."

"Did you try Imrie?"

"No, sir. He's prickly on protocol and you were on your way."

"Right. Go get your breakfast. I'll cope now."

"It proves you were right, Hal!"

"It proves," said Hal severely, "that we have one more piece of evidence . . . " He stopped at the contrition in Henderson's face. He was sounding like Joe Collet and not enough like him. Joe was always patient with ardor.

He put Dawson on the duty desk with orders to call him for anything further from Tech Center and for the official appreciation of last night's raid when it came through. The significance of one jet's bursting out of the cocoon to bomb London would be another kettle of fish and a hot one. It would be handled however by Enemy Attacks, Britain. He wanted the time before calling Joe to think about American Attacks, Germany.

He returned the Litard gen to the library because he did not need to reread it. Then he took his old seat on a bench in the bullpen, staring down at the same old scratches on the table.

The Litard gen was a mixture of Overt, Certain from the Ministry of Economic Warfare, and Not Verifiable from the many and dubious sources in semi-German Strasbourg. The plant was a small manufactory that had supported a five-generation dynasty of Litards in opulence. It had combined general metal fabrication with bold innovation in light, heat-resistant alloys.

The Litards had prospered on political as well as mechanical acumen. Etienne's marriage to a Stuttgart heiress had protected them through the long German era from 1870 to Versailles. With French flexibility Alexandre had procured a contract to make cylinders for DeWotaine French fighter planes in the 1930s, even though the factory itself was within rifle range of the German side of the Rhine.

After the fall of France, Litard had been integrated into German war production. It was known to have made a series of Focke-Wulf engine cowlings, a run of Panther tank visors and to have reconditioned Gnome Rhone and Daimler-Benz engines.

This added up to low priority on the Allied target list. Strasbourg had been bombed on other counts with grievous loss of French life. The Free French in London were vociferous against further attack. Though the Germans sometimes exploited such compassion cunningly, it influenced thought on low priority targets.

In the summer of 1944 an informant initiated contact with a loyal Frenchman in Strasbourg whom he rightfully suspected of harboring Allied air crew on one of the organized escape routes. The informant, who insisted on being known only as Eighty-three, had volunteered verifiable gen about other industrial activity in Strasbourg.

With growing confidence on both sides, Eighty-three had disclosed that he had worked at the Litard plant. That summer increasing segments had been walled off under heavy security guard. All French labor had been dismissed and replaced with German technicians from the bombed-out factories of the Reich. Luftwaffe officers and high civilian officials came and went. Eighty-three asserted that the new work was on components for the new jet planes.

Aerial reconnaissance confirmed physical changes in the plant. The dismissal of French workers was also verifiable. In a troubled meeting of the Target Committee, Hal had cast the decisive vote to bomb Strasbourg-Litard.

Cloud cover spoiled the first attack and cost a lamentable toll of civilian life in the industrial neighborhood around the factory. The second devastated the place, again with heavy civilian casualties. Photo reconnaissance confirmed total inactivity thereafter, and Litard was returned to the watch-recon list.

Eighty-three's last report had been dated two days before the second bombing. When his disappearance was indisputable his contact had been moved to safety. Thereafter the reliable gen on Litard had been limited to aerial reconnaissance.

Hal had requested permission to visit Strasbourg personally as soon as Allied recapture of the town was foreseeable. The advance of the Allied ground forces had doubtless accelerated the German decision to move their surviving mechanics and salvageable machinery back across the Rhine. The other centers of jet production, bombed and unknown, were deep in the Reich. It was just possible that trained investigation in Strasbourg could find a clue to where they were.

Hal's request had met an adamant invocation of the Rule, so sacrosant it was not even written. Men who had worked beyond certain levels of Intelligence were not exposed to capture. Strasbourg even in Allied hands was within sniper range of Germany. Half of its people would always be German in blood and sympathy. The disappearance of Eighty-three spoke for itself. Until last night there had been only his unverifiable gen to connect Litard with jet manufacture. Disappointed as he was, Hal had not blamed Joe for concurring in the Rule. Now there was hard evidence.

Rising from the bench he made his way to the small private cubicle of Group Captain Imrie. Even in the Hole it was policy that the left hand knew as little as possible of what the right hand did. Imrie's small section was the only visible part of the substructure in which knowledge of the agents had to extend beyond their numbers and accuracy ratings.

Hal had worked in the Hole nearly a year before meeting Imrie. A tap on the shoulder one day had brought him to belated attention before the four stripes on a balding little man with fierce black eyes. He had followed an imperious nod to a quiet corner.

"Is Forty-six concordant with your gen, Brett?"

Hal had not known whether the amorphous Forty-six or he himself was under examination. He had cited the two demonstrable flaws in the Forty-six gen objectively. It was full-time work for Imrie's people to get the raw gen into the Hole. Others had to evaluate it, and Hal was becoming one of them. Imrie had nodded bleakly and departed without comment. That week the Forty-six file had gone dead.

Weeks later Hal had paused one noontime for a nostalgic look at the ducks on the pond in St. James's Park. His thoughts were on the birds. It had surprised him to discover Imrie close by in equally rapt contemplation. To speak seemed more natural than not to.

"At home we'd call that black and white one a scaup, sir."

"You'd be mistaken: it's a Tufted Duck." And turning on his heel, Imrie had walked away.

He had seen Imrie in the park frequently since and had avoided him with care. Time had begun to teach him why a man of Imrie's other preoccupations wanted to look at ducks on a pond without intrusion. This morning Imrie indicated the other chair in his cell with baleful eyes.

"You're here about the new Litard gen." It was a statement.

"Yes, sir. Nothing further on Eighty-three?"

"Nothing."

"Do you suppose our bombing got him?"

"I should like to. I do not."

"This imprint warrents further effort there, sir."

"Agreed, but you know the Strasbourg problem: every other one's a goddamned German."

"Could Eighty-three's contact help us?"

"He returned to Strasbourg against warning. Now he's missing."

"Dead or captured?"

"Can't learn. Often we don't."

For a second he thought pain was softening Imrie. The man sighed instead of glaring.

"I appreciate the stakes, Major. I am reviewing available personnel, right now."

"This isn't just . . . garroting a guard, sir. It's a cold trail. Whoever goes will require special knowledge."

"You will be asked for a briefing."

"I'm going to ask again to go myself, sir."

"You won't. Quite out of the question."

He had suspected that anyone with the rank of Group Captain wore more than one invisible hat in the Hole. The finality of that voice convinced him that he had just heard from Security Policy as well as Certain Sources. He thanked Imrie for his time, and the reply was bleak as usual.

"You'll hear from me, Brett."

Joe was never personally available to the phone until after morning meeting at eight thirty. Hal bit his nails, trying not to think about Number Eighty-three and his contact until he heard Joe's placid invitation to scramble.

"Anything hot, or do you want my troubles first?"

"The boss's troubles always come first," said Hal.

"The G-2 report is here from Strasbourg: all negative. No one down there wants to talk about working for Litard."

"So Papa was right all along?"

"About that." Joe was unruffled. "They're taking the wraps off more jets, Hal. Yesterday, while you were in Target meeting, nine 262s jumped a column of Patton's over behind Metz. The Ninth had Mustangs there and couldn't close on 'em enough to read the markings. Shaef's sitrep has smoke coming out of it this morning. Now what have you got?"

He had adrenalin surging through his veins as he reported the new gen to Joe and waited through a perceptible silence.

"This is firm, Hal?"

"Pukka. A second tech report just now believes the engine was a Jumo 004 out of the Magdeburg-Ilesheim run made before we bombed either place. The Litard exhaust imprint is very clear."

"All right," said Joe. "I'll bend the Rule now. Keep your mouth shut till I do."

You could concentrate on the German Air Force to the point of forgetting that you were an infinitesimal digit in the complicated alliance of the American and Royal Air Force. Hal had clearer knowledge of the chain of command under Hermann Goering than of the one over himself. Above Joe Collet ascended level after awesome level of authorities strained by ancient rivalries of ground, sea, air, nationality and professional conviction. It was late afternoon before he was summoned to confront Joe's weary face.

"You go tomorrow. I had to accept some strings."

"I'd go in handcuffs, Joe."

"Firstly, you take an R.A.F. type; someone very hush hush that Imrie's dug up. I gather he's a linguist with experience of Alsace. You meet him at Imrie's at seven for final briefing."

"Good. I read Kraut and Frog better than I speak."

"Secondly, you promise not to cross the Rhine alive."

He had to think a minute before he got it.

"Pills?"

"If you want. Usually it's too late, if they *do* snatch you. They know about pills, too. But your promise stands."

"I'll swear. Never mind about the pills."

"Thirdly, you go and return under a cover plan."

He expounded it patiently. Hal and his companion would carry written orders, signed at the very highest level, that represented them as joint investigators of bomb damage for Air Force Public Relations and the Ministry of Information. Their orders would enjoin all branches of every Allied force to furnish them with whatever supplies, support or assistance they requested. This specifically included signals communication with London. They would memorize a simple code to embed the name of any target they might discover in what appeared to be news copy for press release.

Cameras, typewriters and notebooks would be carried for protective coloration. Hal would be given enough francs for medium scale bribery; his orders would procure whatever more he wanted from the local ground commanders. He and his companion would surrender their passes to the Hole as they left it and would carry only dog tags and normal identification cards. They would be flown to Paris where a Shaef jeep and briefing on the road situation would meet them.

"How tight is this cover order, Joe?"

"Absolute. Our troops are hand in glove with the French divisions and Free French, and you know what that means in Alsace. If you should be snatched alive this cover gives you a chance of being just another P.O.W."

"It fits the snooping and signals need nicely, anyhow."

Joe nodded and for the first time looked at a pad.

"Oh, yes. You'll carry a gas mask and wear sidearms."

"Joe, I've shot that .45 three times at Fort Dix. They stopped me because I almost hit the instructor."

"Protective coloration." Joe smiled wanly. "All pencil soldiers wear arms. And you can get four bottles in a gas mask case. Now what can you think of?"

He thought of the stories that had come back from France after the invasion.

"I'd like one of the new barracks bags full of PX candy and cigarettes and powdered coffee."

Joe buzzed for a sergeant, threw a five pound note across the table and gave the order. Then as the man reached the door Joe's face expanded with a smirk Hal had never seen.

"Put in some prophylactics and silk stockings, too, Sergeant. Major Brett is going on leave."

The man departed with a knowing smile and Joe sobered.

"That's the story around here, Hal. You don't even tell the other bods in the Hole."

"You had trouble with that Rule, didn't you?"

"There are people who don't want to lose you. Now let's get to work on that code."

5

"I deplore this, Major," said Group Captain Imrie.

"I understand that, sir."

"Do you? Tell me the name of your opposite number in Berlin."

"Oberst Christian Gutman Wulfe, sir."

"Do you imagine he doesn't know as much about you?"

"We're not going to Berlin, sir, or even into Germany."

"So we hope," retorted Imrie. "Unfortunately I still have no one reliable in Strasbourg. Flight Lieutenant Vane has visited there and is otherwise qualified."

He pressed a buzzer and glowered through a short silence until the door reopened to a surprise that strained his official compsure. Flight Lieutenant Vane wasn't over twenty-five. She had a ring of short, ash blond curls just circling the severe set of her cap. Its visor made her blue eyes look a little more recessed and her nose a little more uptilted than they probably were; its darkness enhanced thin pink and white cheeks. Under the blanket-stiff folds of R.A.F. battle dress she looked skinny and, perhaps, flat breasted. The long trousers made all legs shapeless.

She was armored in the severe formality that was the pride of her service. At Imrie's introduction she turned her head for a brief inclination to Hal and then refocused unblinking eyes across the desk.

"Vane's orders match yours," said Imrie. "You may complete her briefing en route. I'm adding a verbal order, Vane."

She twitched her head ever so slightly in response.

"Major Brett is in command. You will take his orders as ours."

"Very well, sir."

"Your transport is waiting," said Imrie. "Good luck."

Hal thanked him and waited, until he remembered, and then stepped through the door ahead of her. In the corridor a portable typewriter was stacked beside a camera and a small, regulation R.A.F. kit bag. Vane overtook him just as he was bending for them.

"Thank you, Major. I manage nicely."

Scooping them up in stride she fell in to his left and half a pace behind, with parade ground precision. At the street level where they surrendered their passes to Watkins she balanced the whole load on one arm until a blowsy Amazon sprang from the little car to help them.

"I'll stow this; get the Major's gear from the pillbox," said Vane crisply.

He was grateful that the overwhelming presence of the WAAF driver precluded conversation as they darted through the connecting-rod rattle of the big busses and the metropolitan monoxide toward the cleaner suburban air of Northolt. He was torn between rage and hysterical inclination to laugh. After thirty months in the Hole he was on his way to the front, or at least the Rhine, with the unmistakable fragrance of expensive scent emanating from his comrade-at-arms.

Vane sat with unbending rigidity on the right side, where protocol placed her, blue eyes focused severely now on the driver's unkempt back hair and dirty red neck. Hal wondered if she was considering putting the hoyden on report. She, too, had a right to be tense about this.

She did not even avert her eyes to decline a cigarette with a crisp: "No, thanks." WAAF officers were usually fanatical about punctilio and hers made it easier for him to study her furtively. Her profile was prettier than it had been under the harsh glare of Imrie's neons. In spite of her formal repose there was a muscle knot at the end of her long jaw.

On the tarmac at Northolt she jumped from the car first, giving him no chance to repeat his offer with her gear. She was already addressing the driver.

"The Major has more. Help him and do move."

Thanks to his bulky bag of trade goods, he did have more. He made his way to the steps of the courier plane flanked by two laden females who passed the gear up to the yawning G.I. in the door. A sense of absurdity made him forget himself again, indicating the steps to her.

"After you, Major."

Inside, she settled swiftly to his left in the long row of bucket seats and belted up without a glance. Of the seven officers beside themselves three carried that unofficial symbol of staff duty which is the typewriter. None accorded a second glance at Brett and Vane until the pilot emerged from the cockpit with a rumpled cap askew on an unshaven face, chewing a candy bar to punctuate the routine speech.

"The Paris express is about to fly, folks. We got solid glue from here to Le Mans, so keep your belts buckled and I'll try not to stick the Eiffel Tower up anyone's ass."

Too late, his complacent gaze caught the ring of curls

under Vane's cap. His young face flamed. He made an instinctive turn toward his cockpit and then lowered his candy bar.

"Hey, Miss, pardon me."

She was suppressing a giggle and she did it well. "I found it most reassuring, Captain."

"I didn't know we had a dame aboard." He was studying her hopefully now.

"Hazards of war. I shan't trouble you."

He returned the candy bar to his mouth for a long bite.

"You can trouble me all you like. Stopping in Paris?"

Across the aisle a graying chicken Colonel, holding a cigar unlit until takeoff, began to smoulder. Vane saw it and beat his explosion with a negligent wave of her hand to the camera. Her voice was soft.

"No. I'm after combat types."

The pilot flushed savagely and retreated in raunchy disorder to his controls. The Colonel glared and returned his angry concentration to his cigar. As the first prop spun Vane turned to Hal with amusement still lingering under false penitence.

"That was rather below the belt."

"You saved him a hiding." Hal indicated the Colonel.

"Not about me; that poor man is dying to smoke. I like pilots but some of them do want the odd squelch."

The windows showed only moisture trickles until they banked for descent, and Hal had a brief glimpse of red tile roofs, gray stone buildings and dun wintry fields under the dim saffron of shrouded sunlight. Vane didn't even bother to look.

They descended to black tarmac spotted with opalescent puddles and a dim horizon of bombed hangars. A Captain waiting beside an almost new jeep greeted Hal by name with a negligent salute and helped them pile their gear into a back seat already crowded with K ration boxes, canteens, regulation blankets and helmets. His manner let them understand that he didn't have to bellhop trippers from London. He drove in resentful silence to a small field office improvised of plywood in a corner of one of the damaged hangars, and there enjoyed baring his teeth.

"I'll see your identification, Major."

He returned their blurred photos with disappointment and led them inside to a table already spread with map sections of 1 × 500,000 covering the area from Paris to the Rhine. A heavy crayon arc swung east and a little north from Paris to Nancy and then curved abruptly southeast. Above the line from Nancy on were infantry, armor, artillery and reconnaissance symbols.

"You can't take this map," said Captain Lenn, "but you can mark this smaller one. No problems to Nancy. Anywhere beyond Lunéville you could run into fugitive Krauts from patrol to battalion strength. You will take the south fork out of Lunéville and feel your way down through Baccarat to St. Dié and then up. We tried to leave the bridges through there"—Lenn spoke as if it had been his personal order—"but the Krauts may have blown them. If you're blocked keep south to the Seventh's supply line and go in along that."

Hal copied symbols; Vane traced the map with a gloved hand.

"What about the Vosges through here?" She indicated Schirmeck.

"Ours. Full of *their* stragglers," said Lenn happily. He took a list from his pocket and scowled.

"Water, blankets, sixty K rations, two five-gallon jerricans of petrol . . . Oh! You will wear side arms, Major."

"They're in my musette bag."

"You can put them on outside when you put on your helmets." Lenn patted his own .45. "This isn't Piccadilly."

Vane's innocent voice just beat Hal's anger.

"Very good of you to remind us, Captain."

"Well, I got nothing against Limeys but . . . up here near the front things are different."

"How far did you say to Nancy?" asked Hal.

"About two hundred . . . " Lenn blushed and glared. "I'll check your side arms and helmets at the jeep."

Outside Vane tossed her cap into the crowded back and succeeded in not smiling while Lenn instructed her about the chin strap of the helmet. Hal indignantly buckled on his .45.

"Shall I drive, Major?"

"Do you know jeeps?"

"Quite."

"Can you find the main road?"

"Yes, sir."

"Good. You take it to there."

She shook out one of the blankets, spread it expertly over the driver's seat and tucked her waist and surprisingly long legs into it before he could move to help her. He imitated her, far less skillfully. Through the whirr of the starter Lenn bent forward confidentially.

"Got piles, Major?"

"No."

"You will have," said Lenn happily. Then under a correct salute Hal could see his lips frame a disgusted: "Air Corps!"

A hundred yards beyond the gate guard Hal ordered

Vane to pull up to the side. Mirth played with her eyes and lips as he took off his .45 and helmet and offered her the blue visored cap.

"Oh, good. Helmets always deafen one."

"We'll save 'em for the final push on Berlin."

Her smile opened to show even white teeth. She fluffed her hair carefully before the mirror, replaced her own cap at a slightly jaunty angle and meshed the gears silently. The tension knot at her jaw was gone.

2

VANE drove fast with a bold confidence that made the best of both cobblestone and the deep chuckholes in thin concrete stretches. The traffic was all army jeeps and trucks at first. Then at their closest tangent to the outskirts of Paris were swarms of bicycles and an occasional French truck, lumbering along under its bulbous sack of producer gas. The rare civilian cars wore the same testimony of petrol shortage.

Crumbling plaster walls concealed most of the small houses through a grimy industrial district. The few shop windows were covered with steel shutters. Corner bars and brasseries were closed; bare trees dripped moisture onto vacant parks.

The jeep top flapped and banged, enclosing them in a noisy isolation that inhibited talk. As the factories became garden patches and small fields, civilian traffic ended. The constant thunder of passing army trucks intensified their seclusion in the noisy jeep and the encompassing smell of wool, wet from the showers and splatters on their blankets. He found himself edging closer to Vane before he realized that it was not entirely to facilitate conversation. Two hours from the Hole had burned their bridges. They were on their own.

"That was a fast trip to Paris."

"Your first, Major?"

"Yes."

"Pity. It's sad now. Did you notice the park benches?"

"No."

"There aren't any. Fuel."

"They're all rations and coupons, too?"

"Quite. Nothing at all left, really, except black market scent, shockingly dear. I shall buy some on the way back."

The sudden tilt of her head made it affirmation of the human within that drab uniform. He let another ten miles verify the pattern. Vane would not speak until addressed. The garden patches became fields, vineyards and expanses of plow land between narrow streeted villages in which children and teams darted out from blind, walled corners. After her third deft passage of these he stopped her in open country, took over the wheel and got to work.

"How much do you know of what we're after, Vane?"

"They gave me some reading last night, sir."

"Tell me what you read."

She reprised the Strasbourg-Litard gen without omitting a significant detail and concluded simply:

"We're to find out where they were shipping those exhausts."

"Have you worked on aircraft production or other targets?"

"Never, sir."

"You must have studied late."

"I wanted the Litard background, in case."

"In case of what?"

"Accident."

"You'd go on alone?"

"No use crossing bridges, Major. But Imrie is rather keen on this so I got the essentials. They said you'd know the rest."

"There isn't any rest. You've got all we know, so far."

"May I ask a question, Major?"

"Anything: but my other friends call me Hal."

"Thank you, sir. I'm Elsie." She hesitated and then continued, striving for an even tone.

"If we bungled this . . . or they made one of us talk . . . would it start the hare for good?"

"The hare's already started, Elsie. They know we're after jet production. That's why it's so hard to find. If they were sure we had a solid new fix they'd have to decide whether to try to defend it or move. Even a move cuts production now and there's a limit to where they can move, between us and the Russians. Dispersal itself means a nightmare of transport and you finally have to assemble in one place anyway. Our guess is that they've got most of their new eggs in one basket somewhere. Maybe we get a clue, maybe not. But don't worry about bungling. We've got nothing to lose. The whole thing's a piece of cake."

Her faint head shake rejected this before she spoke.

"I should prefer the truth."

"What truth?"

"They didn't send us for fun. I'm not much, but we have you to lose and Imrie says you're good."

He snorted to cover the surprise and the glow: "Imrie never called anyone good in his life."

"He has done: just once before."

"Tell me how you got into this, Elsie."

"My father was a wine buyer and broker, in trade, you see . . ."

It was a familiar scruple. Every American clerk in uniform had been an executive, every janitor an engineer. Britons boasted in reverse with the emphasis on humility. Elsie's father had risen from apprenticeship in a big firm to the ownership of his own. It had provided a detached villa in Watford "with a rather sweet garden, really," and private schooling for her in Sussex: "some of the girls were dreadfully pompous."

Elsie and her mother had spent summers on the continent with Mr. Vane who had specialized in moderately priced Moselles, Alsatian whites and some of the German hocks. Travel had given her fluency with languages. The R.A.F. had used her first for translation with French missions and then, after the collapse, she had worked for a while with the fugitives who became the Free French.

"They were pathetic, but it was really too futile. I was glad to be posted to Imrie."

"Posted to Imrie means you volunteered."

"That's just the form. They needed people to run errands . . ."

"That's enough unless I should know more, Elsie."

"Errands" in that world probably meant delivering grenades and Bren guns and counterfeit Marks and bringing out gen. The less you knew about the details of other forms of Intelligence work, the less danger there was of divulging them.

"You should know I haven't been in Alsace since vacation days before the war."

"You'd better brief me. What's Strasbourg like?"

"Grubby and inbred. The faces are blocky and gross and the figgers like lorries . . ." Unconsciously her eyes went to the mirror. There was vanity as well as pride in Elsie and the clean lines of her jaw and nose had a right to it. ". . . there's no grace or proportion. It's those fifty German years and of course hundreds more, intermittently, before 1870. Everyone has cousins in Paris as well as Berlin, but neither country trusts them. It's made them think of themselves as Alsatians and they don't even trust each other. That's the alphabet of Alsace: distrust."

"Do you know many of them?"

"Only one family really at the hotel where we always stopped. Daddy knew him in the other war and he's absolutely top-flight French. Their name is Pourvalle."

"Will he help us?"

"To a point."

"What's the point?"

"The whole point, with the French: the reason we couldn't just turn this over to them in London. One Frenchman will burn alive for you. Then you find out he did because his brother was a mouton."

"What's a mouton?"

Her eyes widened and he began to realize how insular the Hole had been.

"Informer, stool pigeon, counterspy. To date the record is one in every cell. But Edouard Pourvalle himself is pukka."

"You never met Alexandre Litard?"

"Heavens, no! We had nothing to do with . . . people like that."

"Like what?"

"Big industrialists. Some of them did play the Vichy game for us, but more played it for themselves. Litard was dealing with Krupp and Stuttgart Metallenwerke right up to Munich."

"He's one-quarter Kraut and all Germanophile?"

"Money-phile, I should call it. Profits have no flag."

"I imagine he's skipped across the river, don't you?"
"Unless the Resistance got him; and men like that don't catch easily."
"What will become of them afterwards?"
"They'll hide awhile and then whine awhile and then . . . business as usual. Daddy was wounded three times in the last war. Next thing you know we're in bed with those Huns again, even in our little wine business."
"The war must have been rough on that."
"Finished ours, right off."
"What does your father do?"
"He's dead. Heart failure, fighting a fire in the blitz. Mother lives with my aunt at Bournemouth." The jaw-line whitened again, the words came clearly. "My brother was killed at Tobruk."
"I'm sorry. I didn't mean to intrude."
"You have a right to my . . . credentials."
"Imrie's people don't need credentials."
"You don't mind being stuck with a female?"
"Not now that I'm sure you are one."
"Whatever else would I be?"
"You acted like a consecrated Amazon, till you remembered about getting scent on the way back in Paris."
"Sorry. One's always a little tense at the start."
"I still am. I shall need your help very soon!"
"How?"
"Next village, you buy us a bottle of wine for lunch."
"Oh! Jolly good. Red or white?"
"I scarcely know the difference. Tell me about them."
"It begins with the grape, you know . . ." She talked with an easy precision that reduced complexities and mystique to comprehensible fact.

A raw low fog obscured most horizons. The foreground of plow land, vineyard, streams and groves might have been Iowa or Indiana, except that the houses were all stone and red tile roof that clustered in little villages far from the dividing walls of the uninhabited open acres. Little crows sprang from the tree lines of the roads with melancholy cawing, and once he saw immense gray and white wood pigeons settling into a cabbage field. When the horizons opened briefly he observed a pattern that would not have been the same at home. From every considerable rise of ground either a church or a great château proclaimed its brooding sovereignty.

The villages as they neared the front showed more of steel shutters; the rainy little squares became emptier. Occasionally a fire-blackened house or burnt-out truck validated the sense of desolation. He watched the jeep, stamping his feet against the increasing chill in one of the village squares until she emerged from a store pink-faced and smiling with two unlabeled bottles and a corkscrew.

"Alsace has come to meet us; it's Gray Pinot, I think."

"We should use the daylight, Elsie."

"Of course. Shall I drive or cope?"

"We'll pull off long enough to set the table."

Beyond the town he drew off into a lane under dripping trees and they laughed to find themselves half shouting in the new silence. She opened one of the bottles and divided it into canteen cups. He stripped out a package of K ration apiece and turned the keys on the tins of cheese and meat. Her eyes danced as the other little parcels became hardtack, gelatinous fruit and chocolate bars, powdered coffee and cigarettes.

"It's like a picnic, Hal."

At least she would use his first name over lunch. "It's going to be a cold one; not even hot water to mix the coffee. Do you mind?"

"I don't mind anything we have to do."

He drove while she passed him his canteen and spread cheese on his hardtack with a formidable knife she produced from the long blue trousers.

"That's quite a chaperone, Elsie."

"Firearms either bruise or burn one. Are you good with that pistol?"

He told her of the extent of his experience and she laughed.

"You're honest: most men love weapons."

"I'm strictly a paper soldier."

"Good. The derring-do types always make trouble."

"Have you a cloak to match that dagger?"

"We both have. The cover story is our cloak."

"I think it's absurd, don't you?"

"No. I helped to invent it."

"Why?"

"I told you. Alsatians don't even trust each other."

At Nancy whole avenues were blocked off for supply lines. The city reverberated with the incessant rumble of trucks going forward. Along the permitted streets cold fog and intermittent snow flurries intensified a macabre hilarity. Soldiers in stained fatigues, mud-caked to the knees lurched along the cobblestones. Music echoed from bars and brasseries. The uniform of the day seemed to be a bottle in each hand and a girl on each arm. M.P.'s afoot and circulating in jeeps were scanning it all with patient vigilance.

At a corner one red-eyed G.I. rocked with his load and plunged headlong to the pavement. The girls who had been supporting him bent swiftly to his pockets. Before Hal could stop his jeep an M.P. materialized behind them. The impact of his boot on her broad Lotharingian rump lifted one of the whores off her feet. Her partner joined her in profane reproaches while the policeman picked the man up rather gently, whistled up colleagues in a jeep and tossed him into it.

At the next corner an M.P. directing traffic stopped them for a passing truck. An immense bearded rifleman lurched to the jeep, scrutinized Elsie through bloodshot eyes and then turned them contemptuously to Hal as he put a hand on her shoulder.

"A thousand francs for her, Shaef."

Hal struggled to get past her to the man's arm. Elsie pinioned him, hand locked on the wheel, elbow holding him back while her other hand disengaged the soldier's arm expertly.

"You can do better," she smiled. "Look what she's got."

The man turned his head following her eyes. Elsie gave him an easy shove just as the alert M.P. closed on him. Half a head shorter than the rifleman, he spun him around and his voice crackled.

"Keep moving, hero!"

The man lurched on, the M.P. spoke apologetically.

"Sorry, Major; they're just back from eighteen days."

Hal drove ahead, seething with a sense of ineffectuality.

"Sorry, Elsie."

He thought she checked a retort before replying equably.

"So am I—but only for them."

At the gate of an immense transport depot a bored sergeant shook his head at the cameras and typewriters in their jeep.

"Our gas is for combat troops, Major."

"Can you read orders?"

"Well, yes, sir."

One glance at Hal's orders was enough. The man refueled them himself while Hal studied maps, eyed the darkening winter sky and asked about accommodation in the town.

"We got a fine hotel for officers, sir. Just go four blocks that way and then ask anyone for the Clap Exchange."

In a quieter street he studied map, watch and sky again.

"We'd better spend the night here."

"We've got some usable daylight left. There are hotels at Lunéville and Baccarat."

"We don't know about them: here we're safe with the Army."

She hesitated, coloring and choosing her words slowly.

"If I were a man would you stay or use this light?"

He felt his own color rising as he ground the gears.

"I'm sorry."

She didn't speak again for ten miles. Then she had to lean toward him and shout above the banging of the top.

"That *was* bitchy but chivalry isn't flattering here."

"From now on I'm just another Jack the Ripper."

To prove it he sped through Lunéville and immediately regretted it. They had lost all military traffic. Even the bicycles and pedestrians were widely spaced. They had turned away from the front as marked on the map. He could not forget the warning about German stragglers and their jeep had only low blue blackout lights. It would be a narrow squeak to make Baccarat without slowing down to a pace any soldier could overtake. As dusk deepened Elsie moved a little closer to him, slipping a glove and burying her hand in the knife pocket.

"We'll stop at Baccarat for the night."

"Good. How's your French?"

"I can read." He grinned. "As for conversation, I'm told all you need over here is 'Voulez-vous coucher avec moi'!"

"That would make us a very short conversation."

"Can you persuade 'em a healthy man and woman want separate rooms?"

"That wants some doing in France" – she chuckled now – "but it has been done."

He entered the blacked out village with a relief he hoped she could not discern. They had to drive deserted streets between gray walls till they found the sign above a dilapidated little hotel. Its door opened reluctantly to a small lobby with a single candle. A swarthy proprietress with a high black pompadour and a little whisker sprouting from a mole on one cheek emerged from the kitchen with cold, defiant eyes. Hal left Elsie to negotiate and took up guard over the jeep in the empty square outside.

Elsie reappeared shortly with a cadaverous old man struggling into a long coat. She had got rooms and M. Daivren would show Hal to a garage where jeep and gear would be safe overnight. She took her own musette bag, and Hal followed their sullen host into the alley where he keyed the big padlock on what had manifestly been the hotel stable.

Hal had had time to plan some phrases. Emerging with his .45 in his musette bag he inquired again for the safety of their gear. The old man replied with a disgusted: "Very safe." At a question about the proximity of German troops his host spat and brushed the horizon with disdainful hands.

"Soldats Americains . . . poof!"

He had expected welcome from the liberated French. M. Daivren was closer to hostility even as he acknowledged that Americans had chased the Germans over the horizon.

The lobby was smaller than it had seemed at first. A little ell off the main room held a small bar and tables from one of which two domino players regarded him stonily over aperitif glasses. Both wore the dirty white collars and seedy neckties that proclaimed a notch above day labor. While M. Daivren struggled out of his long coat and wiped the mist off white mustaches, two blue-jeaned workmen entered the bar by a side street door. Madame hurried to take their orders. His host beckoned Hal impatiently toward the stairs.

The single upper floor had a short corridor with four doors showing. Candlelight illuminated one and Elsie appeared in it, toweling a wet face still ruddy from the cold ride.

"You're next here. I asked him to unlock the door between."

"Good. Come in when you're ready."

M. Daivren ushered him into a large room, lit a solitary candle stuck in a Benedictine bottle and gestured angrily toward the lightless electric fixtures: "La Guerre!" The war was Hal's fault. Candlelight came up to reveal a brass-bound four poster of heroic dimensions under acres of lace and billowing feather bolsters. The walls were of a faded floral design, offset by a single steel engraving of the Sacré Coeur.

M. Daivren knelt grudgingly to a double handful of twigs in a small fireplace. The scrap of paper under them responded slowly. Madame appeared in the door with a pitcher of tepid water and a severe pronouncement that dinner would be in one hour. Hal washed and was stretching his hands to the last heat of the twigs when he heard Elsie's faint knock on the connecting door. He called and kept his distance as the doorway framed her hesitant figure.

Candlelight turned the changeable hue of her short curls nearly golden. She had fluffed them out from the crushing embrace of her cap. A faint trace of anxiety made her glowing face look younger. She had removed several layers of undergarments from beneath the shapeless battle jacket. A soft white shirtwaist showed through its open collar and the new tightness of the jacket corrected an earlier misimpression. She was not flat chested. A desirable woman lived under that official severity. The nonregulation white shirtwaist, like the scent, bespoke feminine independence. She came up slowly to share the fire with him.

"There's something sticky here."

"They hate my guts. But why?"

"Mine too. I haven't a clue except that this is Alsace."

"Are they Krauts?"

"The name and dialect aren't." She shrugged.

"Well, this isn't a popularity contest."

"If you won't misunderstand, I'd like that door ajar tonight."

"I'm afraid I understand perfectly. Open it stays. Now let's go get a drink."

"Thanks, Hal. I'd love one."

In the little bar two more blue-jeaned workmen with dirty hands had taken another table so that the single remaining one was surrounded by the other three pairs of customers. Madame shook her head indignantly at Hal's request for cognac and addressed a stern answer to Elsie who translated the baffling local idiom.

"Nothing but wine or Mirabelle – it's a plum brandy."

They settled for Mirabelle and Madame departed.

"No cognac in France?"

"They have it; we just don't rate it," said Elsie.

The Mirabelle was as clear as water with a tasteless fire that reminded Hal of the worst California grappa; in the stomach it was welcome after the cold drive. Elsie made a further conciliatory effort at conversation which Madame squelched with a grunt before leaving them. Their presence had stopped other talk. The domino players moved their pieces silently. There was a uniformity about them that eluded Hal for a few seconds.

"Every one of them is over fifty, Elsie."

"Young men are still hiding out from the labor draft or off with the Maquis now."

He had called Madame twice without result to request another Mirabelle when M. Daivren shuffled in bearing a tray laden with napkins and silverware and passed around Hal to his rear. The first intimation of trouble was a gasp from Elsie. Hal looked around to see that their host had drawn a small nickel-plated pistol from under a napkin and was holding it, irresolutely, to his head.

"What the hell is *this?*"

The other drinkers were on their feet. One shot home the bolts of the side door; two hurried purposefully to the front door. The others surrounded Hal and Elsie so closely that he could smell a reek of garlic from one before their host spat out a blast of unintelligible idiom.

"Hal! He thinks you're German!"

He spoke angrily to Daivren who merely blinked without lowering the wavering little pistol.

"*You* tell him!"

"I'm trying but steady on: they mean business."

"Ask him where he thinks a German got that jeep."

Conversation became a hopeless jumble. She was spluttering French at Daivren who seemed half willing to listen. The others interrupted with angry expostulation. The nickel-plated pistol was not even cocked, but one of the workmen had slipped a wrench out of his pocket and another had out a short-handled, ball pein hammer. Through a pause in the babel Elsie blurted:

"They think we're stragglers who stole the jeep. You're a German and I'm your French tart."

"Tell him we've got orders . . . photos on our cards . . ."

"I'm trying. Do be careful, Hal."

The garlic-eater, close behind Elsie, drew a knife and spoke roughly with a toss of his head. She arose slowly, very white.

"They want us to go into the kitchen."

"No!"

Hal arose with a half turn toward the uncertain Daivren.

"M'sieur, I demand . . ."

He never finished. Elsie had tried to speak again and the garlic-eater with the knife closed his other hand over her mouth. Hal swung on his left foot and got Daivren full in the mouth with his left fist. The man sprawled backward and the pistol clattered to the floor. Then as he tried to pivot toward the others Hal felt the impact on the back of his head, and the dancing lights in his eyes went slowly out.

He knew recurrent waves of pain and peace. The pain was a hot throbbing in his head. The peace was cold that relieved it. Presently he was sure that the cold was wet. He opened his eyes to fresh waves of pain from a flickering candle above them. He made himself hold them open, and the pain receded as a white-faced Elsie eclipsed the light and then applied a wet rag. She turned away quickly for colder water, and he realized that she was kneeling over him on the floor. Then her face showed that she had seen his open eyes.

"Don't move," she said. "Just don't try to move."

"I'm all right," he said. "How about you?"

"Fine. It's all over. I convinced them."

"How?"

"Just be quiet now."

She turned for fresh water, and beyond her he could see the ringed faces of the Daivrens, the garlic-eater and one of the white-collar men peering down on him anxiously. Shame flooded through him like adrenalin. He lifted himself on his elbows.

"Hal! Do be careful!"

"Stop talking like a governess!"

A flush ignited her pallor. "You may be badly hurt! Must you be heroic?"

Reaction was turning her solicitude to anger. He compared the fire in her face to the abating pain in his head and put tentative fingers on the back of his skull.

"So I goofed; it's my head."

Daivren unleashed a flood of French, unintelligible and apologetic in tone. Hal saw a bruise under the white mustaches, with a consolation that became shame at his childishness.

"Cognac!" he said firmly.

Daivren vanished. Hal struggled to his feet, rocked for equilibrium, found it and extended a hand to the kneeling Elsie. She disdained it, springing up as Daivren returned with a bottle of Martel and two glasses. Hal handed the first one to her.

"This is one way to get what you want."

"You could have been killed." She was implacable.

"Not with you defending me."

He managed a belated smile to cover his humiliation and then indicated the bottle.

"Tell Ali Baba to set 'em up for the other forty thieves, and then I'd like to know what the hell happened."

Through the rest of the brandy and a stringy, overcooked chicken, Elsie translated for him the idioms and velocity of an extensive postmortem.

M. Daivren was the leader of a cell of the underground resistance, composed of the cronies in the room and others. Baccarat had been host not only to the normal German occupying forces but to a regional headquarters of the Gestapo. Daivren's cell had first helped the local young men, demobilized from the defeated French Army, elude conscription into the work draft called Service Travail Obligatoire. They had been hidden out in rural houses and mountain retreats, protected by a human warning net.

The German defeat at Stalingrad had given the cell's work a grimmer urgency. To recoup the lost armies of Von Paulus the Germans had declared that all blond Alsatians were ipso facto Teutonic and subject to conscription for duty on the Russian front. There, the simple challenge of kill or be killed resolved all question of loyalty. Fourteen thousand young Alsatians had vanished into that abyss.

The garlic-eater reappeared, pushing before him a thin-faced ten-year-old boy whose dark eyes shrank back from the sight of Hal's uniform. At a command the boy drew off a long mitten to reveal a knotted red stump of hand that made Hal choke on his food.

From assisting Frenchmen, Daivren's cell had progressed into activity in one of the escape chains for shot-down British and American air crew. They had harbored fifty-six men along the routes to Spain and Switzerland. The garlic-eater, whose name was Ambroise, had worked at this zealously with a twin brother, Hyacinthe.

Inevitably "bad ones" in the village had suspected them. Both had been arrested, interrogated and beaten without result until one day a surprise search of Hyacinthe's garage had yielded an American flying boot. Hyacinthe had been beaten to unconsciousness with a chain and revived three successive times without speaking. Then the Germans had put the little boy's hand in the vise in his garage and tightened it until his father broke under the screaming. Even after that, he had been able to maintain that he worked alone and had been shot without compromising the others.

Ambroise had seen the jeep draw up at the hotel. Fugitive Germans had trapped other jeeps with road blocks, killed the occupants, donned American uniforms and made their way through the wide open spaces in the Vosges lines. Some had even brought their local mistresses to assist disguise. The shortness of Elsie's hair had inflamed suspicion that she had already paid one installment on the classic punishment for horizontal collaboration. Ambroise bowed again in apology to her and directed a similar tone to Hal.

"He says he's killed four Germans and was hoping you would be the fifth. He's glad they realized their mistake."

When they had regained the privacy of their own rooms Hal found a substantial fire crackling in the grate and jugs of very hot water on the washstand. As Elsie knocked and then opened the connecting door he saw behind her the flicker of a fire to match his own. Her face was pale and drawn again.

"How's your head?"

"I can't even feel it," he lied.

"Hal, you have to know something: I broke our cover."

He had a light-headed inclination to laugh in the face of her gravity. It seemed the last touch of comic opera unreality. Then he felt his head again.

"Tell me about it."

Daivren's cell had been undecided about them up to the moment of Hal's attack on their leader. The intention to remove interrogation to the kitchen had been for their own security. The entrance of an American patrol would have been embarrassing: the arrival of a straggling German unit would have been fatal to all. Hal's assault upon Daivren had confirmed Ambroise's wishful surmise that he was German.

Elsie had been studying their vacillation between discipline and anarchy. When it was apparent that there was no other way to save the unconscious Hal, she had challenged Daivren with one of the standard greetings pilots used to make contact with escape chains. Daivren had responded instantly, tested her with counterquestions and then accepted them at once as allies. Her manifest remorse intensified his feeling of ignominy.

"I never broke cover in my life before."

"Were they actually going to kill us?"

"You, certainly. I might have got by with a head shaving but I was scared for myself, too," she insisted.

"Then you did right. Forget it."

"They know we're going to Strasbourg and we're *not* press."

"What's the harm in that?"

"I told you: there's a mouton in every cell."

"You didn't tell them our real purposes."

"Of course not. But Press wouldn't know the identification I had to give them. It rips our cover."

"You take that damned cover too seriously."

"Did you see that little boy's hand?"

"Yes." He winced.

"You'd better start growing up."

He took a long breath and tried to speak lightly. "Should I have let him choke you—for our cover?"

"I should have managed better."

Her assumption of responsibility grated.

"Forget that damned cover, Elsie. You're just tired and borrowing trouble . . ."

He had not intended condescension: he saw his mistake too late.

"Will you turn off that chivalry! Of course I'm tired but I don't have to borrow trouble. You're quite enough . . . lashing out like a hero in one of your juvenile films . . . thinking you can beat up half of France!

"You're all alike, you Americans! Everything is going to be safe and easy and happy! No rules for you! You come over here at the eleventh hour with half the good men in Europe already dead and think you'll just romp through our little war with your voulez-vous coucher and candy bars for starving people . . ."

"Elsie!" She blinked as he intended. "Go to bed! I'll call you in the morning."

She glared through incipient tears and then, turning sharply, went into her own room and slammed the door. He undressed mechanically down to shorts and T shirt and then stood staring into the fire. His head throbbed in painful reminder of his inadequacy. Comic opera or not, he had been unequal to the emergency and his failure had touched something deep in Elsie, some memory he could not match.

2

Five minutes after Mme. Daivren had lit Hal's candle and put the hot water jug on his washstand, Elsie was in the connecting doorway again, shapeless in battle dress, flushed of face.

"Hal! I said unforgivable things . . ."

"Forget it. Let's get cracking."

Downstairs, Daivren with a white chef's hat accentuating the blue bruise above his mustache gave them the best ham omelet and the worst imitation of coffee Hal had ever tasted. Their hosts thought all bridges on the St. Dié – Strasbourg road still serviceable. American patrols policed the region irregularly and Daivren opined they would have no trouble if they limited their stops to areas of wide visibility.

He and Madame alike shook off all mention of payment for the night with unequivocal refusal. When Hal and Elsie were blanketed again in the jeep he reached back and poured into their delighted hands a generous offering of cigarettes, candy and powdered coffee. Elsie kept her face averted through their exclamations over the presents. Then as they crossed the square Hal saw her look from the barracks bag behind them to the affectionate waves and nod slowly.

It was wet and raw again with flurries of fog, sleet, snow and rain. This morning he was grateful for the banging of the top. Elsie was in seclusion. She held the map as before, in a ready hand; the rest of her had withdrawn from communication into some armor deeper than the artful layers of blanketing.

The road wound through dun little pastures patched with snow and flanked with running brooks. Beyond these were foothills rising with the green shade of fir trees. As they ascended over the gradual Vosges the air became clearer, the distant vistas of green on white snow more constant.

Three times at switchbacks they passed roadblocks of boulders and heavy timber. Vehicle paths had been bull-dozed through them. The timbers were charred with flame and some had been shredded with shell burst. Behind two of them burnt out German tanks sagged in rust and ruin. On the approach to the last one an American M-4 lay overturned, its treads gaping at the empty sky like the legs of a dead beetle, its ports flame-gutted and spectral.

As they rose there was perceptible increase of interval between the little farms. Some showed smoke at the chimneys; all looked as if barricaded behind the fort-like stacks of firewood reaching to the eaves. The only living soul they passed in the first hour was an ancient woman driving an older bullock hitched to a cartload of firewood. She did not even look up at them.

Isolation began to thaw the constraint in the jeep. Continuous switchbacks in the road lowered speed, reducing the intrusive clamor of the banging top. He had not stopped at any of the roadblocks for fear of ambush, and after the third one Elsie had drawn as close to him as the divided seat permitted.

Abruptly they climbed through the overcast into open sunlight. Frost instead of murky puddles glinted from road edges. The little stream that shared the pass with the road sparkled. Some of its cutting exposed bold faces of red sandstone, and occasionally it widened into little blue and silver lakes.

The high point of the pass was a mountain meadow, dazzling with new snow through which the road was far from trees. He thought it safe to stop for a long look at the lowering overcast east of them and the red, green and white world that enclosed their solitude.

"You're very silent."

"I'd like to bite my tongue off, Hal."

"I told you to forget it."

"That American tank stabbed me. We *do* know that you've had appalling casualties, too."

"You saved us a very silly one last night."

"You were rash, but fighting *is* basic for men."

"You believe that?"

"We've had five years to learn it."

"At least you've learned to fight with your brains."

"Underdog has to." She shrugged.

"We've missed that, too. Last night seemed like comic opera to me. I couldn't believe it was dangerous. I've always had a safe chair, on the winning side."

"You'd better lose that guilt. Weakness is not virtue; it's just bad luck."

"You get over thinking that safety is good luck. What was it like, being underdog?"

She frowned and shook her head: "Hindsight is too easy. At the time you're too busy to think. We knew we hadn't an earthly till they attacked Russia. We weren't sure of survival until Pearl Harbor. And then, inside, we knew that nothing would ever be the same, anyway."

"At least you know that you can cope."

"Most people can; the sticker is why."

"It always is: worst word in the language, Elsie."

She nodded and even her silence became more companionable as he drove on. She seemed to be emerging from a shadow of fatalism. Abruptly they could see the end of the meadow and the vista ahead dimmed into lowering fog. There was still safe clearance to the sides and he stopped for a last look at the green and white around them.

"I'm afraid we've had our sunlight."

"It was beautiful." She rallied now.

"It could be the Sierras, below timberline."

"Tell me about your home and family."

"I have no family except parents."

"Fancy! We think of all Americans as married. Before you ever came we were warned." She chuckled.

"We were warned about you, too." He thought of Joe Collet's severe injunction and chuckled himself. "How do we measure up?"

"Surely you know the going gag in London?"

" 'Overpaid, overdecorated, oversexed and over here'?"

"Oh, that too. I was thinking of: 'When you go out with an American you spend the first part of the evening looking at pictures of his wife and children and the last part reminding him of them.' "

"I've met that one. Do you know our counterpart?"

"I'm not sure."

" 'Over here there's a dead hero in every bed.' "

Her quick start and then the change of subject corroborated the other evidence.

"It must seem so. What do you do in civil life?"

It was a long time since anyone had asked him about himself. He responded diffidently, factually at first about the little college where he taught Freshman composition, setting subjects, grading papers, trying to maintain expectancy for talent that did not appear. Elsie wanted to know more. Under the stimulus of her sincerity he found himself remembering how the clean white buildings and red tile roofs contrasted with the feathery green of pepper trees, the pervading scents of orange and eucalyptus trees, the liquid notes of quail calling from the foothills at sunrise and dusk.

"It sounds idyllic. What's the name of the college?"

That had been Lois's first question. She had frowned ever so slightly at the answer. Elsie glowed.

"I love classical names. Will you become a don?"

"No. They understand that: they're good people. I'm trying to learn to write."

He had never told Lois that at all. Elsie took it as casually as if she had been expecting it.

"Do you work at it?"

"Yes. Not well enough for bread and butter yet."

"You will: you're fundamentally sympathetic, Hal."

"I thought I would once; I'm not so sure now."

"War turns everything upside down."

"I never knew which side was up. I was taught the Golden Rule and the Ten Commandments and sportsmanship and service. I wind up in the Hole planning ways for better men to kill Germans."

"Would you rather turn the other cheek?"

"No. Their record is clear. But you can't help reflecting on what it's done to ours. You have to protect the Sixth Commandment by killing its transgressors. After the whole journey up from the slime we're still at the mercy of our worst. If one man wants to fight, the others have to kill him.

"I was brought up on a romantic dream of progress measured in moral terms. It's nonsense. You were right. fighting *is* basic. It's not just a perversion of politics or profit. You can't even rationalize it with talk about the instinct for survival. We fight to prove something in ourselves that no other measurement satisfies. For men it's the ultimate quest. The guilt you just needled me about is self-doubt."

"You'd better lose it," she retorted. "You're on fire to get yourself killed and you're just the kind that does."

She stopped. The flame died out of her face and her voice was sad.

"Let's go on."

They descended into a darkening gloom of fog and rain again. Then, from one of the long spurs of mountain, some caprice of meteorology opened fifty miles of horizon before them. Sunlight shafted down on a vast plain of ancient riverbed. They could see small farms and patchwork fields, a jumble of rooftops surmounted by the spire of the cathedral upthrusting into mist above serpentine flashes of the Rhine. Far beyond it they could just discern the darkling smudge of the Black Forest.

As capriciously the overcast closed to shroud the very road before them. Switchbacks became sharper. Hal had to decelerate and their pace became uncomfortably vulnerable to ambush from the underbrush flanking the road. At one reverse turn a small ancient Citroën emerged from the fog and swiveled to a stop that blocked the road. Hal fumbled for his .45 as two men with rifles jumped from the car and advanced on them. Elsie put a restraining hand on his arm.

"They're just Fifi, I think."

Closer up he could see the bright tricolored arm bands on civilian coats. If authentic they were the going identification of the irregular Forces Francaises Intérieures. They were easily counterfeited by fugitive Germans. The first words of these men were unmistakably French. They apologized for blocking the road, assured Hal that the interruption would be brief and then, with exuberant pride, invited him and Elsie to watch the passage of their prisoners to a connecting road.

Hal had expected to see captive German soldiers. Rounding the turn with the Fifi guards they beheld a long file of civilians of both sexes and all ages plodding wearily from the pavement into an even steeper intersecting mountain lane. The first shock was their diversity. Brightly polished boots glinted among pearl-buttoned cloth tops and clanking sabots. Fur-lined coats elbowed shivering figures in open-throated cotton shirts. Expensive hand luggage swung arcs beside rag- and paper-parcels.

A gray-haired old woman dropped a bundle wrapped in wet newspaper. It exploded into dirty garments from which sprang three bright apples. Her neighbors scuffled avidly for them. As she screamed and protested a guard entered the column and kicked her forward. The garments were trampled out of sight in a second; the victors of the scuffle wolfed her apples as fast as they could bite. She walked on with tears streaming down her face.

Interspersed through the column were young women with bare heads shaved down to the white skin on their skulls. Like the others they walked with faces downcast, heedless of the rain running down their necks. There was no conversation in the column and the first impression of diversity was slowly supplanted by that of uniform despondency. Most of the eyes were on the feet just ahead of them. They didn't even bother to look up as they left pavement for wet mud and gravel.

Elsie had been conversing with the guides at a rate Hal could not follow. In the first short silence he nudged her.

"What was their offense?"

"German blood."

Strasbourg was still readjusting to the reversal from German to Allied occupation. Each of these captives was known to have been a German or German sympathizer. Many were suspect of active assistance, collaboration, or denunciation and betrayal of loyal French. Proven traitors had been shot out of hand in the first blood-letting of the liberation and the process was continuing. The file passing now was the second category of suspects. They were being taken for custody, interrogation and, perhaps, ultimate trial to the German-built concentration camp at Natzweiler.

"Where the French *they* betrayed were tortured and killed," Elsie concluded.

"An eye for an eye and a tooth for a tooth?"

"Exactly. How does it look, close up?"

"Elsie, I didn't say I liked war. I said that's the way things are."

"They're that way because men do like it, Hal."

3

The Strasbourg they entered cowered under a spiritual oppression as penetrating as the wet fog that shrouded it. The blank, dark dormers brooding over steeply pitched gray slate roofs were death masks. The steel shutters and permanent iron grilles on every lower window suggested as much of evil lurking within as of peril from the narrow deserted streets. The flash of eyes withdrawing from upper windows seemed a continuance of medieval legends, of siege, assault, repulse. Hal would not have been surprised to see their jeep enveloped in cascades of molten lead or Greek Fire.

"Merry as a morgue," he frowned to Elsie.

"Germans dehumanize everything, and altogether they've had hundreds of years here. Wait till you meet Edouard and Felice Pourvalle. When they laugh you love the whole world."

The prospect had restored her to eager excitement. She craned her neck out of the jeep, pointing out old landmarks and explaining the junction of rivers that had been reshaped to form a circular canal enclosing the center of the city.

Anciently, the purpose of the canals had been defensive. Time had adapted them to water-borne commerce. To Hal the ring still suggested a hostile seclusion from the rest of mankind, a web of entrapment into the inner darkness. Once within the ring, however, they passed swiftly from the ominous desertion of the outskirts to turbulent activity. Here, too, all shop windows were barred. The rust on the shutters of the shops dated a long interruption of normal commerce. The pulsating life of the streets was the life of war again.

In every alley bars, bistros and Bierstubes were open. French soldiers wandered about them in morose silence. G.I.'s with dumpy, dough-faced girls cuddling close to their pockets circulated happily under the watchful eyes of white-helmeted military police. It took Hal a second to comprehend the difference between the open abandon of Nancy and the noticeably sober atmosphere around him. Nancy had been a leave town. Strasbourg, though militarily quiescent, was front line. Only the narrow river and a tacit truce separated the festive from the entrenched Wehrmacht.

A seething civilian activity offset the military languor. Every other native wore the tricolored arm band and many carried weapons that ranged from foot-long flintlock pistols to modern target .22s. As individuals approached each other these were brandished, compared and avidly discussed under the amused eyes of the American soldiers.

"Who do they think they're fighting?"

"Each other now." She sighed. "In the Occupation possession of a weapon was death. Now it proves the owner was on the right side all along . . . or he hopes it does."

Hal had to burn his brake bands as a group of men emerged from a bar in a churning knot that carried them heedless across the foot-wide sidewalk. Two of the gang were holding another by twisted arms. Two more were beating his bloody head with pistol butts. He screamed and struggled. An M.P. appeared and thumbed them sternly off the pavement without interfering in the violence. They dragged their victim into a dark areaway on the far side of the street and the M.P. motioned Hal briskly to proceed.

"Collaborator?"

"Presumably. He could be just an unpopular landlord."

They came to a large open square. In its center the bronze equestrian hero of another war glowered haughtily upon contemporary pedestrians and cyclists. Beyond him, Hal could see the majestic tower of the cathedral truncated now by low cloud. Its windows from which the old glass had been prudently removed gaped as blankly as the open scars of recent bomb damage. He remembered the afternoon the Target Committee had decided to bomb the Litard plant. By the democratic device of the vote he bore personal responsibility for those scars.

They lost the cathedral in a foreground of lower buildings as Elsie directed him through a labyrinth of narrow streets and alleys. They burst from one of these, scarcely wide enough to pass the jeep into a self-contained little square, and she leaned forward, expectancy illuminating her face now.

"There . . . on the corner . . . Oh! No . . . no . . . NO!"

He pulled to the curb and looked first at her stricken face. On the opposite corner what had once been a modest four storey building was now a fire-blackened ruin. Its roof and interior floors had burnt out so cleanly that only a heat-stained shell of stone and brick remained, silent and spectral among its undamaged neighbors. When he looked back Elsie had a handkerchief clenched tightly in her hand. She dabbed twice at her eyes and then pointing across the square she spoke in a low voice.

"Go there: he was a friend of Edouard's."

The Hotel Gustav had evidently been a modest rival to its more imposing neighbor. It was recessed from the square proper in a little walled courtyard of its own. Hal turned into it through a low arch. At its apex the rock was carved in black Germanic script: 1543, as if to confirm the impression that to move fifty feet from the Place Egalité was to move back four hundred years in time.

The yard was of cobblestones with moss in the deep cracks and around the lower masonry of the building. A massive chestnut tree spread its bare branches in symmetrical pattern over a long watering trough, a wrought-iron pump and hitching posts of oak with heavy iron rings inlet into the carved horse-heads at their tops.

The ground- and first-floor windows were all criss-crossed with heavy, permanent iron grillwork. Small leaded panes looked out through them suspiciously and yet managed to lighten a gray facade of stone, plaster and heavy sagging beams. Modern metal down spouts and rain gutters were a jarring anachronism against the ancient slates and dark dormers of the steep roof. On the oak front door at the top of a little stone stoop were iron strap hinges three feet long. At its very center, a small glass peep window was recessed behind iron grilling.

Studying the building Hal had a sense of coming to the end of a quest, of the very core of the concentric circles of mountain, plain, rivers, canal ring and inner streets through which they had made their way to ultimate secrecy. Elsie's voice was trying to reassure herself as well as him.

"Edouard always said Antoine Gustav was a true Frenchman."

Together they climbed the narrow stoop and pulled the ancient bronze bell rod. Hal had a flash-bulb impression of blue eyes under thick white eyebrows through the bars of the little peephole. A bolt clicked inside and the door opened to a small parlor of antiquated elegance. Heavy brocades, fringes, tassels and cushions of plum color helped to mute the illumination of a solitary candle behind the wire mesh grille on the desk.

Antoine Gustav was of the generation that had immortalized Marshal Joffre. Nature had assisted sentiment in his conscious emulation of that hero. He had the same bell-shaped figure, the same sharpness of eye and severity of ponderous mustaches, the same snowy mane of abundant hair.

His faded, immaculate frock coat had an empty left sleeve. He had come from the desk to open the front door for them; unexpected agility had returned him close enough to it so that his remaining arm now rested within easy reach of a German P.38 automatic on its top. Beside it sat a tricolored arm band he had not bothered to don for indoors or for the guests to whom he now bowed. Elsie turned on a torrent of French to which he listened gravely. He answered with a move of the head to include Hal in his slow precise English speech.

"Mademoiselle must prepare herself for a sadness."

He indicated two of the overstuffed chairs and sniffed through the forest of hairs at his nostrils as if to clear them for an effort. His observation had immediately grasped Hal's deficiency or ignorance of French. He waited until both were seated before continuing in his slow English.

It was no longer dangerous to confide that Edouard Pourvalle had been the leader of a cell of the Resistance. M. Pourvalle had not embarrassed his old friend with this confidence, nor had their host burdened M. Pourvalle with disclosures he might have made upon his own account. In such times men fried their own fish. Especial discretion was imperative for two who were known to esteem each other. The most trustworthy of friends had other friends.

M. Pourvalle's cell had been active from the first in helping young Alsatians elude the S.T.O. and the subsequent military conscription for the Russian front. It had progressed from that to harboring fugitive Allied air crew. It was impossible to keep such work entirely secret in a close community; the audacity and ingenuity of M. Pourvalle had spared him anything worse than routine suspicion and abortive searches until shortly after the second bombing of the Litard plant. That had intensified the German search for airmen known to have been shot down in the operation.

Gustav thought his friend's misfortune was attributable to an informant. Without warning, the Gestapo had surrounded his hotel while a meeting of the cell was in progress. M. Pourvalle and his colleagues had killed the first intruders and attempted organized resistance until darkness should offer some hope of escape. Grenades and flame throwers had terminated this hope. M. Pourvalle had been able to shoot Mme. Pourvalle before the rest of them and three innocent guests were incinerated.

"Altogether they killed six Germans." It was a requiem.

Elsie nodded numbly, pale face downcast.

"Relax a minute while I talk to him."

"I'll be fine in a minute."

Hal took Gustav to the desk and explained that he and Elsie were on an Allied press mission. They required separate rooms, adjoining, the use of this or another parlor to interrogate people and a secure garage for their jeep and supplies. They had intended to stay with M. Pourvalle; he hoped M. Gustav would find it convenient to keep them here.

The flicker in those blue eyes seemed sympathetic; it was nearly impossible to fathom that inscrutable reserve. Then, in measured sentences, M. Gustav declared that he would be honored to house France's allies. He must advise them that he was not on the American billeting officer's list, that his hotel was of the third class, though but for the war it should by now have been second. He had rations only for his own people and, so far, no electricity, hot water or heat. The departing Germans had enjoyed disabling their lost city. Restoration of its services was in the hands of a committee on which M. Gustav did not serve. A regrettable number of its functionaries were fractions of pigs. One could only hope for their improvement.

Separate rooms, a secure garage and the freedom of the parlor were available. If M. Gustav could presume a suggestion, he had also a suite with adjoining bedrooms and its own parlor and bath. Though unprepared it could be made ready within an hour. In that time

M. Gustav could make formidable representations to the fractions of pigs. He could promise nothing; he would try. The Boche were barely gone, but all would march yet.

Hal shook his hand and after a beaming, "Accord, Major," recrossed the room.

"Elsie, this is home. You rest while I check in with the American Command Post."

"I didn't come to rest," she said.

Gustav banged an ancient hand bell. A pretty young woman with blond hair, flawless skin and hideous steel bridgework showing among white teeth appeared at once. She bowed to Hal and Elsie with a flicker of fear in her eyes and then hurried to the jeep. A boy of seven or eight rushed unheeding through the parlor to help her.

By the time Hal and Elsie got outside they were already heavily laden with gear. Gustav was reaching his single arm for more when a white-haired woman bounded down the steps. Her natural dignity shook with agitation. She was carrying the tricolor arm band and with an apologetic glance at Hal and Elsie she began to try to tie it around Gustav's one good arm.

He shouted angrily at her, evading. She followed relentlessly, screaming admonitions. He dodged, turned, exploded French and then in an extremity of passion began hitting her over the head, rather gently, with his empty sleeve. Through this she succeeded in tying on the arm band despite a final blast which ended in a detonating "VERDUN!"

She retreated into the house. He looked at the arm band, shrugged apologetically and shook his august white head.

"My wife is a woman of many virtues but excitable."

They stripped the car leaving only cameras and typewriter for protective coloration. Inside, Hal found the little boy standing guard over a neat pile of their gear by the desk. He slipped a hand into the trades good bag and asked the child sternly if he spoke English. The eyes widened, the lips framed a shy: "Non, M'sieur."

Hal tossed a candy bar into the air, the boy eyed it incredulously, whipped out a hand and caught it running. Gustav's thunderous voice overtook him at the door.

"Gervais!"

The boy stopped, reflected, smiled quickly and bowed: "Merci beaucoup, M'sieur."

Gustav nodded, pacified, and the boy was through the back door with two steps.

"My grandson inherits the impetuosity of his grandmother's temperament . . . but then he is young."

Gustav marked the American headquarters on their map and repeated that within an hour all should be worthy of his new guests. As they drove out of the arch and into the square Elsie averted her eyes from the Hotel Pourvalle. Hal avoided the ruin by taking the other street of egress from the Place Egalité.

"What the hell was all the row about the arm band?"

It helped: for the first time since she had seen the fire-blackened ruin, Elsie smiled.

"His wife insisted that he wear it for safety. He told her that anyone who doubts his patriotism may go and dig up his other arm at Verdun."

3

THE American Command Post, Forward, in Strasbourg was a skeleton staff that had taken over the lobby of one of the many hotels fronting the Place de la Gare. A young Captain of Infantry put a bottle of Riesling hastily under his desk at the sight of Hal's gold leaf and settled to a skeptical perusal of his orders with intervals out for furtive scrutiny of Elsie. Then he spoke briefly into a phone. An immense corporal with hand grenades clipped to his jacket and a tommy gun half concealed under one arm ambled out from a back room.

"Driscoll will take you out to Colonel Graves."

At the curb Driscoll contorted his huge frame into the back seat and cradled the tommy gun so that it did not quite touch Hal's ear.

"Just drive where I say, and we won't have no trouble, Major."

"What kind of trouble are you anticipating?"

"A body can't hardly tell anymore, sir. The Captain, he said he didn't know nothing about you. Second place, the onliest thing these Frogs 'druther do than kill each other is step in front of some poor devil's jeep."

"You sound experienced."

"All the way from Marseille, sir. I'll be glad when we get over that Rhine. This France, it's worse than Frontier Days in Amarillo."

They drove out a broad avenue flanked by imposing residences as tightly shuttered as those in the poorer areas. Garden patches became open fields again before they reached a small, heavily wooded hill rising abruptly from the plain. Driscoll directed him into a turn forking up a narrow gravel road and then leaned forward.

"When the guard says: 'Stop,' you stop, Major."

A sharp turn brought them to the muzzle of another tommy gun and an upraised arm. Driscoll exchanged a few inaudible words with the sentry, and they were waved through heavy iron gates to a parklike yard. Terraces, geometric flower beds and statuary rising from pools surrounded an incongruously modern mansion of severe rectangles and glassy panes.

Driscoll had to speak for them again before turning them over to another sentry at the porte cochere. He led them into a long hall and with the faintest twitch of his tommy gun asked Hal to leave his .45 on a waiting bare table.

"If someone kilt the Colonel, I'd get hell, sir."

At the end of a long corridorlike hall a quick: "Come in!" answered the boy's knock. He maneuvered so that Hal and Elsie went in with the tommy gun at their backs.

They entered what had obviously been a drawing room of magnitude and graceful proportion. Now all the furniture had been removed except for three chairs grouped around an elaborate desk topped with intricate inlay. On it were a telephone and two hobnailed boots. Colonel Graves was reading with his back to large glass windows framing a magnificent panorama of the city, the Rhine and the dark smudge of the Black Forest far beyond. Now he looked over his boots with annoyance that faded at his approving estimate of Elsie. With deliberation he took his feet off the table, gave a reluctant glance at *Guns Along the Pecos* and rose. Erect, Colonel Graves was both tall and thick, with a weathered face leading up to a half-bald, bullet-shaped dome.

"We'll accomplish your identification."

His outstretched hand forbade other conversation. Only when it was full of their credentials did he scratch his forehead and indicate the other chair.

"The little lady may sit there."

"Thank you, Colonel. I'm comfortable."

They stood at ease while Graves dismissed their escort, seated himself and examined their orders and cards. Twice he raised his gaze for comparison of faces and photographs; at the end of the process he shook his head.

"Now I *have* seen everything."

The observation pleased him. He repeated to himself with relish: "everything," and then turned to the left and jerked his thumb. Following his gaze Hal saw that an impassive soldier holding a paperback book on his lap had been covering them with a tommy gun from a little alcove that provided a clear field of fire past the Colonel.

"You can get lost, Swanson."

Swanson arose with visible perturbation.

"Excuse me, sir, but Major Smathers says we got orders from Seventh Army itself . . ."

"Swanson." The voice was patient. "Would you rather be in trouble with Seventh Army or with me?"

"Yes, *sir!*" Swanson skated out the door.

Colonel Graves came around from behind his desk and moved one of the chairs about three inches.

"I'd like for the little lady to be seated. You, too, Major."

They sat. Colonel Graves indicated the departed Swanson with an air of apology. "That's a good ol' boy, Deaf Smith County. Our Security folks caught a couple of Krauts in G.I. uniform last week and we've been hoping for more."

"Sorry to disappoint you," said Hal.

"Oh, we'll get more. Strasbourg's good hunting for singles."

He seated himself, took another wistful look at *Guns Along the Pecos* and tapped thick knuckles on their orders.

"Public Relations and Press deal, Major?"

"Yes, sir."

"Well, I'll hand it to you flyboys," said Graves thoughtfully. "You'd won this war three times before I hit Africa and twice before I hit Marseille, and here you are before I've met that first Fräulein. There's just one thing I would like to know: with all this victory through air power, what in hell . . . Pardon me, Miss Vane . . . What are us dogfaces doing out here in the mud?"

"I don't make policy, Colonel. I obey it."

"Well now . . . come to think of it that's the way I've always worked it out with the War Department myself." His smile forgave Hal. "Now what do you want from me?"

"First, a signal contact with London."

Hal elaborated his need to report his arrival to his superiors and to be assured of continuing communications with them. Graves opened a drawer, took out a scratch pad and pencil and began the patient doodling of a star.

"What else?"

"Face and, maybe later, some support, sir."

"Tell me more about the face, Major."

It was the first time he had to work through the restrictions of the cover plan. Improvising, he told

Graves that daylight would limit the hours they could spend afield photographing bomb damage. He had chosen a hotel in which he could interrogate civilians away from the military atmosphere of the official billets. If Colonel Graves would deliver some gas and rations to the Hotel Gustav it would amount to public notice that Hal and Elsie were under the protection of the Army. Later, Hal might request help in rounding up civilians he wished to question. Finally, he requested the Colonel's opinion on the safety of Strasbourg and the feasibility of his proposals.

"That's a lot of different wants, Major." Graves glanced at the orders before him, "but these beat four of a kind if they're the McCoy."

"You can verify that with one signal."

"We'll start with *your* problems, Major."

He sharpened the last point of the star, put down the pencil and took up Hal's requests in sequence. His own headquarters had no signal contact with London. Hal could leave a message with a copy of his orders. Graves would send both to Division, for their action. He could not tell what that would be. On the strength of the orders Graves would have a weapons carrier deliver gas and rations to the hotel that afternoon.

"You savvy the gas deal here, Major?"

"I understand it's in demand."

"The going black market's a hundred and fifty bucks worth of francs a can. If you bootleg mine you'll break a lot of rocks. Next, I'm not kidnapping any Frogs for you, so don't get yourself out on a limb.

"The safety of Strasbourg is a guess question. My guess is they're over the river for good. The Krauts pulled out so fast we didn't even have to shell the city. We're keeping everything but patrols and river pickets out of town so *they* got no excuse to shell it. So far it's working. I don't think they want this lousy place any more than I do, but I could be as wrong as those ol' boys up in the Ardennes. If they recross the river in force, you and the little lady are on your own. I might even have to tear the town up myself.

"Your real danger is Frogs, shooting it out to find out who's new boss. They're real trigger happy and I didn't come over here to mess in their politics. They understand that anyone who hurts a G.I. gets clobbered, but you could be dead before I got to the clobbering. That 'feasibility' is a long word and it's not my problem either. Now write your message and I'll send it to Division with these orders."

He tore the star from the pad and pushed a clean surface and the pencil to Hal.

"May I ask where Division headquarters is?"

"You did ask," said Colonel Graves. "It's where we shoot spies. If you don't learn that way, I'll tell you when I know more about you."

Hal wrote the message and handed it back to him. "I hope this will tell you very soon."

"So do I." Graves put the papers together and began a new star on a new sheet. "If you *are* a Kraut spotting for that battery of 88s over behind Kehl, tell your boy friends to go right ahead and tear this joint up. It belongs to some Kraut tycoon the Fifi had hanging off the end of the porch the day I homesteaded here. All I got invested in this spread is a field phone."

"If I'm a spy, I'll tell 'em. Any other advice, Colonel?"

"Now you are making me suspicious." Graves grinned. "Air Corps never asked no one for advice yet."

"I'm asking."

"How long is your mission going to take you?"

"Can't tell; shouldn't be more than a few days."

"My advice is: 'Get on with it.' Things change in war."

His eyes went back to *Guns Along the Pecos*. He arose and made the barest suggestion of a bow to Elsie.

"If you and the little lady are on the level, I'm real pleased to of met you."

2

When they had returned Driscoll to the Command Post, Hal drove back to the main square and pulled up in the mist before Marshal Kléber's statue. Regardless of Elsie's feelings, they had to face the loss of assistance from the Pourvalles.

"What does the little lady make of that?"

"Is what he calls 'the McCoy' the same as our 'Pukka'?"

"Yes. Joe Collet will straighten him out, very fast."

"I do hope so. Meanwhile, we shall need local help."

"That's why I settled at Gustav's."

"I thought so. Shall we see what he knows?"

"He'll know more after Graves sends that stuff in."

"Will he send it? Graves was skeptical, Hal."

"If he'd been skeptical we'd be under arrest. He's just playing us by the book."

"Yes. I'm sure you're right."

She had said it too quickly; it sounded as hollow as his own reassurances. She had suppressed her grief about the Pourvalles; the shadow of it still overhung them. He looked at the shrouded light and fished among their maps.

"We've got an hour of light. Navigate me out to Litard's."

"Litard's now . . . alone?"

"It's what we came for."

She compressed her lips and thought before speaking.

"Hal, there is a . . . form. Whenever possible someone should know where one is."

It was there again, the unconscious assumption of his inadequacy. Only the truth could sting like that. He answered more sharply than he had meant.

"We're making our own form here."

She bent to the map with instant acquiescence; her voice was steady over the instructions.

They drove through another stately square dominated by a large opera house. Yellowing, wind-torn notices announcing the *Meistersinger* mocked boarded doors and an air of mortal decrepitude. Beyond it they passed the municipal theater of almost equal size and a similarly moribund melancholy. The smile on the mask of Comedy looked derisive under the dark skies.

Beyond the canal ring, a progressive decline in the pretentiousness of houses, bars and stores led them past shabby cottages and factories. The linear trail of a bomb pattern had swathed these with devastating, albeit erratic effect. By helicopter he could have flown straight down the trail to the factory.

In the Hole, civilian casualties to bombing were just another statistic. Hal had arrived in London long after the first blitz. Through the smaller ones and the isolated raids that had followed, he had gone often to the closer strikes, following the soot and fire flickers through the din to where patient men cleared the way for ambulances, warned each other of falling walls, delved in the wreckage to carry out limp figures or lead bleeding ones to help. He had seen the vacant faces of shock, the distortions of rage, heard the plaintive echo of humanity; ". . . and 'oo is to get 'ubert 'is tea, with *me* in your bloody 'orspital? Just you answer me *that!*"

Around him now, as cold as the treasures of archaeology, were the mute evidences of other fires, blasts, mutilations and pitiless extinctions suffered in another language because of his own vote. No matter how good your bombing, there were always people living near factories. Elsie didn't miss much, but he owed her warning.

"If I lived here, I'd want to lynch anyone connected with our bombing."

"Yes. We must expect hatred."

They came to the Rhine. From the hills to the west it had flashed silver and golden in the changing light. Close up, the water was oily and gray, the far shore a dark blur. Railroad and highway bridges had spanned the river nearly side by side before the French had dynamited them in the early days of the war. Through the Occupation the Germans had replaced them with wooden bridges. Now these were gone. There remained only the crumbled masonry of the earlier approaches. From the glassy sheen of the water some of the ancient steel structures still protruded, forming permanent riffles in the swift current.

Through the mist they could see the outlines of little islands, dark and still with inactivity. Beyond them was the long smudge of an opaque and shrouded shore which he judged to be scarcely more than two hundred yards away.

From the bridge wreckage their road turned north, paralleling the river through a wasteland that was partly uninhabited swamp and flood plain, partly industrial jungle overhung with the fetid air of long disuse. Old canals and stagnant ditches crisscrossed the whole area.

They rattled over wooden bridges through roadside underbrush and low, sickly trees until a turn by one of the larger canals brought them full view of the Litard factory.

From the ground it looked larger than photo-reconnaissance or strike prints had suggested. Hal estimated five acres, almost entirely surrounded by canals and ditches that gave its isolation the character of an ancient moated fort.

Its structures ranged from four foot thickness of old fieldstone to anachronistic supplements of sheet metal and sawtoothed glass roofing. Most of the glass had been shattered in the bombing. It lay where it had been swept by half-hearted efforts at clearance, in windrows reminiscent of dirty snow. Bomb craters filled with water pocked the yard. One of three main brick chimneys lay in crumpled ruin along a whole crushed bay. Another tottered drunkenly against the low moving cloud.

The steel mesh fence, bulging here and there with blast shock, was largely intact. The older masonry walls showed gaps through which he might have driven the jeep. A turn over another rattling wood bridge brought them to a surfaced driveway and spacious grassy lawn, now sere with winter, fronting the main entrance and administrative offices. Here sections of relatively undamaged wire mesh fence sat firmly astride drive and sidewalk, its gates secured with chains and heavy padlocks. Close behind them a trickle of smoke plumed from the cinder-block box of a new guard's shed. Hal stopped and began memorizing the main configurations.

"Do you suppose witches dance here by moonlight?"

"I've been expecting Charon to row up that canal."

Her voice was light and firm again. There was still

wariness in her face and it came to a full frown as he reached for their cameras.

"Hal, I'm going to natter you again."

"Shoot."

"If this fog lifts, we're in range of snipers."

His mind had to agree; it was one of those facts emotion resists. The plant was not more than three or four hundred yards from the French shore. From the slightest elevation German field glasses could probably read the maps in their hands.

"Graves told us there's a tacit truce."

"Not for patrols. This factory's an ideal hide."

"I spooked you at Baccarat, didn't I Elsie?"

"We're after a target; impetuosity won't find it."

He took a long breath and said: "Thanks, I'll remember."

Then, with another appraisal of the lowering overcast he took out a camera, left the jeep motor idling and walked slowly toward the fence. Instantly she was out of the jeep with her own camera, chatting and pointing like an enthusiastic tourist while they aimed their lenses and clicked shutters for the benefit of anyone who might be watching.

Smoke still plumed from the guard house. Retracing his few steps. Hal picked up a small rock and arced it onto the tin roof. An elderly man in a thick blue jacket and wooden sabots emerged and hobbled angrily up to the locked gate. Close up he had a lean unshaven face and antagonistic eyes that widened when Hal asked for M. Litard. His replies exploded with a velocity Elsie had to translate.

All of Strasbourg knew the factory was closed and M. Litard was away. No visitor was allowed inside. If the soldier threw rocks again, the watchman would have to inform the police. Turning his back contemptuously, he hobbled to his shack and slammed the door. Hal looked thoughtfully at the open gaps in the wall beyond the mesh fence and then began to laugh. It was already too dark to read, even if there were records inside.

"Go ahead and say it."

"Say what?"

" 'I told you so.' We do need local help."

"It isn't funk, truly. It's elementary that someone should know where one is."

Dusk was enclosing the river road as they drove back. By one of the crumpled bridge piers the first of several American trucks was dropping machine gun and mortar squads along the shore. Behind them other trucks with generators and batteries of searchlights awaited nocturnal patrol duty.

Not a candle was showing among the workmen's cottages. In town curfew had ended the parades of Fifi and victims. Streets and sidewalks were deserted. Dance music issued incongruously from behind the blacked-out doors of one of the larger bistros. By the dim blue lights of the jeep they could see M.P.'s standing a stolid guard below a heavily chalked sign: Gonorrhea Gardens.

The Place Egalité before Gustav's courtyard was empty and soundless; the enclosure within the arch funereal. They groped up the stoop and awaited scrutiny before the barred window until Gustav drew the inner bolts for them.

Inside, the lobby blazed with a resurrection of candles and a bright fire of logs crackling in the big hearth. From the kitchen came a welcome fragrance of cooking. Gustav's austere formality was modified by a twinkle of complacency.

He had informed the fractions of pigs that his hotel was now in the service of his allies. A certain fraction had arrived to verify this at the very moment when the weapons carrier of Colonel Graves had begun to unload petrol and rations for the Major and Mademoiselle. The hotel's problems of light and fuel were already eased. All would march yet.

Their suite was prepared. Gustav would put away the jeep for them or escort Hal to the garage, as desired. Hal sent Elsie to the suite and, with Gustav guiding, drove a circuit of alleys that brought them to the massive barred doors of another converted stable. At spaced knocks from Gustav bolts rumbled from within and the doors were swung by young Gervais. The boy had been plucking two dead pigeons in the immaculate main section of the small enclosure. Gustav indicated them with pride.

"He is artful with the trap, that one. Now he guards, too."

Leading Hal to a box stall, he pulled aside dusty horse blankets to disclose jerricans and ration cartons. Graves had been generous as well as prompt. Hal gave the boy more candy and insisted upon Gustav's taking two cartons of the rations at once. The hotelman thanked him gravely. One could not deny that food was welcome. Nevertheless the Hotel Gustav desired the honor of giving M. le Major and Mademoiselle their first dinner in Strasbourg.

Unlike the Daivrens' this garage connected with the hotel itself. They went through a series of laundries, sculleries, kitchens and pantries to the main lobby. By the improved light Hal saw that it was built around a glass-roofed inner court. Near the fire a table glistened with candles, linen and silver for two.

Gustav apologized for the Interdit sign before the tiny ancient elevator. Wreckage of the gas and electric plant had been a farewell gift of the Germans. As the Allied advance made their evacuation inevitable they had placed every candle in the city under requisition; to withhold one invited the death penalty. When the last fugitives were across the Rhine and the bridges dismantled a battery of 88s had systematically demolished the city's utilities.

"What good did it do them?"

"No military good, Major; it was spiritual. The German must either possess or destroy."

Mademoiselle had gone up. The Major would find candles on the staircase and another burning before their door. It was painful to speak of absurdities but he must remind the Major that blackout rules were severe. Any window showing light must expect bullets.

"Another corruption of the Boche, Major. One understands their malignance. For us the blackout is preposterous. Have we moved Strasbourg so that they cannot find it? They have it surveyed to the inch under cannon muzzles that need no light. But precisely because *they* enjoyed shooting out windows when they were here, our fractions of pigs must now grant the same recreation to every Sunday citizen with a pistol. Accord?"

"Accord," said Hal.

He made his way up the winding staircase to the fourth floor and, after a knock and responding call from Elsie, let himself into the heavy door. Their parlor, like the one downstairs, contrasted the fragile grace and the ponderous opulence of other eras.

Brocades, fringes, tassels and thick rugs almost smothered the elegance of white wood paneling that retained its delicacy through peeling paint. There were high Gothic windows, fitted with inner shutters reinforced by blackout curtains, and a brass trimmed fireplace aglow with a bright coal fire. On a table beside it awaited a bottle of Blanc de Blanc, two glasses, a dish of biscuits and a small tin of pâté de foie gras.

Above it was an immense wall painting of nymphs and swains in multicolored silks, dancing on a greensward below circling birds. Then he saw a flash of new light in the six by four gilt-edged mirror on another wall, and Elsie came through one of the inner doors.

She had fluffed out her hair becomingly. She had removed the enshrouding battle dress for a blue service skirt, the white silk nonregulation shirtwaist and a fleecy angora sweater. He could feel the impact of a femininity dainty and desirable: the hand-stitched run in the stocking around a shapely calf, the respiratory rise and fall of firm breasts, the throbbing pulse at the little hollow of her neck. Excitement had brought her glowing face close to his. Without premeditation his arms went up to embrace her. A lift of her own was responding to them, and then with a return of thought she flushed more deeply and stepped back.

"What do you think of home?"

"Nothing like champagne and K ration. How's the rest?"

"Heavenly. We even have balconies that must overlook the Rhine and that battery behind Kehl by daylight. I hope you don't mind ghosts."

"Ghosts?"

She took his hand to lead him through a bedroom, ornate and spacious on the scale of the parlor. They rounded a vast four-poster billowing with snowy counterpane and bolsters to a big closet which she opened gingerly, with her other hand. On wire hangers were two freshly pressed gray-green German officers' uniforms. As he reached for one her hand held him back.

"They could be booby-trapped."

In the parlor they cranked the little handle beside the ancient wall telephone and found that it worked. Gustav appeared breathing heavily from the stairs, his somber face red and solicitous.

"Your other guests left some property," said Hal.

At first sight of the uniforms Gustav swore, muffled it with an apologetic glance at Elsie and snatched them from their wires as if he had never heard of booby-traps. It was his own fault. He had entrusted final inspection of the room to Josette. She was one of many excellences but unhappily afraid of pigs; she had not dared touch the uniforms.

"Does she expect their owners back?"

"Strasbourg always expects the pigs back," replied Gustav.

Hal felt himself reddening and Gustav saw it.

"Since one sees the confidence Colonel Graves reposes in my guests, it is possible to be more candid. Two pigs were billeted in my hotel. When your Armies approached I removed these on the pretext of having them cleaned. Unfortunately those pigs had just enough cunning not to return for them. If the Major wonders why they were here at all, he must recall that all of us were at their mercy for rations."

He bowed and departed with the uniforms draped over his single arm.

"Do you believe him?"

"Yes," she nodded. "But I'd like our parlor door locked and that one open again tonight."

She indicated the connecting door between the bedrooms.

"I was going to suggest it for the duration."

"Thanks. I had them put your things in your room. When you're ready, we might try their peace offering."

His bedroom was identical to hers. The bathroom, obviously a converted closet, was between them. Beyond the ell it formed, another door connected the bedrooms directly. A slight wisp of steam on the mirror was the only trace of her. Even the towel she must have used had been fastidiously removed to her own room. He washed up in a Stonehenge of nineteenth century porcelain fixtures. Only the cold water ran. Elsie had left him three quarters of a capacious jug of hot.

She was seated by the fire in the parlor and arose to join him at the champagne tray. He picked up the bottle and corkscrew and then, as their eyes met, put them back on the tray and took her in his arms and kissed her. She submitted passively at first; then her arms tightened and she returned his second kiss.

"I wanted to do this in Imrie's office."

"Conditioned reflex, Major?" Her eyes were merry.

"You were so severe. I wondered if a kiss would make you look . . . just the way you do."

"I thought you were hating me."

"Not for yourself; it was just the governess aspect of it."

"I'm glad you don't." She frowned ever so slightly. "Sometimes you need a governess, Hal."

She disengaged herself deftly and put the bottle and corkscrew into his empty hands.

"Would you like to know what you need?"

She flushed. "At the moment what I need is a drink."

"I preferred what we were doing."

"So did I. That's why it's time for something else."

He studied her crimson face and the pulse throb at her neckline. Then he loosed the wires on the cork, popped it and filled the two glasses.

"Here's to our mission."

She clicked rims and drank with him. He pushed the chair closer to the fire, waved her to it and began to open the tin of pâté de foie gras.

"Tell me about Blanc de Blanc, Nanny."

"You're a nice guy, Hal."

3

The Hotel Gustav was a despotism modified by tempests of anarchy. Antoine gave the orders. The gaunt and sorrowful Madame, the pretty Josette, a squat little woman named Gabrielle whom Hal and Elsie instantly nicknamed Four by Four, and the boy, Gervais, received the orders, considered, protested, debated, defied and reproached until they were sent scurrying by commands and slaps from the empty sleeve . . . to do exactly as they had intended anyway.

Gustav never spoke of his affliction except in angry reply. To his face or behind his back it was the favorite topic of his lugubrious wife.

"He is a just man but of an imprudence. One has only to reflect upon the thousands at Verdun who did not lose an arm!"

A similar freedom of speech obtained throughout the ménage.

"If M'sieur *desires* his guests to have cold plates . . ."

"Was your fire *planned* to burn Mademoiselle's pretty skirt?"

"Grandpère *promised* I should pull the cork . . ."

"The soup of our allies *curdles* while you talk . . . !"

"Be gone, woman, and stop dulling my knives!"

Through this Hal and Elsie were served pâté de foie gras in aspic, onion soup completely encrusted in melted cheese and bread, Gervais's pigeons in individual casseroles with carrots, potatoes and mushrooms, a salad of endive and apples, and a compote of preserved berries and peaches in kirsch. The bottle of Burgundy made Elsie exclaim.

"This is irreplaceable!"

"It has aged for you under the noses of the pigs."

Hal insisted that Gustav and Madame bring glasses to their table. It was a helpful elixir. He praised the pigeons and inquired about Gervais's method of trapping. The boy glowed with pleasure, shot a question at his grandfather and vanished. He returned with a crude box trap, over which they held a solemn critique with Elsie translating the bewildering and rapid idiom.

The trap had provided many meals through the Occupation. Now it was no longer reliable. Everyone trapped pigeons. The competition in bait was becoming ruinous. One must risk scraps of a size for soup. The time was costly. Gervais's trap had only a crude post and string apparatus for a trigger. He had to crouch for hours in one of the dark dormers to spring it.

"Where did you leave your chaperone, Elsie?"

He was starting for the stairs. She checked him with a gesture. Her hand slid under the table and reappeared with the knife to a gasp from Madame and a delighted "La-la!" from the frankly eavesdropping Four by Four.

Hal took some kindling sticks from the fireplace, carved for a few minutes and presented the awed boy with a figure of 4 trigger that tripped at the slightest touch on the bait spoon.

"Formidable! On a larger scale one could catch pigs!"

"Gervais! If you call Germans pigs they will shoot you!"

"Grandpère calls them pigs, Grandmama."

"And where is his other arm?"

"It is at Verdun! Women comprehend nothing! To call a German a pig is to compliment him!"

"They will return and kill us all," replied his wife.

"Madame forgets that two can play that game!" Four by Four was ready for confidences. A ferocious glance from Gustav silenced her.

"Why do you call some pigs and some fractions?" asked Hal.

It launched a long discourse on the complexities of citizenship and nationality in Alsace through which Hal paid more attention to his host than to the disquisition. Apparently after Versailles had returned the province to France, restoration of full citizenship had been contingent upon proof of having four full-blooded French grandparents before 1870. Gustav's contemptuous "fractions" summarized the lesser status of mixed ancestry.

Obloquy and injustice had attended it. The German capture of Alsace in 1940 had turned the tables cruelly; their recent expulsion was turning them again. Both sovereignties had been helpless before romance and biology. Under both flags the fractions had multiplied until the only alternatives were acceptance or extermination.

"I say people should not be shot for their grandparents!"

Over a pretense of crumbing the table Four by Four glared at her employer.

"It is not shooting to remember that they *are* fractions!"

"Hatred will make us as bad as them!"

She flounced out with her crumb tray. Antoine nodded ruefully.

"A sharp tongue sometimes penetrates to truth."

"May I ask if you know Alexandre Litard?"

The geniality chilled. Gustav exchanged a glance with his wife who paled ever so slightly and replied for both of them.

"All of Strasbourg knows M. Litard, Major."

"We should like to talk to him."

"I think you must learn German for that," snorted Gustav.

"Antoine!"

For the first time he remained silent before the echo of fear that always haunted her voice. She did the explaining in sentences that might have been measured by the expectation of their being used against her.

"Others do not understand our problems here. Fate has made us the frontier. It was the bourgeois like us who held the wall, who would not compose with those Germans. The great industrialists like Litard thought only of their profits. The working people, like Josette and Gabrielle – though only Gabrielle is an unofficial fraction and that only one-sixteenth – thought only of their jobs. Why should they care who paid them?

"It is unjust to blame those who were hungry. Litard never knew want and in his case great antagonism remains. Antoine meant only to tell you that he is now a fugitive. His name is high on the list of the new Committee. Even other fractions would arrest him on sight."

"So despite the liberation he will not return?"

"It was the liberation he fled," replied Antoine. "There are Frenchmen as well as fractions on the Committee."

"Antoine! They will report you an anarchist!"

"We are living in anarchy," Gustav shrugged. "M. Litard will not show his face until we have a new government, sufficiently stable for effective bribery."

"We are not concerned with his politics." Hal took out a copy of his orders and handed them to Gustav. Madame stared anxiously as the hotelman perused them with deliberation. When he had nodded with respect and glared at her a silent "I told you so," Hal continued. He and Elsie had been sent to investigate bomb damage at the Litard plant among others, and to ascertain, if possible, precisely how that damage had extended to the detriment of war production inside Germany.

They had already been refused admittance to the plant. They could force it easily with help from Colonel Graves. It was their wish to pursue their purposes amicably. In addition to physical inspection they desired to interrogate workmen from the plant. Hal wondered if their host had time to help them.

"I am at your service, Major."

Hal listened with a straight face while Antoine went on to explain the history of the factory. In every way it confirmed the London gen, including the change of work and workmen, the secrecy and, after the bombings, the removal of the salvageable machinery and imported workmen to the Reich. All of this, Antoine acknowledged modestly, was common information in Strasbourg. Unfortunately there remained in the town only French workmen who had been excluded from the secrets.

"Can you find them for me to question?"

"Easily."

"Can you make the watchman admit us to the plant?"

"It will be a pleasure."

"Antoine! They will murder you there!"

"Peace, woman! No one has murdered me yet!"

"We shall expect to pay you."

"In francs, no."

"Then how?"

Antoine glanced at the orders again and proceeded cautiously. Work of such manifest importance as the Major's would require additional assistance. Antoine could furnish Frenchmen of unquestioned loyalty, beginning with the husbands of Josette and Gabrielle. They were men of virtue. One had a small motor bike, the other a little truck, immobilized by fuel shortage. With a little of the Major's abundant supply of petrol . . .

"All you want, if these men suit me. What else?"

There was a point of greater delicacy. It was a time of turmoil and distrust, even among Frenchmen. Unless the Major and Mademoiselle worked under constant guard of the soldiers of Colonel Graves, other precautions should be considered. Even among the innocent Strasbourgers there was fierce resentment of the American bombings. If the Major could procure suitable weapons for the friends of Antoine, they would be used to serve him and France.

"I have no weapons, Antoine."

"One supposes that Colonel Graves might."

"I shall tell him that good work from your men would merit them. I cannot promise."

"Accord, Major."

"Gustav is leader of a cell," said Elsie when they had locked the door of their parlor.

"How do you tell?"

"In this case by their women. Women are usually brave for themselves. They're always terrified of losing their men. Madame Cassandra is worried about the boy, too. Antoine has been active enough to give them all bad scares. What's more, he's at outs with the Committee and that could mean betrayal."

"To what, now?"

"Private malice or, if the Germans return, worse."

"I suppose that's why he wants to arm his men."

"Probably. I hope you'll give your private army a hard dekko. This could be sticky."

"It's wonderful, now that you've explained." He extended his arms. "Tell me you're terrified of losing your man, too."

He saw her arms lift and then check. Her face went red and suddenly it was all wrong.

"Hal, I don't want to lead you up the garden path. I'm not going to play."

"Someone else?"

"No."

"You weren't offended before dinner."

"I'm not now. It's just that . . . kissing leads one on."

"That's exactly what I was hoping."

"We're here to work." It was unequivocal. "If this proximity disturbs you, I'll get another room."

"You've already disturbed me. Changing rooms won't cure it. Leave that door open and I'll see you tomorrow."

"Thanks, Hal."

She turned swiftly and was gone.

4

As requested, Four by Four banged on their parlor door an hour before daylight. Hal called to Elsie and admitted the maid who had waited patiently with both arms full of hot water, coffee, rolls and kindling.

She greeted him with good nature indifferent to his underwear, disposed her burdens and knelt industriously to revive their fire. Not until her chores were completed did she arise to confront him with easy assurance. For all that she looked like a cut off phone booth, her round face had the serene confidence that women take only from proven success with men.

"Will the Major accord me a personal request?"

"Of course."

"I desire to place myself at the disposal of the Allied espionage."

"I have nothing to do with that, Gabrielle."

"One is not a child, Major."

"How does an adult draw such conclusions?"

"Since you test me, I must be candid. Certain ones say nothing of you downstairs. You do not come with the soldiers of Colonel Graves. It is evident that sage governments do not send male agents to Strasbourg alone. There are too many light-hearted girls with German friends. One must praise the discretion you and Mademoiselle preserve, but the use of two rooms deceives no one and merely increases the laundry. Madame maintains that the Americans and English are always eccentric. I say no one is *that* eccentric.

"One must admit that your Mademoiselle is très chic. Nevertheless her endowments are not to the German taste." Gabrielle glanced complacently at the mirror and then her face clouded. "My sixteenth of that evil blood is a cross, Major. It has compensations. Those pigs fancy their diversion by the armful. You will find me loyal and discreet."

"I'm afraid you don't understand our mission, Gabrielle. Mademoiselle and I work for the press."

"It makes a good masquerade. German spies are always of the press, too. Will the Major test me as he chooses?"

It was not a personal overture: it was a plea. He told her as kindly as he could that he would ask if Colonel Graves needed a counterspy. Her face beamed. She didn't believe a word of Colonel Graves: they had advanced to negotiating by indirection.

Over coffee and rolls he gave Elsie a suitably edited version of the conversation. To his surprise she was tart.

"Fancy. You're making a conquest."

"Don't be ridiculous. It shows what our cover's worth."

"It's orders — even if I did rip them."

They set out to work a little stiffly. Downstairs they found Antoine a changed man. The frock coat of yesterday had given way to a poilu's surcoat of World War I, its faded blue offset by the brightest of new tricolor arm bands. Around his equator of a waist stretched the polished black belt and holster of the German P.38.

"In a war, careless soldiers lose things," he replied with bland satisfaction to Hal's question.

His eyes were twinkling expectantly as he ushered them out the front door. The keys and distributor rotor of the jeep were in Hal's pocket. The vehicle itself had been pushed from the garage around the alleys and into the courtyard. In a temperature that put skim ice on the puddles it had been hand washed until it gleamed. Two fifty-year-old Frenchmen in berets and the ubiquitous faded jeans beneath short navy blue jackets stood at something like attention. Tricolor bands brightened their arms. In holsters of home-sewn cloth one wore a nickel-plated .32, the other a single-shot .22 pistol.

"Marcel and Alphonse await in hope of serving you," said Gustav.

He would have accepted their pathetic appearance and earnest eyes on sight. He prolonged examination to appease Elsie's suppressed suspicions. Marcel, taller and probably dour when he was not so eagerly on the make, was the husband of Gabrielle and a stone mason by trade. Josette's simple and rather jolly Alphonse was a carpenter. Building, like all other activity in Strasbourg, was paralyzed by shortages of currency, transport and material. Hal gathered that they made common cause by pooling their rations and contributing labor in the communal life of the hotel.

Marcel, after a respectful question to Gustav, led Hal out to the ancient arch of the entryway. With pride he pointed out the black Germanic script letters. Hal had to look closely to see how deftly 1843 had been transformed to 1543.

"Gustav's place lacked the antiquity tourists desire. With half a day's work I gave him three hundred years. Alphonse here does beautiful worm holes in the woodwork."

He would have hired them on the spot except that protocol suggested final commitment to Gustav himself. As they regained the stoop Marcel vanished and Gustav beamed to propitiate the chafing Elsie.

"They wish your confidence, Major, and will give you theirs, if you will spend a minute with Alphonse."

He walked with the carpenter a little uncertainly out

the courtyard and around the still dark alleys toward the half-open door of the garage.

"Imagine yourself a pig, Major," ordered Alphonse.

There was movement in the gloom beyond the doors and then he had a clear glimpse of Gabrielle. As their eyes met she lifted her skirt to show a vast white thigh, chuckled throatily and receded into the shadows. He entered the room, tripped hard over a stretch of wire and would have sprawled to the floor but for the quick embrace of Marcel. He looked up into the razor edge of a mason's pick and roars of laughter from all three.

"We did four of the pigs just so," Gabrielle exulted.

"Josette says you may tell the whole story. I shall not listen." Alphonse vanished through the inner rooms.

Pacing their idiom to his ears they told him that early in the Occupation Josette had been caught on her way home in that alley one night and raped by two drunken Germans. Finding resistance futile she had managed to make them believe that her sister, freshly widowed from the war, would welcome such gallantries the next night.

The trap had been sprung exactly as it happened to Hal. Alphonse had an ancient horse and a wood-hauling permit. They had been able to float the bodies down the Rhine the next evening.

It was Gabrielle who insisted on changing luck to procedure. Prowling overtly she had brought in first a young corporal and then the captain whose pistol Gustav now wore. In both these cases, too, they got the naked bodies into the Rhine without an incriminating clue to the hotel.

Unhappily other citizens had begun to enjoy the same game. One day the occupying commandant had fifteen native Strasbourgers seized on the street and shot in the market without even the formality of questions. Gustav had insisted on terminating his friends' avocation.

"They're hired," said Hal to the hotelman when they had regained the courtyard. He gave them rations and cigarettes on the spot, authorized the use of one can of his gas and dispatched them to find the most intelligent and communicative of the ex-Litard workmen.

Gustav disposed his enormous bulk over the little back seat and rode like the caricature of a postillion behind Hal and Elsie. The morning light was better. Hal reappraised the damage to the factory itself with an approving eye. His previous scrutiny had apparently missed some details. On the upper outside balcony facing the river someone had actually emplaced a ladder to cope with high, shattered windows and then apparently abandoned the job in despair.

At the gate Gustav rattled the padlock and then shouted to the plume of smoke still rising from the guard house. After a few seconds of unresponsive silence he drew his German pistol and raised a puff of dust from the cinder blocks. Immediately the watchman emerged, cursing angrily only to be silenced by a countertirade from the hotelman. At the end of it he hurried to unlock.

"I explained that the kind Major hopes not to shoot him."

Gustav now introduced the watchman as Jean Valéry, a man of modest virtues, regrettably clouded by excessive loyalty to M. Litard. Valéry endured these sarcasms with sullen silence.

"Not truly bad, that fraction: merely venal and timid."

"What is truly bad in these parts, Antoine?"

"The Boche, Major."

Inside the factory Hal devoted an hour to validation of their cover story, by photographing bomb damage.

There was compensation for the wasted time in orientation to the plant itself and in confirmation of the gen. Broken glass and the lighter rubble had been swept to the walls. The rest was craters, holed partitions and twisted steel structure half supporting roof sections over a yawning emptiness. Not a machine was left. Wall marks showed where the overhead chain hoist and trolley system had been removed.

"When pigs depart, one is left with fresh air," said Gustav.

"Tell Valéry we'll examine files and records."

"He inquires whether technical or administrative."

"Both. We'll start with technical."

Valéry led them to a less damaged second storey bay in which at first glance Hal estimated a hundred line feet of four-tiered filing cases. The ease and magnitude of the find was fair warning. A platoon of investigators could spend weeks of reading here, and premonition told him that the departing Germans had hoped it would.

A sampling was imperative. Dividing up, he assigned Gustav to Arado and Heinkel, Elsie to Focke-Wulf and plunged himself into the Ms for traces of complicity with Messerschmitt. Three hours of hard work in the icy air yielded nothing of use.

"We'll eat and then do administrative," he said.

Now that Valéry knew they were reading records, Hal wanted to complete the sampling before turning their backs. Antoine nodded thoughtfully over this explanation and barked commands at the watchman.

Glowering, Valéry led them back to ground level and across the plant to the high Gothic doors of the board or meeting room. A caprice of the bomb pattern had left its modern opulence little damaged. Gothic windows reached to high carved ceilings. Here plywood and sheet metal had replaced the shattered glass to protect the rich interior woods from the weather.

They removed enough of these to light a table for twenty flanked by wood and leather chairs, a neat bar open to empty cupboards, a secretary's desk behind a discreet screen and a large fireplace. In this they built a fire from wood wreckage to toast potted cheese, meat and hardtack, and boil water for the K ration coffee.

Hal insisted that Valéry share their lunch and worked hard at conciliating the old man with assurances that they intended no harm to him or the factory. The watchman remained sullen, insisting that he had no idea where Litard was or when he might return. Elsie had attempted to distract Gustav from some of these questions. His bland comment indicated sharp observation.

"The requirements of your press are exacting, Major."

Behind his back Elsie's head shook warning.

"A paper soldier must take paper seriously," Hal replied.

They began the administrative search in the office of Litard himself. Adjoining the board room, it was comparably lavish. The ancient wood-carved desk was as empty as the personal files. Four hours of eye-straining work among the general administrative files were as unrewarding as the morning's efforts. Hal took notes only to validate their pretenses. He got perfunctory thanks for a generous present of K ration to Valéry and then they drove back to town in a dejected silence.

Darkness was increasing the raw cold and curfew had emptied the streets again as they reached the Place Egalité. He dropped Elsie at the front door before he and Gustav took the jeep around to the garage. Gervais opened it with the only bright news of the day.

"Three pigeons, Major; your trigger is of a perfection!"

He offered them eagerly for the dinner of their guests. This time Hal declined. He and Mademoiselle would not eat pigeon again until everyone in the hotel had had a turn. Gustav's eyes were warm as Hal overruled him, too. In the lobby Madame informed him that Marcel and Alphonse had not returned and there were no messages for their guests.

Candlelight and the crackling fire made their parlor a sanctuary after the cold day. It was the presence of Elsie that pervaded its creature comfort with a subtler excitement. All day, surrounded by others, they had worked together as impersonally as men.

Homecoming, nightfall and firelight had reawakened or released her femininity. She had changed into the white shirt, sweater and blue skirt and was bustling over a kettle and teacups borrowed from Madame. Powdered coffee waited close to the boiling water. Studying it, he thought her deft activity a shade defensive, as if she, too, knew they were going to need a continuing barrier against the spontaneous combustion that had flared so briefly between them the previous night.

"It isn't tea but this will help." She held up a bottle of brandy.

"Good work. Where did you get that?"

"Cassandra. She's sweet in spite of those lamentations."

"I hadn't thought of you as so . . . domestic."

"I want to be of some use."

It might be veiled apology for last night; it might be another declaration of limit.

"You did more than your share today."

She only smiled until he was comfortably seated with

the coffee and brandy supplementing the welcome warmth of the fire. Then her voice was rueful.

"Today was total failure, wasn't it?"

"Total. That's the end of the paper chase."

"Bodies next?"

"If our private army can find them."

Until now he had made the excuse of insufficient privacy to withhold from her the confidences he had received in the garage that morning. However disquieting they were, it was safer for her to know them. At the end of the recital her slow nod was sympathetic.

"This happened all over Occupied France, Hal."

"Then why are you frowning?"

"Killing Germans is fine. Telling us about it is something else."

"I thought so. I thought: 'Too much, too soon.' "

"We *are* alike." Her face glowed and then sobered. "They're after us for something."

"More than gas or weapons," he agreed. "But what?"

She shrugged and then spoke bluntly. "There was no message at the desk from Graves."

He had hoped to keep that from her. He might have known it would not elude her instinct for essentials.

"Army paper work always takes time," he evaded. "Sometimes it fails altogether. Antoine is at outs with the Committee, which makes our private army only as strong as the shadow of Graves. Strangers in a community create a kind of displacement. Our ripples are still going out and they're going to arouse a lot of curiosity. Things could turn sticky if Graves disavows us. Remember how he warned us to get on with this . . . fast?"

"Can you suggest anything we're not doing?"

"One notion; it may be silly."

"Shoot."

From Cassandra, Elsie had learned that Strasbourg had been an official evacuation refuge for Germans bombed out of their own homes, beginning with the earliest British attacks upon the Ruhr. Besides the congestion, confiscations and downright thieving that had marked the advent of these immigrants, their mail problems had swamped the local post office. Elsie proposed inquiring whether any of the Germans imported to work in the Litard plant had left forwarding addresses at the time of their return to the Reich.

"That's a damned good notion!"

"Litard workmen left while Strasbourg was still in German hands. Of course they were under security rules, too, but people do break them for black marketing or love affairs or family emergencies. It's just possible some of those technicians knew where they were going in Germany. Is this too obvious?"

They were in perfect, unself-conscious accord again over a discussion of the possibilities of her notion when Gustav and the dour Marcel presented themselves at the parlor door.

"We have found your man but we cannot find him," reported Gustav.

Over coffee and brandy the mason made his own report.

Francois Monet, a quarter fraction, was the highest ranking of the former French foremen of Litard. He had served his apprenticeship in the factory and risen through the ranks to the close confidence of M. Litard. There had been mutterings about Litard's success in keeping him out of the French Army though Marcel thought these originated in pure jealousy.

Through the early German periods Monet had turned a blind eye to the sabotage of his countrymen and helped to protect them from their German masters. Excluded like the others from the secret work, he had been the last Frenchman employed in the plant. He had survived the bombings and assisted the final German removal. Since then he had lived at home by odd jobs, suffering the same stringencies as the other unemployed.

Preliminary inquiries had kept Marcel and Alphonse from reaching the Monet house until mid-afternoon. They had found the ex-foreman absent and his wife near hysteria. She said Monet had gone out to seek work as usual that morning. Customarily when he found a few hours of odd jobs he returned to lunch or sent word by some boy anxious to earn a few sous. Today he had neither returned nor sent word.

Marcel and Alphonse thought her disturbance over such a trifling delay ridiculous and said so. She had burst into a tirade, declaring them imbeciles for not realizing that the best of men had been murdered or kidnapped. Only yesterday, she had fumed, an Anglo-American delegation headed by a British female engineer had come to reopen the Litard plant. Either the Germans had sent a kidnapping patrol to deny her husband's skill to the Allies or jealous ex-colleagues had denounced him to the Fifi in order to get his job when the plant reopened.

"We'll go talk to her at once," said Hal.

"Likely enough he has only another woman somewhere, but it could be more than meets the eye," summarized Marcel. "She asked me to leave Alphonse there to protect her."

The blue jeep lights made for a slow journey back to the Monet cottage at the most desolate end of the industrial wasteland near the Litard factory. The house as befitted a foreman's was slightly larger than its few neighbors and enclosed within garden plots by a waist-high stone wall and head-high shrubs.

Madame Monet had been a young girl of beauty. Remnants of it had survived the attrition of peasant life upon her figure and her hands. She still had striking black hair and the florid coloration of active work. Tonight fear distorted a naturally volatile temperament. She seemed to want to believe that Hal and Elsie were responsible for her husband's disappearance. Her first outbursts alternated abuse with pleas for his release.

Through these Hal studied the evidences of a solid marriage and industrious lives. The single room combining kitchen and parlor was immaculate. Cabinet work of cunning skill separated show pieces of good glass and china from earthenware. There were well made tables and chairs. A hand-fashioned, ultra-modern stove of one of the lustrous new alloys was cleverly fitted to a special alcove flanked by utensils of the same material. A sizable screen before the big open hearth reflected an extravagant blaze upon iridescent surfaces. The display was too public for theft: Monet had either bought or been given some of the special Litard metals.

The Monets had much to show for a lifetime of work, much to lose. As they convinced Madame that they knew nothing of her man, a perceptible guilt began to pervade her fear. He was the best of men, the dearest of husbands. It had been no more than her duty to prod him in hard times. She had done so only for the children. Even so she had told him never to take risks; it was not her fault he had forgotten his St. Christopher. In her distraction she produced the little silver badge from a drawer and eyed it reproachfully. He should have carried it.

"Where was he traveling, Madame?" asked Hal quietly.

"To look for work. Now the bad ones have killed him."

"May one ask Madame who are the bad ones?"

They seemed to encompass her whole world. It could be jealous neighbors who had denounced him for spite. It could be his partner in the asparagus patch who desired to steal their joint treasure from a defenseless widow. It could be the Fifi who resented his forced labor for the Germans at the plant. It could be the English or Americans avenging themselves . . .

"I can find out about the Americans," said Hal.

"We should bless your name, Major. He is a good man."

"We have wasted your time," apologized Antoine as Hal retraced the dark road to town.

"She wouldn't tell us the truth. Why?"

"She's not worth another question." Gustav was evading.

"I don't agree," said Elsie. "He *is* missing; that fear is genuine."

"Your men thought she lied this afternoon. Tonight she obviously wants help and yet holds out on us. Why?"

Through the darkness there was a false note in Gustav's chuckle.

"The reasons for deceit are always the same. The truth would be damaging."

"How? Why?"

"You ask me to recite the imperfections of man: philandering, black marketing, collaborating . . . we can easily find you another workman, Major."

"I want to talk to this one," said Hal.

At the American Command Post in the Place de la Gare, the duty Captain read Hal's orders, opened his own records and then summoned the Lieutenant in charge of the M.P. section. At his request the Lieutenant phoned the municipal police, with the same negative result. Nothing was known of Francois Monet.

"Fifi might have got him, sir. But our orders are not to mess with Frog politics."

"Who's in charge of them here, Lt.?"

"No one, sir. There's no one in charge of this whole damned country yet. They're still shooting it out for a new boss."

Hal went out to the jeep at the curb and asked Gustav about the local committee only to meet with further, transparent evasion. At best the committee was only a kind of clearing house for independent cells. It would be impossible to institute a search among them at this time of night.

"Could I meet them in the morning?"

"With orders from Colonel Graves."

"You have read my own orders, Antoine."

"They are signed by impressive authority, Major, but that authority is far from Strasbourg."

Over Antoine's protests he insisted on returning to tell Madame Monet he had learned nothing so far. Elsie refused to be dropped at the hotel. They made the cold ride again in a silence now surcharged with unspoken discord. At the house Madame Monet seemed to have recovered self-possession. She thanked them with a dry-eyed stoicism manifestly anxious to terminate their visit. Even her gratitude was guarded.

At the hotel he and Elsie made a late dinner of warmed up C rations in an atmosphere very different from that of the previous night's banquet. Madame and

Antoine politely declined to join their guests for wine at the table. Their answers to even the most casual conversation were distant.

After dinner Hal signaled Elsie to retire and then resumed the matter bluntly with Gustav. He did not wish to bother Colonel Graves unless it was necessary. He wanted every effort made to ascertain whether Monet was in the custody of one of the innumerable Fifi cells.

"Without orders one must use other means, Major. Is your petrol available for bribery?"

"As much as you want. I trust you."

He thought the man looked mollified; he was still uneasy.

"Inquiries invite counterquestions; are you sure you desire this?"

"Earnestly, Antoine. I feel responsible."

"Because his wife lies to you?" The eyes were skeptical.

"Because he disappears exactly when we seek him."

"France has fractions to spare," Antoine shrugged. "But . . . accord."

Elsie unlatched their parlor door to his knock and then, leaving him to lock up, preceded him in to the dying fire. As he came up she moved, ever so slightly, and he could feel the tensing of a faint wariness. It was not fear of him. It was acknowledgment, however unconscious, of the relentless chemistry astir between them, of a compulsion her mind and spirit were still resisting. He kept his distance and got his own mind back to work.

"When did Antoine start dragging his feet?"

"We do think alike!" She relaxed.

"You noticed it, too?"

"Unmistakably. Our ripples have struck something, Hal. But I didn't expect opposition from Antoine."

"It's not exactly opposition. He did take us to the Monets' after all. Then he froze up. Why?"

"What put the cat in the pigeons was your catching her out on travel and the medal. His mustaches twitched at that. I'm afraid the whole place knows we're too intense for press. Naturally they have to ask themselves what we're up to. They may think we're trying to help Litard. They all hate him and they've seen his kind come out on top too often."

Unity of thought had disarmed her wariness and, briefly, drawn them closer. Now the reminder of the tragic plight of the Monets, of all of France, seemed to engulf her in that impenetrable fatalism he had met in her before.

Her eyes were more sad than distant. He wanted to lighten them, to embrace that wan fragility, to comfort and console, and the very strength of his impulse knew it would never stop at that. Sympathy was immemorially a stalking horse for passion. It made his voice more brusque than he intended.

"That's not our problem. I'll call you in the morning, Nanny."

4

ANTOINE banged on their parlor door half an hour before dawn, with urgent purpose. Two cans of Hal's petrol had been enough to shed light on the disappearance of Francois Monet. The ex-foreman had been taken into custody on the previous morning.

"Whose custody?"

"As I told you, we live in anarchy." Gustav was still evading.

"Whose anarchy?"

"A cell of pigs that aspires to rule France."

"Will they let us interview Monet?"

"With an order from Colonel Graves."

Four minutes after Hal had called Elsie she was in the parlor fully dressed with only a patch of undried soap beneath one ear to attest to the haste of her effort. Downstairs Madame Cassandra, blinking under an ancient nightcap, was struggling to tie the tricolor badge to the empty sleeve while Antoine's single arm was whipping the German pistol belt around his massive girth. It made for a frenzy of commotion through which her reproaches shrilled: new frost on the streets would precipitate a fatal car crash; one could perish of pneumonia in such temperatures; to go out without coffee was certain invitation to cancer of the stomach . . .

"Peace, woman! They could shoot him while we drink coffee!"

He caught and snapped the buckle, beckoned to the others and led something between a charge and a retreat to the garage. Outside it was well below freezing. Early light just tinting the eastern sky promised a clear day.

"Which way, Antoine?"

"To Colonel Graves."

"No. I'm trying my orders first."

Antoine protested and then, finding Hal determined, settled into a silence broken only by the utterance of directions. They went through the Place de la Gare and out the Boulevard Woodrow Wilson until they reached a long enclosure contiguous to the main city market.

Once the place had been a freight depot complete with switchyard and sidings. Now it was a detention camp. Under a long line of bare chestnut trees the old stone and iron grille walls had been topped with barbed wire. The gates were guarded by arm-banded sentries carrying a miscellany of weapons that ranged from percussion cap fowling pieces to modern tommy guns. Other patriots patrolled the bare streets outside the wire and kept order in a long line of civilians who waited patiently for permission to take inside the bread and pots of soup they had brought for prisoners.

Hal parked at the main gate and, with a feeling of butterflies in his empty stomach, saluted the guard and demanded directions to the commanding officer. An unshaven, irresolute sentry who looked as hungry as Hal felt waved him and Elsie and Antoine toward a hut in the center of the enclosure.

Their first impression was of a parade. A continuous stream of prisoners, both men and women, in civilian clothes marched apathetically around nearly a mile of perimeter track along the walls and fences. They plodded wearily, doggedly, heads downcast, bodies moving mechanically with the solitary purpose of keeping warm. Just inside the procession Hal dropped a cigarette butt. Before it had bounced three men were fighting for it. The incident had raised other heads. Instantly the visitors were surrounded by the hardier prisoners, clutching cuffs, rehearsing memorized excuses, begging more cigarettes.

A guard appeared and began kicking the supplicants back to the circular parade. At a shed before the main hut a line of prisoners was trading cardboard discs for small dippers of soup from an immense cauldron over an empty fire. Others who crept toward the warmth were booted away by cook's helpers. In all Hal estimated that there were several hundred captives in the enclosure. From their filth, apathy and length of beard it was obvious that many had been here for weeks.

"What are the charges against them Antoine?"

"Various, Major; they all mean Collaboration."

The little hut at the center was as dismal as its surroundings. The Commandant, seated behind a packing crate desk, was a small roundish man whose hair and clothing were arranged to emphasize a remote likeness to Napoleon. He had a petulant face and a pursey little mouth that tightened as Hal asked to see the prisoner, Francois Monet. The Commandant eyed him and Elsie doubtfully, scrutinized Antoine's arm band and pistol with great care and addressed himself to the hotelman.

"They are officers of Colonel Graves?"

Gustav replied that they were a special mission, resident in his hotel. He wished to add his personal observation that the mission was supplied by Colonel Graves.

"One must congratulate them," said the Commandant bitterly.

There followed a resentful outburst against the Colonel. The American Army had no sympathy with the problems of France. One could see by the very number of the prisoners in the compound the significance of what the Commandant's brave volunteers were doing. And yet Colonel Graves had refused to supply them with modern weapons. He had had the impudence to say that his weapons were for use against the Boche. It was the obtuseness of all Americans; they could not comprehend that the most dangerous of enemies did not advertise themselves with uniforms. But then perhaps the Commandant was hasty; perhaps M. le Major had been sent with an offering of weapons to rectify the earlier mistake?

Hal regretted that he had none to offer. He was on official business for which he requested a short interview with Monet.

"Impossible! He is a dangerous enemy of the State!"

"This is important Allied business, Commandant."

"Pray tell our allies and the frugal Colonel Graves that Monet is French business!"

Hal passed a copy of his orders and a pencil to the Commandant. He hoped that official would be kind enough to read the orders and then write out the correct spelling of his name.

"Why does the Major wish my name?"

"To avoid error in my report to my superiors."

The Commandant recoiled from the orders, pushed them back unread and exploded at Gustav. Velocity made the idiom unintelligible; the effect on the hotelman was obvious.

"Monet was taken to Natzweiler this morning, Major."

"How long would it take to have him brought back?"

"He would not live to get here."

"Is this Commandant telling the truth?"

"He is now. Your request for his name frightened him."

"Find out the charges against Monet."

A lengthy, acrimonious colloquoy produced the assertion that Monet had been arrested for being discovered in a canoe on the Rhine. This was considered prima facie evidence of treasonable communication with the Germans. It was punishable by death. Monet had been held here briefly in the hope of making him disclose the names of contacts or accomplices. His intransigence had been softening when the camp had been electrified by rumors of an effort to free him during the previous night. He had been sent at once for safekeeping and further interrogation at Natzweiler.

"We'll go there," said Hal.

When they fought their way through the supplicants to the street again Gustav's heavy face was troubled.

"We should have orders from Colonel Graves."

"We didn't need them here, Antoine."

"Natzweiler is easier to enter than to leave, Major."

"I must see Monet while he is still alive. Mademoiselle and I know the way if you prefer not to come."

"Natzweiler is not a suitable place for women, Major."

He heard Elsie's inhalation and saw her lips lock.

"Mademoiselle is on duty as I am, Antoine. We do not wish to coerce you but we are going there."

"My one wish is to serve you." Gustav yielded.

Elsie's eyes thanked him over a long sigh. Then she

broke out K ration boxes and they munched a cold breakfast as they crossed the plain and ascended the low mountains to the west. Twice they passed small columns of prisoners plodding their doleful course up the snowy road. The guards of both groups were certain that Francois Monet was not among them. Antoine's face lengthened. Conveyance to Natzweiler by auto was an ominous honor.

The little river Bruche winding along the road seemed to complete a Christmas card beauty of blue water, snowy mountains and the eternal green of fir forests. Beyond Schirmeck they forked away from the main road. Pace slowed for the switchbacks of a steeper ascent, and through the growling of the low gear Hal interrogated Antoine about the Natzweiler-Struthof concentration camp.

The place had been a combination hotel and sanitarium until the Germans converted it to their own purposes soon after the Occupation in 1940. It had been overcrowded from the first with Alsatian victims of the Gestapo's unrelenting war on resistance. Death, deportation to the Reich and the progress of the war had refilled it with the whole galaxy of Nazi conquest. Poles, Czechs, Norwegians, Greeks, Yugoslavs and Russians shared its international infamy.

As German experimentation with penology advanced, gas chambers and cremation ovens had supplemented its gallows. Prisoners had been used to test the toxicity of phosgene. Female prisoners had been sterilized for subsequent use in field brothels. Others had been slowly frozen alive and driven through progressive insanity by drinking sea water in the name of scientific experiment. One Commandant had systematically helped hardier prisoners to escape in order to train police dogs on their recapture. When the Germans took over the Department of Anatomy in the University of Strasbourg, female prisoners were asphyxiated in the Natzweiler gas chambers for use on the university's dissecting tables.

"And even this, I think, is not the worst." Antoine hesitated.

"Go on," said Elsie through white lips.

"Now we imprison Germans here. They have made us like themselves."

They rounded a bend from pristine serenity of snow and evergreens to confront a rectangular jungle of high barbed wire surmounted at close intervals by guard towers from which machine guns covered the prisoners inside. All the fences were double with a three-foot alley between the two rows. Through this ran a separate barrier of electrified live wire. The first sight that met their eyes through the heavy grilling of the main gate was the spectral half-cross of a gallows, brooding patiently over the platform trap of its base.

A succession of low wooden barracks sprawled down a steep hillside, and from their dark silence not a single wisp of smoke broke the icy mountain air. A parade much smaller but similar to the one in the town detention camp had been walking the trampled snow of a sharply sloping perimeter track within the wires. At the sight of the jeep by the gates it broke into a frantic rush, augmented by half-dressed recruits pouring out of the cold barracks to shout through the gates for help, liberation, mercy, food and cigarettes. Instantly the guards in the towers stopped beating their arms against the chill and deflected the muzzles of the machine guns suggestively with angry shouts.

Slowly, apathetically, the clamorous mob dispersed to its previous listless tramping. The ones with fewest clothes limped back to the barracks, and through the crisscrossing of the gate grille Antoine pointed out the low, sinister outlines of the gas chambers and crematoria. A single involuntary turn of Hal's head changed the prospect to miles of green and white valley framing another cluster of little buildings beautifully grouped under plumes of blue smoke rising to tranquil winter air.

"A sanitarium that escaped this perversion, Major. Here misery may at least look down on mercy."

2

Commandant Gelan received them skeptically in a headquarters that was simply the best guarded of a row of shacks outside the barbed wire. Like his numerous and officious sentries Gelan wore only the arm band over civilian clothes for uniform. He was over sixty, with a spade of white beard sharpening a thin, intelligent face and a defensive hostility more bureaucratic than military. He bowed coldly to Hal's introductions, scrutinized the arm band on Gustav's empty sleeve and then applied himself studiously to the orders Hal handed him.

When he had read these twice, following the lines with a well manicured finger, he waited through a chill silence until Hal requested an interview with prisoner Monet. Then the white head shook firmly.

"Monet is charged with treason against France."

"We wish only to talk to him."

"At present he is making his confession."

"May we see him when that is done?"

"When that is done he will be shot."

"Then I will see him at once."

For a long second the angry blue eyes locked with his own. Then the Commandant put a finger on the signature of Hal's orders. His other hand pulled thoughtfully at his lip.

"That might improve the Major's understanding."

He led them out a back door and along the rear of the little row of shacks to one of noticeably high windows and a double guard with modern tommy guns. As the sentries stepped back Gelan pushed open the solitary door and spoke half defiantly.

"This was built by the Germans."

Entering, Hal heard Elsie's gasp and then locked his own teeth to restrain an instinctive retch. The room was low ceilinged and nearly square. A heavy iron pipe had been mounted about two feet out from one wall and seven feet above the floor. Handcuffs on short chains had been welded to it. At the moment they enclosed the wrists of a prisoner bare to his waist, with a long ugly welt already showing on his white back. One of two inquisitors was just raising a four-foot whip of cloth-wrapped chain for another blow.

At sight of the Commandant both torturers stepped away from the prisoner and came to attention. Hal could see now that their victim had to stand on his tiptoes or simply hang from the chains. At his feet a trickle of water from a wall faucet ran slowly through a cemented gutter, caked with ancient blood.

Close to the prisoner a school desk chair waited with an open pad and pencil for the confession the Commandant had so confidently prophesied. Along the wall beyond the chair hung a wide choice of further stimuli: whips of knotted rawhide and of unraveled rope, wooden clubs, and sections of rubber hose and of uncovered chain.

At the end of the room was a small fireplace with a brick hearth on which was spread an array of pokers, burning irons and long-jawed pliers. Along another wall were four comfortable armchairs and behind them a dozen school chairs for what must have been audiences. Gelan waved a proprietary hand at the whole institution. His voice had a measured self-justification.

"Does the Major see why we do not love our enemies?"

"I see. I still want to talk to that man."

Gelan strode over to the chained figure and addressed the reddening welt on his back.

"Traitor Monet, have you found your tongue?"

"I am innocent. I was fishing for my family."

The voice was strong, albeit infinitely weary. Its very resolution provoked the inquisitors to coarse laughter. They were both muscular young men with short cropped hair and gross, lumpy faces so alike that Hal thought they might be twins.

"Fishing for German bribes, with French blood!"

"He will sing a different song very soon, Commandant."

The Commandant lowered his voice to Hal.

"Those little ones volunteered for this. Their father was beaten to death in this room, very slowly, by Germans."

"This won't help him. Take that man down."

Gelan's eyelids lifted; his voice was cold.

"He is only there because he refuses to speak. If the Major and Mademoiselle prefer to wait outside . . ."

"No! Tortured men say whatever they think one wishes. This man may have information of value."

"Evidently!" snapped Gelan. "That is why he is here!"

"Nevertheless, I must talk to him alone."

The inquisitors had perceived the contention if not its causes. Now they moved to range themselves beside the Commandant, glancing at each other and then, with unmistakable wistfulness, toward Hal, Elsie and Antoine. As if reassured by them Gelan recovered his temper for icy hauteur.

"I must remind the Major that it is Allied policy not to interfere with the internal safety of France. Colonel Graves has issued local orders in support of this."

"You have read my orders, Commandant."

"The Germans counterfeit orders cunningly," replied Gelan. "You could be agents, rescuing this traitor."

Gustav had visibly paled. Hal could feel hackles on the back of his neck as he held the Commandant's gaze. Then, unexpectedly, one of the inquisitors blurted.

"Would M. le Commandant like to question *these* visitors?"

He heard a long soft intake of breath from Elsie, and with an effort managed not to turn his head. It was three or four seconds before the Commandant's gaze broke away from his own. The man's lip twitched, his left hand stroked it; then he barked angrily at the inquisitor who had spoken.

"Not at present: release the prisoner."

The two men turned obediently to Monet and began manipulating his handcuffs. Unlocked, Monet collapsed to the floor and then with a prodigious effort of will raised himself to his feet. Hal jumped to place one of the desk chairs beside him and as Monet settled into it the tension in the room broke. Gelan's final words were an infuriated salvage of face.

"Any attempt to escape will be fatal, Major."

With a gesture he beckoned his guards ahead of him

and walked huffily out the door. Gustav shook his ponderous head.

"I must endeavor to placate that one, Major."

He followed the others out, and Hal could hear the long slow expiration of Elsie's breath. Her voice shook faintly.

"Good show, Hal."

"We aren't through." He tried to cover his pleasure.

"I don't care. I'm proud of you, no matter what."

"I want you to translate. Tell Monet he will not be tortured by us or for us. We'll help him if we can: it will depend on whether he can help us."

He gave the man a cigarette and studied him through Elsie's opening speech. Monet was in his mid-thirties, dark-haired and with the slight stature and delicate bone structure of his predominantly French blood. His face had the sallowness of the indoor worker. Today its pallor was accentuated by a heavy cheek bruise and a black eye.

The skin of his upper torso was incongruously white against dark, shop-stained trousers. He listened to Elsie with intense concentration apparently unaware that he was shivering. Hal found his shirt and jacket on the floor where the guards had thrown them, and helped the man into them. Monet flashed him an absent smile: his attention was fixed on Elsie's careful words.

"I expressed sympathy and told him we're Allied press. He's grateful and wants to help if he can. What next?"

There was no time for indirection now; Gelan was angry.

"Ask him straight out where Litard shipped those exhausts."

The tone of their voices through fluent interchanges prepared him for disappointment before she turned back to him. Monet was sure no one in France knew where the Litard exhausts had gone. Shipment had been handled with security as meticulous as manufacture. Unmarked boxes left the plant in Luftwaffe trucks that showed no trace of destination.

"At least he's not inventing lies to please us."

"We can't just . . . give him back to them!"

"Ask if our arrival and his arrest were coincidence."

He focused every pulse beat of concentration he had on Monet's face. He could see it tighten with defiance before Elsie got the verbal answer.

"He says he is innocent and was fishing for his family."

"He's lying, Elsie."

"How would he dare, with what he faces?"

"The truth may be worse for him, but I've got to have it."

He had to repress active nausea in his stomach now. No matter how you tried to rationalize it his next step would be torture. For all that the Germans had originated it and the French happily adopted it, he was going to be the conscious beneficiary of it, as morally culpable as if he held the whip.

"Tell him I know he's lying. If he won't tell the truth I'll have to give him back to them."

This time in spite of the sympathy of her voice Monet turned, involuntarily for a long look over his shoulder at the handcuffs dangling from the pipe. For a second the trickle of the water faucet was the only sound in the room. Then Monet wet his lips and spoke in a low voice.

"He will make a statement, in confidence, to us only."

"Repeat it, word for word, Elsie."

He gave Monet another cigarette and settled again to a study of his face as the man began.

"The Allied officers will realize," Elsie translated, "that I speak the truth because it puts me in their power to be executed, even legally.

"When the Germans closed the plant and offered M. Litard refuge in Germany, he needed a trustworthy man. Valéry is a dotard capable of frightening away only mischievous boys. I had worked for M. Litard all my life. To continue now was my only chance to retain after the war the position I had earned. I agreed to watch the plant and report to him any significant developments.

"He was able to arrange through his German friends for me to use the bridge freely until the Allied approach made the Germans destroy it. After that he arranged for me to cross the river by canoe in darkness without being fired upon by the German sentries . . ."

"How?" demanded Hal.

"The placing of a ladder on the upper east balcony alerts them. At night a hooded lantern can be shown from the same level without being visible on the French shore."

"All right. Go on."

"For weeks the factory lay idle. There was nothing to report. Then when the Germans had gone some American officers came to my house and gave me cigarettes and rations and asked me, as you have, where the products of the plant had been shipped. I could not tell them either, because I do not know. But that night I canoed over to Kehl and told M. Litard."

"Is he living at Kehl?" inquired Hal.

"Not really. He sent his wife and children to Switzerland long ago. Sometimes he visits them there. Most of the time he stays at a hunting lodge he owns in the Black

Forest. That is fairly close to Kehl where, between ourselves, he visits a woman whose husband is on the Russian front. She will not leave her house for fear of compromising her pension when her husband is killed, so M. Litard has to come to her. From her house you can see across the river to his factory."

"He comes there regularly?"

"Yes. She is in some respects a most amiable woman. M. Litard was much excited about the visit of the Americans. I was to keep their interest aroused by telling them that I might be able to find out, through correspondence with other French workers who had moved away, where the Litard products were shipped. Then I was to report back to M. Litard at once.

"Unfortunately I was unable to do this because those Americans did not return and I had no idea where to seek them. Then when Valéry told me that you two had been there I felt I should report that. Valéry believed from the very way you took pictures that you were going to rebuild the factory for Allied use.

"So night before last I raised both ladder and lantern because it was nearly dark when Valéry told me of your visit, and then I paddled across. For such trips I always take a fish line. The river is badly polluted now, but since the food shortage many do fish from the banks and no French jury would convict a man of fishing for his family. That is why these patriots wish to beat a confession out of me before a jury can hear me.

"Luckily M. Litard was again in Kehl and again greatly excited by your visit. He says Valéry is an idiot; the Allies have plenty of factories without bothering to rebuild one within rifle shot of the German shore. Nevertheless he ordered me to stay near the factory and learn what I could if the Allied officers returned."

Monet had been addressing both his narrative and his attention to Elsie, pausing at intervals for her translation to Hal. Now at the explicit confession that his spying had been directed against them, his eyes went to Hal in apology and appeal. A nod and half smile were enough. Relief lightened his face and strengthened his hoarse voice.

"Since American soldiers now patrol the French shore it is more difficult to recross than to go to Germany. The fog was patchy that night and starlight is dangerous. With dawn, however, mists and fog usually return for a while and the American patrols withdraw since their artillery observers, like the German ones, cover the river all day.

"At dawn yesterday a heavy mist covered me safely to a certain swampy sector of river front which soldiers usually avoid. I had dragged my line all the way without catching anything. I landed and had put away my canoe when I was seized by two neighbors wearing the arm band of that accursed Fifi that now blossoms on every coward and criminal in France. I do not know whether Valéry betrayed me to them or whether they had been watching me.

"One was a wretch who had cheated me in the reckoning over an asparagus patch I own. The other was a man I had discharged from the Litard plant even before the war for stealing sheet aluminum. Now both are heroes of the Resistance, though no one saw their noses when the Germans were here."

He spat as if to rid himself of the divisive poison that infected the veins of France.

"They told me they had seen me land my canoe and would keep quiet about it for certain accommodations. I defied them as extortioners. Then it occurred to them that I was worth more dead than alive. At pistol point they took me to the market detention camp and denounced me for trafficking with the enemy.

"The penalty for that is instant execution. Even so, those now claiming authority desire precautions against subsequent investigations. They spent most of yesterday trying to frighten and beat a confession out of me.

"For the sake of my family I was able to hold out against them. My accusers became nervous, fearing I would live to confront them with their vileness. Last night inquiries were made for me and my accusers easily persuaded the authorities to cover their own tracks by sending me out here. The rest you know. I swear to you that although I have broken trifling laws I have never been disloyal to France."

"Is M. Litard still in Kehl?"

"He promised to wait there till I learned more about you."

"Why did he leave his own country?"

"He feared exactly what has happened to me. The Litard plant, if you must know, has a bad odor in Strasbourg. We had to work for the Germans or be conscripted into their slave labor. Some Litard workmen were conscripted anyway and there were rumors that this was done with the secret complicity of M. Litard—to rid himself of malcontents. Conversely, it was rumored that those who remained at the plant were German sympathizers. This, of course, is a malicious lie. M. Litard is sure the Allies will win the war. But he does not dare return to France until victory has given her a government he can trust."

Hal knew he was going to do it again now and this time it was already easier. He had never imagined holding the literal power of life or death over another man.

He held it now, unless Gelan chose to exercise the same power over him.

"Would you risk taking M. Litard a message for me?"

Monet merely glanced at the whipping rack and shrugged.

"As alternative to that . . . of course."

"Elsie, will Gelan play?"

She cogitated before replying slowly: "I'm not sure. Petty men with power can be very sticky. But we've got to try."

"Yes."

Their first bad moment came right outside the door. The waiting guards had been instructed not to let the prisoner pass them. To leave him while they spoke to Gelan would probably be to find him dead upon their return, even if they got back. Hal listened patiently to their explanations and then drew a notebook from his pocket.

"I must have the names and next of kin of men who defy the American Army," he said quietly.

Both men would have resisted weapons with their lives. The appearance of paper and pencil was too much for them. They wavered, argued and then brightened at his suggestion that they accompany him to the office of the Commandant.

"France gave the world the expression, 'red tape,' " whispered Elsie.

He had the impression upon entering the office that Antoine had reached a precarious accord with his pompous host. Their arrival with the white-faced Monet and the troubled guards shattered it. Gelan was so furious at the sight of his victim without handcuffs that Hal's demand for Monet's custody was lost in his first outburst.

Gelan would remind his allies that they stood upon the sovereign and sacred soil of France itself. Let them remember that! As Commandant he was entrusted to preserve the honor, the dignity and the internal security of the nation. M. Gelan was answerable to a committee, the committee was answerable to the French Army, the French Army was answerable to its government, or would be when a government had been formed to safeguard the eternal rights . . .

"Shut up!" said Hal.

Gelan blinked as Hal turned to Elsie.

"Tell him the only thing that took France out of slavery was British and American soldiers. Monet can save the lives of some of them and he's going with me, right now."

Gelan blinked at her crisp accents, glared at Antoine and Monet and after a long pull at his upper lip fished in a drawer, drew out pencil and paper, and wrote furiously. He then passed the page to Elsie with an angry blast of French.

"It's a document accepting responsibility for you to sign, Hal."

"If Colonel Graves confirms your authority this will not harm you, Major," said Gelan.

Hal signed with a steady hand, thanked the Commandant coldly, and then in French ordered Monet to come with him to the jeep. Though his release had certainly saved him from being beaten to death, Monet now looked so fearfully at Antoine's arm band that Hal wondered if he would obey. At a further command he did. Hal turned his back on the Commandant and, with hackles rising, ushered the ex-foreman, Elsie and Antoine out of the door ahead of him. Once outside

Monet took another cringing glance at Antoine's arm band, and then, jumping into the jeep, crouched as far from his bulky companion as possible. He spoke not a single word on the cold drive back to town.

Antoine had become an embarrassment. He preserved his own thoughts and feelings in icy silence. It was evident that Monet was in mortal terror of him, and Hal had promised to hold his confession secret. Driving first to the hotel he told Gustav that he and Mademoiselle would take Monet home alone. The hotelman acceded readily. Then after alighting from the jeep he tugged Hal's sleeve and led him out of earshot.

"Gelan is angry and afraid, Major."

"We did him no injury."

"Anger and pride make dangerous enemies. He will report this at once to Colonel Graves."

"Let him."

"Without the Colonel's support this could be grave for me."

It was both true and perceptive. Intuitively Antoine had understood Hal's uncertainty about the support of Graves. For him and Elsie trouble with Graves could be resolved by investigation. For Antoine it might not.

"I shall report it to Colonel Graves myself."

"I was hoping so; may one offer a comment, Major?"

"Always, at any time."

"Monet has certainly been abused by Sunday patriots. In itself that is not proof of innocence."

"Innocent or not, we need him. We are grateful to you."

"If Colonel Graves shares your gratitude, Major, we could use some weapons. M. Gelan could be a formidable adversary."

"I'll do my best to get you some."

On the way to Monet's he told Elsie in low-voiced English of the conversation.

"What if Graves won't play? What if he orders you to give this wretched man back to them?"

"I'm getting him started before I tell Graves."

Their arrival at the Monets was a resurrection. The windows were still shrouded with blackout curtains in full daylight. He had not stopped the jeep motor before Madame burst from the door crying with incoherent relief. When she had ascertained that her husband was not injured, her embraces extended to Hal and Elsie. Leading them all into the house she produced a trembling little boy and girl from the back room and then returned again with an infant in her arms for another hysteria of hugs and kisses.

Monet made light of his troubles, reassured them all that he was truly safe now, and then got out a bottle of unlabeled wine and the most ornate glasses in the cabinet. At a curt word his wife vanished with the children and he addressed himself submissively to Hal.

"I am at your service, Major."

Monet was certain that Litard spoke English. Hal wrote him a simple note, regretting that they could not meet in person and explaining that the bearer would present some questions. The British and American Press looked forward to the day when circumstances would permit appropriate expression of their gratitude for his answers. He enclosed the note in a copy of his orders for further validation of their cover and then, with Elsie's help in translation, spent half an hour coaching Monet on the questions.

When they considered the ex-foreman letter perfect, they reviewed their plans. Monet was certain of his present safety. Every pair of eyes within a mile would have witnessed his return to his own house under the sponsorship of Allied officers in their own jeep. The fact itself forestalled further persecution by his neighbors.

"More likely those two are hiding themselves," he said.

"What about your canoe?"

"They would have been too crafty to steal it until my death."

Even if they had, he continued, he knew where Litard kept another one hidden, and he would use that. He would set the signal ladder and lantern on the factory balcony by the last of the afternoon light and depart as soon as he judged it safe. His return would depend in some measure upon the wishes of Litard and, after that, upon favorable crossing conditions.

"It may be two or three days but you can trust me, Major."

Hal and Elsie made a conspicuous operation of carrying a windfall of rations into the Monet house, so that the whole neighborhood could witness his new eminence. The return drive to town was the first time they had been alone since he had awakened her before dawn.

"Tired?"

"Exhilarated. This is progress, Hal."

"Will he deliver our message?"

"Of course. You saw him with that family."

"It bugs me. First we make him talk under threat of returning him to torture. Now we're capitalizing on his hostages to fortune."

"Field Intelligence can be very dirty work," said Elsie. "You said it all when you told that Commandant it was for our troops."

"Yes. I'm going out to see Graves now."

"Will you need me?"

"No. Want to rest?"

"Of course not. I want to try that post office."

They had reached the center of town again and the bright sunlight had filled squares and streets with strutting, arm-banded patriots. The warning of Antoine came back to him.

"One condition: you take Antoine or one of his men with you."

"Just to the post office?"

"Anywhere you go, from now on. I'd worry about you."

She was silent for so long that he stole a glance at her and saw that the little muscle knot along her jaw was tense again. When she did reply her voice was low and warm.

"Righto. I don't want to be a worry."

3

Colonel Graves removed his boots from the inlaid table, put down *Guns Along the Pecos* reluctantly and frowned.

"Where's the little lady, flyboy?"

"I made her swim over to Kehl to give that Kraut battery your coordinates."

"I wish you could." Graves scowled. "Those bastards haven't lit a match for a week."

"Colonel, did you signal London for me?"

"Division did, that day. I told 'em nobody but Air Corps *could* be as crazy as your story."

"We've had time for an answer."

"Check," replied Graves evenly. "I repeated your

signal red line urgent this morning. You got me wondering if I'm crazier than you are."

"Not a chance; wait till you hear what I've done."

Maintaining the pretext that his objective was a press story, he gave Graves a full account.

"You've saved yourself a lot of trouble, flyboy, by telling me first. I've had two beefs this morning about your wheeling and dealing."

Both the Commandant of the market camp and Gelan had already lodged emphatic protest against the highhandedness of the Allied press mission.

"All I had to do was warn you," concluded Graves. "Dawg if you haven't done ever' single thang I told you not to! You couldn't get out of here fast enough to hire yourself a private army and start kidnapping Frogs. Two more boxes of K ration and you'd run for king of France."

"I'll make you a field marshal," said Hal. "You can have a statue in the square and share those pigeons with Marshal Kléber."

Graves was not amused.

"Flyboy, don't overplay your hand. French brass hasn't got gumption enough to scratch its own crabs, bat team in the Army. Or at least it was the best till those

"Could you brief me on the local law?"

"The law here and now," said Colonel Graves, "is me — by virtue of the best goddamned regimental combat team in the Army. Or at least it was the best till those bastards in Shaef decided to cool me off and let those ol' boys up north catch up. When they do decide to get on with the war again and send for me, the law here is gonna be just what it is in the rest of France. It's gonna be the Fifi gang with the most guns."

"Colonel, my gang needs guns."

Graves listened patiently while Hal explained that Gustav, Marcel, Alphonse and others unknown to him had incurred suspicion and enmity in his service.

"This country lives on suspicion and enmity," said Graves.

He had seen enough of the French dilemma to understand it. He remained unshakable in the opinion that true sympathy was letting the water find its own level. He considered the French soldiers able and willing. The same commanders and politicians who had led them to disaster in 1940 were vitiating their present usefulness. The current high level squabble with Shaef was nearly a mutiny against their liberators.

"I'm not setting up any new armies, Major, and you've founded your last one; unless I get confirmation on you from London, you go back to Shaef Main, under guard, tomorrow."

"With luck I'll hear from Litard tomorrow."

"You'd better. Now just to show you there's no hard feelings I'm giving you a present to take the little lady."

He led the way to a nearby room and waved a proprietary hand. What had once been a spacious library was crowded from wall to wall with orderly tiers of wine, cognac and liqueur cases, each one heavily branded with German insignia.

"We liberated these from a Panzer Grenadier outfit that got homesick. Pick a case of what you want and Swanson will put it in your jeep."

"I pick what you want to give me, Colonel."

Graves's headshake was rueful. "You know, if I could believe a word you say, I'd like you, Major. Swanson!"

The guard with the tommy gun materialized from behind them.

"One case of brandy and one of Frogpop in the Major's jeep." said Graves.

The Colonel walked him out to the little parklike yard and they stood together looking off across plain and river to the dark scar of the Black Forest. It reminded Graves of his obsession. He spoke bitterly of the hidden battery while Hal looked at the first early stars and remembered that Monet would be crossing the Rhine soon. Then, as Swanson reported the jeep loaded, Graves's voice veiled a note of solicitude.

"Get on with your work, flyboy; fast."

"I'm trying, Colonel. Thanks for the presents."

"Puts me in mind of home." Graves chuckled. "My daddy used to be sheriff of Bexar County. He always said the part he liked best was watchin' prisoners gobble up that free chicken dinner the night before he hung 'em."

4

A starry dusk was softening the death masks of the dormers as he drove into town. Forty-eight hours ago he had found the fog-shrouded town sinister and oppressive. Tonight he reentered it with an elusive glow of expectancy.

Curfew was as rigid and silent as before. Now it seemed a proper frame for the reflection of starlight from the tranquil waters of the canal ring. The covered bridge and the ancient Vauban fortifications so invincible in their time and so futile in the age of aerial bombardment slumbered now with reposeful disdain of modern violence. The upthrusting spire of the cathedral seemed in the twilight as contemptuous of its new scars, as serene in its proclamation that men were capable of more than killing.

Antoine admitted him to the garage with a report that Mademoiselle had returned and was in their suite. Borrowing a hammer, Hal opened the two cases and gave Gustav most of the champagne and brandy, to soften the tidings that so far it seemed impossible to hold out any hope for weapons.

Even through manifest disappointment Gustav's inherent grace did not desert him. He simulated gratitude for his consolation prize and inquired gravely at what time Hal would desire the services of himself, Marcel and Alphonse next day. It made for an awkward moment. Hal wanted to be free of them, to move with Elsie alone when Monet returned. He could not simply dismiss his private army without incurring suspicion. He told Gustav that he would let him know in the morning.

As he raised his hand to the knocker on their parlor door the expectancy that had buoyed his return to town ebbed. The combustion of love could be imperceptible in its early stages. It was inexorably progressive. Once it had been exhilarating just to sit beside her in the jeep. Now the enforced intimacy of the suite could provoke a pain subtler than physical frustration.

He had had enough of sexual rebuff and compliance to recognize a deeper failure here. Ironically he had touched desire in her and felt it respond in their single, spontaneous embrace. She had drawn back not from that but from its evocation of some standard he did not satisfy.

When he finally made himself knock, her overly brisk greeting confirmed his dejection. Tonight again, she minimized confrontation by hurrying back to the fire while he locked up. At the hearth she was entrenched behind preoccupation with brandy and coffee. The very cup she proffered held him away. His chagrin took refuge in the one certainty in their relation; at work they were unified.

"What luck at the post office?"

Her eyes widened a little at his abruptness.

"That's for you to judge. Sit down."

Her report was brisk and factual. Interviews with the head of the post office and three clerks had produced long lists of forwarding addresses for departed Germans. There were no military ranks or technical titles among them. Most were undoubtedly fugitives from Allied bombing and now fugitive again. The dates of their departure testified that it was the Allied Armies that had driven them back across the Rhine to addresses covering the whole Reich.

One clerk had disclosed a more specific possibility. Shortly after the second bombing of the Litard plant a German of imposing, official appearance had approached her with an incongruously furtive manner.

He said he had been receiving personal letters at the post office through a short, official stay in the city. He was returning to Germany sooner than he had anticipated and did not wish to lose mail. He gave the girl fifty marks for her promise of special attention. She was to watch also for any mail that might be addressed to him in care of the Litard plant. He wanted all letters for Hermann Loeder sent to the post office at Gustel in Bavaria.

"Post office, you're sure, Elsie?"

"I noticed especially. It seems to rule out a return to normal residence or office."

He nodded agreement and then shook a rueful head. Human memory could not hold all the gen. Messerschmitt had had an engineer named Loeder, who, like many another, had had a contention with Marshal Milch. Hal seemed to recall that it had resulted in a transfer from Augsburg to some other post. He was certain that he would have remembered any recent mention of the enigmatic Strasbourg. And without a refreshing look at the files in London he could not put his tongue to Loeder's first name.

There had been no significant gen on Gustel. It was a town on the Danube, notable only for a spa, hospital and sanitarium. Prior to the war it had nurtured no important industry. A small commercial airport had been its only original reason for a card index in the gen. After the German attack on Russia its runways had been extended so that the heaviest transports could fly wounded to the hospital, now similarly expanded for Wehrmacht use.

"The recce photos bristle with red crosses on the roof."

"They'd enjoy making planes under those," said Elsie.

"They would. When we're in touch I'll signal Joe Collet to lay on fresh recce of Gustel."

Absorption in work had eased the tension he had brought into the room. Her sharp glance revived it.

"Hasn't Graves had a reply from London yet?"

"No. And I can't help it."

"You needn't be so cross!" Her face flamed and then, with visible effort, she made her voice conciliatory. "I didn't mean it critically, truly I didn't. Can't you tell me more?"

It was not her fault and it would not be her fault if Graves did send them back on the morrow. He ought to be relieved to be coming to the end of this, but he was not. Suppressing his irritation now, he repeated to her the gist of his interview with Graves.

"Would he really send us back?"

"He might; if I told him the truth and told him how close we are to being done he might let us stay on."

"Stay on independent of him?"

"We're independent of him now."

He could see her stifle a retort and measure her words carefully before she spoke again.

"Would you like to send me back, at once?"

"Why?"

"To open up this signal block. I could."

"It's not that important."

"It could be," she persisted patiently. "It could be crucial. I'm no real use to you here. Until this morning I thought you needed me. You don't need anyone; you're doing wonderfully. Without the Pourvalles I'm worse than useless. I'm a burden and a worry to you . . ."

"Elsie! Will you stop taking things personally?"

"We're in a very personal business." She shook her head slowly. "You heard Antoine this morning. I think he's jealous of our obvious interest in Francois Monet, but it could be dangerous . . . and doubly so if Graves disavows us. If you send me back you could move in with your own troops and be safe . . ."

"Do you want to go home?"

She hesitated, ever so briefly: "I want to do whatever's best for our mission."

"Then stop talking nonsense! We were sent together and we're stuck together, till we're done. After that you'll never have to see me again!"

Springing to his feet he put down his cup and turning quickly from her white, set face went out their parlor door. In the gloomy chill of the corridor he stood very still, ashamed and appalled. This was worse than he had realized and going back to their suite would not rectify it.

With a conscious effort now to immerse himself again in work he made his way down to the kitchen and Antoine. If their host was disaffected it could be dangerous.

He could see no sign of it in the bland, familiar courtesy of their greeting. At his invitation to join in the sampling of some of Graves's largesse the hotelman demurred. In the Hotel Gustav his honored ally would drink the brandy of his host. In a few minutes Elsie came down the stairs and, at his quick invitation, sat down with them as calmly as if she and Hal had never spoken a personal word.

When the announcement of dinner threatened to isolate them again in the deserted dining room, Hal insisted that Antoine and Madame Cassandra come to their table for some of Graves's wine. Elsie seconded the invitation warmly and, after a noticeable hesitation, Antoine accepted. As the cork popped Madame rose to the festivity of the occasion:

"Perhaps it is not poisoned after all."

"Peace, woman! Would you spoil their dinner?"

"Better their dinner than their lives."

Once the issue was raised Antoine had to resolve it. A little sheepishly he confided that while he appreciated the generosity of Hal's present, its intrinsic worth was problematical. Honest Frenchmen considered it a moral obligation to sell the Wehrmacht mess officers the worst fluids that could be rebottled under pretentious labels. Savage reprisals had stamped out the use of actual poisons. Premium prices for execrable wine and brandy had consoled the Gallic spirit.

"One regrets only that the pigs never even knew they were being cheated."

Beneath her unalterable morbidity, Madame was sensitive to atmosphere. Now, with a casual glance at Hal and Elsie, she inquired politely about their day and then took over the conversation for her own reminiscences of the bombings of Strasbourg.

The inhabitants had not even bothered to go to shelter for the first attack. They had become used to seeing American daylight bombers pass their city en route to the Reich. They enjoyed applauding the sight before their German occupants. So on this day streets had been full. Other approving spectators had gone out onto balconies and opened windows to cheer when the lethal cascade began.

"Arms blown to different sides of the paving, legs and shoes flying through windows, intestines hanging from telephone wires like ribbons! A friend of ours was walking her little daughter in a pram. She looked down on the coverlet and *pouf!* a human ear. Unhappily it was French."

By the time of the next attack new regulations had only compounded the casualties. The Germans had ordered all residents within walking distance of the station to take shelter there. The immense square before that edifice was full of hurrying fugitives when an eccentric stick of bombs penetrated beneath the heavy cobblestones so that the explosion threw them around like projectiles.

"Many Germans were killed, too," Madame smiled.

Antoine took over the conversation now with an inflection as innocent as his words were pointed.

"Most of us were consoled for our losses by the destruction at the Litard plant. The bomb aiming was of an excellence and loyal Frenchmen shed no tears over the misfortunes of M. Litard. Nevertheless, blameless people near there were killed and bereaved. There are parts of Strasbourg where it would be hazardous for M. le Major and Mademoiselle to find themselves without resolute friends."

When they had regained the privacy of their parlor, he faced Elsie and spoke firmly.

"I'm sorry . . . and ashamed."

"I don't mind about myself but . . . distractions are no good in this business, Hal."

"The distractions exists. Will you tell me about him?"

"Oh. Is it as transparent as that?"

"It might not be to others. I'm in love with you."

She flushed crimson and then gathered herself and pointed to the chairs before the fire.

"Will you sit over there, away from me, please?"

5

I FIRST began going into France," Elsie told him, "for the Free French. I'd known some of them through Daddy and the business and many more from the time I spent translating for their missions in London before France fell. Even before the collapse they were operating in almost total discord; after there was Satan's own dispute night and day about who were official and who were truly patriotic and who were moutons or collaborators.

"Anyway the top factions of that time in London trusted me. I never parachuted but I went over in some of the very first planes that took them guns and grenades. We had landing strips near Le Mans and at Rennes and other places, too, and I rode with the supplies and carried messages. I could pass for a French woman anywhere and it was much easier for a female to get about in trains and busses. The Gestapo was always on the lookout for men traveling without explicit purposes and papers; at that time they didn't bother women so much.

"I was provided with a personality and a cover and papers and contacts, and I never had any trouble. I was really just a courier. I'd sit around London translating for two or three weeks at a time, and then when important papers were ready I'd whisk over by plane at night, hide in a farm till we were sure it was all right, and then catch a train and take the packet into Paris. Usually there was another packet or answers to pick up. I'd stay in a Paris hotel till these were ready and then go back out to the country and lie around a barn, or even stay in a house for a night or two until the pick-up plane came back.

"It was exhilarating. It made me feel useful and, I'm afraid, a little superior. When I passed Germans in the streets of Paris or sat with them in train compartments I used to think of a silly old song, '. . . if you knew what I know . . .' It was a game, at first, an exciting game.

"In those days I didn't even know that Imrie or his shop existed. The fact was that he already had his own people among the Free French. They noticed that I was lucky. One of Imrie's British men came to my flat in London and asked if I'd pick up some papers in Paris on my next trip over, without telling the Fifi.

"The man already knew everything there was to know about me and what I was doing. It scared me a little to realize how deeply we'd been penetrated. I knew enough to ask him for proof that he *was* official and I got it at once. This was a lot deeper water than just helping to determine which Fifi in Paris could give orders to which ones in Seine et Oise and who got the most francs. As soon as I was sure it was pukka I accepted.

"Imrie's bods were so deep in the Fifi that they could control my movements without even seeming to do it; they could make up reasons for sending me on strictly Fifi business. The very next time I went over I took a load of francs for a cell in Marly. In my head only was the address of the Griffon and Satyr Bookshop in a little alley off the Rue du Bac between the Université and the Boulevard St. Germain.

"Its owner was a young man named Robin DeLand who had a French father and a British mother from a family in Cambridgeshire. He had studied at Cambridge and taken a diploma in agriculture. His mother's people had land that he intended one day to farm.

"He'd done his French military service in their air force, completing his cadetship finally with the rank equivalent to our pilot officer. Then on a leave to England some time before the war, he had most of his left foot blown off in a grouse shooting accident.

"That ripped it for regular service. I'm not sure whether Imrie's people hadn't already found him before that. Robin was wizard with languages and a cousin of his father's already owned the bookshop. Robin was moved into it before Munich and converted the place into a double front. The cover business fitted the Left Bank locale. It was already well established in belles lettres, avant-garde poetry, translations and prints; precious things, really for students and intellectuals.

"As such it would have attracted Nazi attention for potential Communist sympathies. Imrie's people turned that hazard to use. The precious merchandise became a front for sub rosa business in pornographic books and pictures and porcelain figurines. It was above the grosser levels of the street corner postcard vendors. Robin used to say the only real difference was that his wares were gamier. They had aesthetic and cultural pretensions for the elite of psychopathology. He said that some of his items would have made Leda and the swan blush.

"Imrie had foreseen an insatiable appetite for such things among the Nazis. The place was pretentious enough for the highest ranks of both Army and party.

It fitted their preconceptions of French decadence and it supplied their own wants. Illegality gave it the final cachet. The Germans flocked to it and sent their friends. There was even a secret password of introduction about which Robin was severe. It was more than safe; it was fashionable for highly placed Germans to be seen there. Some of those were working for Imrie, even then.

"The normal flow of mail and merchandise made it ideal for handling letters, documents and even blueprints in the safest way, which is always the open postal system. The impediment was getting gen from Robin's to England. I became one of the people who did that.

"I never learned the full scope of what went on in the shop. I only set foot in the place once and that started us off with a quarrel. I went there, as ordered, with a coded introductory speech, and Robin was furious. He said my orders were suicidal; I should have telephoned him for a meeting at some other place. They were orders of course and it made me mad, too. He finally agreed that it wasn't my fault but he made me take back a blistering message to Imrie.

"Robin made me swear that I'd never go near the shop again. The Gestapo always kept an eye on it. For the most part it was an indulgent eye. Their higher ups liked those pictures of the Empress and the Shetland ponies too, and they had orders not to bother him. But he said the German Counterintelligence was well trained and my face was easy to remember.

"Later, he admitted that he didn't want me near the shop for another reason. The Germans regarded the women who frequented it as fair game. They never bothered Sorbonne girls straying in after a copy of Rimbaud. They assumed that mature women who came there understood the atmosphere and were on the look-out for their own kind. Robin said the assumption was usually correct.

"Keeping me out of there was sound, elementary precaution. Robin had more personal reasons. I didn't even learn about pornography until much later. Robin was cringing with shame about it. His brain accepted the value of what he was doing. He'd even accepted the fact that he was so hot they were sure to get him if the war lasted long enough. The cerebral part of him, the disciplined part, could leer and giggle with bona fide customers in the back room. The emotional part of him was one seething revulsion.

" 'It's like pimping,' he told me once.

"Sometimes I think he fell in love with me as a protest, because I wasn't German or depraved, and then of course there was his British blood. He'd been brought up almost as much in England as in France. He was desperately homesick. He used to question me for every detail about the bombings and the rationing and coupons and blackout. And of course he was just one living ache about his foot.

"He was always after me to see if I couldn't get Imrie to bring him over and let him fly in one of the R.A.F.'s international squadrons. He said that if Bader could do it with no legs at all, he could manage beautifully. He had most of the use of that leg and he did all sorts of regular exercises to keep himself fit. He limped, of course, even with a cane and he couldn't run. Otherwise he was as strong and fit as a man can be. I did speak to Imrie for him and I got a savage wigging. Imrie said he was uniquely valuable where he was.

"To see the way he looked up, even at German

planes over Paris, was enough to make you want to cry. Twice we heard our own bombers going out in the dusk. And once we saw a whole flight of Fortresses going home across Paris after a trip to Germany. Robin was so chagrined he couldn't speak for an hour.

"In all I made nine trips to him. On the fifth one we were lunching at a brasserie in the Place St. Michel and he suddenly said:

" 'After the war, will you marry me?'

"I said: 'Yes; or this afternoon, if you like.'

"He said that he would like and it was out of the question. I was due to start back immediately after lunch. We almost always met in bistros or restaurants because there were papers to pass and it's safer with a table and napkins for screening. When I brought the papers he insisted on receiving them as soon as possible so that I'd be clean if we were picked up. When he brought them he wouldn't give them to me until the last minute. Then I'd go into the women's room till he'd had time to get away from the place.

"That day we both knew I could perfectly well have stayed over in Paris. I was going to have to wait at least two days for a pick-up in Le Mans. He would not hear of it. He said we couldn't get married in Paris without being seen together and probably getting into official records. It was too much of a risk and, for that matter, he was a bad risk as a husband until after the war.

" 'Then why did you ask me now?'

" 'Because I won't see you again until peace.'

" 'Are you going somewhere . . . worse?'

"I shouldn't even have asked that. I was suddenly paralyzed with fright. Robin had been to Berlin more than once on the pretext of taking selected things from his stock to very high personages. It occurred to me that he might even be intending to open a branch store in Germany. There was nothing he would shrink from doing.

" 'I'm having you taken off this run; too dangerous.'

" 'Imrie wouldn't do such a thing,' I said.

" 'He will, if I tell him you're affecting my judgment,' said Robin.

"That was where my mistake began, Hal. I thought he was just being masculine and bossy. I told him it was as much my war as his. If I didn't do it some other bod would have to. I said if he really loved me he wouldn't force me into the position of quitting. He said any talk about love was frivolous. Then, of course, I had him because he'd never said anything about having me switched before he fell in love with me.

"He protested that I was particularly vulnerable because sooner or later the Fifi would realize I was frying other fish besides theirs on my trips to Paris. We both knew the Fifi record, and good as some of it was there only has to be one leak. I told him that if I was transferred someone else would just have to take my place and I would volunteer for something chancier, if they had it.

"So I had my way about staying on the Paris run. I didn't have it about anything else. Robin absolutely refused to marry me until after the war. I didn't care about the formality of it. I loved him and I wanted to do everything I could for him. I told him so and he refused that, too. An affair, even an extra hour or so together, violated the rule about our not seeing any more of each other than was essential. He would not violate it.

"The droll part of it was that our cover story—the one to cover a joint capture if they got us together—was a clandestine love affair. I had a personal cover so good that I can't even tell you what it was. They passed it on to my successor and it never was broken. It's in use right now, and not in France.

"So there we were, posing as lovers in Paris and both of us wanting desperately to make it true. Robin still refused to meet me anywhere except in public places. The reason he lasted so long was that he always assumed he was being tailed. Any unnecessary meeting would have jeopardized the whole operation as well as ourselves. No woman alive ever had a stricter chaperone than the rules made for me.

"He got me a beautiful ring which I could at least wear in England. And he gave me a letter to his parents in Cambridgeshire, and made me promise to deliver it if anything happened to him. We both felt I shouldn't go near them while I was on the Paris run, just in case the Germans did have someone among our people who could put two and two together.

"For the rest of it there was nothing we could do except meet for lunch. Usually it was only once a trip. Sometimes he could make me wait over for something coming imminently, and then we could have a second lunch. He would never cheat on that though, and sometime I'd be sitting around farms or barns out in the country for two or three days I might just as well have spent with him.

"Mostly we talked about after the war. He had all sorts of plans. Even before the buzz bombs and rockets he said modern technology had made England indefensible. He thought our best hope was a kind of peaceful, disarming balance of trade and development of our agriculture. He thought a great deal could be done with that, in more or less the Scandinavian pattern. He said it was criminal of us to have ignored it so long for other things, and he was very keen to make his family land a kind of test tube to show the rest of the country what could be done.

"He'd never speak a syllable about the war itself that he didn't have to. Only part of that was security. He was like you in that silly masculine feeling of guilt because he wasn't in the front line or up in a plane. In fact he was like you about everything, inside.

"We had three more perfect lunches together, and right up to the end, the last one was the best of all. That day we had some new hope and he was on fire with it. He would never tell me a detail he didn't have to, but he did say that if the new thing worked out, it could all be over very soon.

"I didn't learn until afterward that he was right. There was a plot against Hitler himself that had begun right after Stalingrad, a year and a half before the Witzleben one last July. A lot of the very top Germans were almost ready. They were insistent upon finding out first how soon the Allies could land troops to support them. Robin knew a great deal about it and the papers he gave me that day were negotiations.

"I should have known from his inner excitement that the new risk of whatever we were up to was proportionate. I'm ashamed to say that by then my mind was more on Robin than on the work. Instead of being cheered by his hope I was dejected and I nattered him. I was tired of giving him a casual kiss and walking out of the room. I told him that even if we couldn't be married I wanted to stay on with him, overnight. He only shook his head.

"'There's a good chance we can be married in a month.'

"We were in a place that was new to me, a modest

little restaurant in one of the streets just off the Champs Elysées. I wanted him to walk down the Champs with me after lunch and he wouldn't even do that. He said the day's stuff was so hot that we were going to receive it right there, so that it wouldn't even have to go into the bookshop.

"Presently another man came in and, seeing Robin, came straight over and sat down with us for a moment. He was clumsy, too. I saw the envelope pass, although I'm pretty sure the waiter did not. The man pretended to be an old friend of Robin's who had just blundered into him there. Robin introduced me under my cover name and made the usual pretense of offering the man an aperitif. He declined, saying he was waiting for someone else and went into the bar.

"The instant he did Robin asked for our bill. He gave the waiter a big enough note to require a lot of change. When the man had gone Robin slipped me the envelope and I got it into my shirt front without any difficulty. I was gathering up my bag and gloves as usual when I heard the door open behind me and saw Robin stiffen.

" 'It's going to rain, Elsie.'

"We'd rehearsed it all very early on. For a second I was too petrified to move. Then two men moved from the doorway into my view. They might as well have been wearing Gestapo badges. They had on porkpie hats and had their hands in the pockets of their trench coats, and they were looking the whole room over, a little uncertainly. Then one of them began to focus on us, and Robin spoke just a trifle more urgently.

" 'It's going to rain very soon.'

"Then, in spite of all my training, I said: 'No. I want to stay with you, no matter what.'

"I was pretending to myself that it would be just a

casual pick-up and inquiry; that my cover plan could help him. The only firm idea in my head was not to leave him. He looked at me just once, and then the one who was looking started for us. Robin sprang up and ran, limping for the front door. He got to it because they had to dodge around other tables, and they both plunged out the door after him.

"I'm not sure how soon my senses returned. I knew he hadn't an earthly of running away from them. He'd made that fuss only to clear me. My first thought was to go into the loo and get rid of the envelope and then try to help him. That was useless. They might not really have anything on him. If they came back, or if there were more of them, and they got the papers it was high jump for him as well as for me. I got up as slowly as I could and walked back toward the women's and then kept on going, right out through the kitchen with all the help staring as if I were crazy.

"He always chose places with an open alley behind the kitchen. I ran up it, listening for shots and there weren't any, and I knew then that they had him alive. I always carried in my mind the name of another hotel to which I'd never gone. He didn't even know it so they couldn't get it out of him, no matter what they did. I went to it and said the right words, and the man at the desk took me straight up to a room. I sat in that room four days, trying not to think what was happening to Robin.

"Four days was the rule. Even though he didn't know where I was he knew enough to compromise the courier planes if they broke him. They never did. Imrie found out afterwards that he was beaten to death in Fresnes prison that first evening, without ever opening his mouth. The Gestapo had picked up one of the conspirators in

Hanover late the night before. They had broken him and telephoned Paris and put them on the track of the man who had brought Robin the envelope. The whole conspiracy was snuffed out without a word of it ever coming out in public. I was carrying the names of men who were dead before I got the envelope to London.

"When the four days were over I initiated contact with the Fifi line to the courier service in the prescribed way. They thought *I* had been picked up on Fifi work. It gave me a wild surge of hope. It meant that Robin hadn't given them away. He might just have been taken in a routine dragnet. The hardest part of the whole procedure was the rule against phoning his shop or apartment. I kept it by remembering that a call to either place, then, might have been fatal to him.

"When we landed in England a car took me straight to Imrie and he told me the truth. He knew it from another source that had a line right into Fresnes. They'd offered any amount of money and even a choice of the Germans we had, for Robin. Because this was a conspiracy against the Führer himself even the people Imrie half controlled didn't dare play.

"Imrie couldn't have been kinder. Since those two men had seen me with Robin, it was out of the question for me to go into Occupied France again. Imrie put me on his own staff and ever since I've just been doing coaching and teaching. He promised he'd give me the first possible thing that turned up. This was it."

"Are you still in love with him, Elsie?"

The muscle knot along her jaw had vanished in the weary pain of the recital. It ridged up again at the question.

"I don't think so. But I'll always think I killed him."

"That's morbid and it's not true."

"Exactly what Imrie says." She made herself smile wanly. "But if I had quit the Paris run when he wanted me to . . . or even obeyed instantly that day . . ."

"Nonsense: he was protecting that envelope as well as you."

"I've exhausted the excuses long ago, Hal. Nothing did any real good. It just had to die by itself, and I thought it had until you came along and I woke up again and it hurt, inside. I'm afraid it's made me bitchy. I wanted you to . . . to like me, quite early on . . ."

"When?" It was greedy and he couldn't help it.

"Outside Villacoublay. Instead of arguing with that pompous fool who briefed us you just waited till we'd driven away and then took off your pistol and our helmets, and I knew you were a sane man in a mad world.

"At Baccarat you *did* behave like an idiot. It was the right kind of idiot though and it stirred me up, and all I could think of was killing you, too."

"You won't. You're going to marry me."

He arose and stepped toward her, arms out. She had sprung up as swiftly, to step away from him, and now for the first time he saw fear in her.

"You mustn't even say that!"

"It's the truth. You know you feel the same way."

"At first I thought it was just propinquity." She spoke slowly, as if to herself.

"Everything has to start. Now it's for keeps."

"Not for me." The headshake was a plea. "Not yet, truly. I'm scared enough already. I have been all along. I'm scared of letting you down."

"You couldn't."

"I'm doing it right now – distracting you."

"Elsie! We're practically through here."

"Then it will keep, till you're safe in London. I'm sorry, Hal. I just couldn't stand killing you."

She hurried swiftly to her room and after a while he put out the candle and went to his own.

He could not sleep. He lay abed, tossing and turning with it until his ears caught the long rumbling approach that rose to a climactic thunder overhead and then became a receding whine. The whine in its turn was obliterated by the heavy crump of detonation. He waited through perhaps a minute of silence. Then from the direction of the crump came the sharper muzzle blast of closer artillery and he tracked the reciprocal rumble high overhead on its eastward course into Germany. Graves's men had been quick with their counter-battery.

He hurried to the window to check the blackout curtain and the angle of the glass panes. Patchy fog obscured most of the stars and intensified the foreground darkness. After a few seconds he was sure he could see the faintest of flashes far to the east before the distant detonation and rising rumble confirmed another westward, incoming shell high above him. This time the reply of Graves's battery was much quicker. Crump and answering muzzle blast were nearly simultaneous. Whether the fog had allowed them the sighting flash for which Graves pined, he could not tell.

His eyes were adjusting. He could see both the shadow and motion as Elsie came through the open connecting door. She had taken time to don the shapeless jacket and long pants. Her approach through the gloom to the faint illumination by the window was wary and tentative until she stopped close to him.

"Just the Kehl battery and Graves, isn't it?"

"Routine searching exercise, I think. An attack barrage would be down around our ears. All these are passing high."

"Will the Colonel think we did spot for them?"

"Maybe; he can't do much about it."

"He can send us back." Her gesture encompassed the suite. "That would be the end of this."

"Who cares? We'll be married all the sooner."

"You'd care, always. This target would haunt us."

"You do understand, don't you, Elsie?"

"Of course. We're both proving something."

"What did you come to prove?"

"Whether I'm alive."

"Did you doubt it?"

"A long time. That's something I'll always owe you, Hal, no matter what."

"You don't owe me anything except the rest of your life. Now go get your sleep. You're going to lose a lot of it when we're done here."

2

The phone awoke him while it was still dark. He hurried into the parlor and lifted the instrument to the hysterical accents of Madame Cassandra. Gustav had had to go out early. Now an insistent man named Monet was at the door, demanding to see Major Brett.

"Send him up at once, Madame."

"Antoine made me promise to admit no one."

"Tell Monet I'll be right down."

Hal hurried into his clothes and belted on his automatic solely to reassure Madame. He was at the parlor door when Elsie came in fully dressed except for unlaced boots.

"Where are you going without me?"

He explained and, promising to return with Monet, left her to revive the fire. Madame Cassandra with her demure little mustache offset by the fluffiest of nightcaps was wringing her hands in the lobby.

"Night is the time of murders, Major."

The shivering figure beyond the peephole in the door looked more frightened than sinister. When Hal unbolted for him Monet looked first to the rebolting. Madame Cassandra had vanished after her futile protest. Enjoining Monet to silence, Hal led him to their parlor. Elsie had the kettle on revived flames, and brandy and glasses waiting in the candlelight of the table. Monet would not speak until he had checked Hal's bolting of the parlor door.

"M. Litard came back with me."

"Where is he?"

"At my house; he didn't dare come into town."

"Drink this and I'll go right out with you."

Monet had made an uneventful crossing of the river to find Litard waiting impatiently at the house of his mistress. Litard had been deeply impressed with the note and the copy of his orders Hal had entrusted to the foreman, reading and rereading them before he would permit Monet to interrupt him further. Then at the first of the questions in which he had been coached, Monet had received only a curt head shake from his employer. This required Litard's personal attention. He would return to the French shore himself.

Monet acknowledged that he had been badly frightened. Two humble canoeists could make as good a pretense of being fishermen as one. To be caught on the French side of the Rhine with Alexandre Litard would be fatal. Litard had shown his own estimate of the situation as they set out. Displaying an automatic he declared flatly that the Fifi would never take him alive.

Litard had been perfectly aware that the battery exchanges during the night would redouble American vigilance along the French shore. He had waited calmly until the optimum moment of predawn mist had confirmed his confident prophecies of success. From the Monet house he had dispatched his reluctant foreman for the dangerous bicycle ride to the hotel with a chilly admonition. Treachery to him would place Madame Monet and the children in acute danger.

"He sounds like an endearing house guest."

Monet had caught the tone if not the English words. "He has the temper of a tiger, that one."

"I'm ready when you are, Hal."

She had laced her boots while he was downstairs. Her battle jacket bulged with underlayers of wool.

"I'm not taking you," he said.

"Why?"

He tried for an easy plausibility. This interview would be like a prisoner interrogation. Experience showed that one questioner got the best results. Respondents talked more readily in the absence of witnesses. He wished to establish a man to man accord with Litard . . .

"I'll wait outside in the jeep," she cut through it.

"I'd rather not take you at all."

"Because it's dangerous; that's why. Isn't it?"

That was exactly why; denial would only make it more obvious.

"You were right about someone knowing where I am. Antoine will be back soon. If I haven't returned in a couple of hours . . ."

"In two hours your body could be five miles down the Rhine."

"Will you turn off the melodrama?"

"When you turn off the chivalry. I came to work, too."

"I'm going to handle this alone."

"Is that an order, Major?"

"If it has to be, it is."

"Very well, sir."

She was white-lipped and silent as he led Monet out. He walked down the stairs with his guts churning. She had been right. He had let consideration of her safety influence him.

The night had put icicles on the eaves and skim ice in dirty crusts over the road puddles. To the eastward a strong dawn was showing promise of a sunny day. As they neared the river fog shrouded it with the saffron tint that foretold its early dissipation. It still reduced visibility to the few yards. He drew up to the Monet wall and hedge with the echo of Antoine's warning in his ears. He was finding himself in an obscure place without resolute friends.

Francois insisted upon preceding him into the house. Remembering Litard's admonition about the safety of Madame and the children, Hal waited by the jeep until Monet opened the door to beckon.

Hall entered the low roofed kitchen–living room to find it vacant. Monet had disappeared. An extravagant coal fire burned bravely in the hearth below a solitary candle on the mantel. He had barely realized that he was clearly silhouetted against the light before his eyes picked up the figure in the darkened inner doorway, the hand in the pocket of a short coat. The voice had an authority so firm it could afford a tincture of irony.

"You will pardon my precautions, Major. I'm unsafe here."

He turned slowly to face the voice, taking care that his open and empty hands were showing.

"You're safe from me," he replied. "Do you want to talk?"

"I have crossed the river to do so."

"Then put that gun on the mantel," said Hal.

There were perhaps three seconds of total, uncertain silence. Then Litard spat a French phrase behind him, strode briskly into the candlelight and put a German automatic on the mantel. The half bow he directed to Hal was as intentionally ironic as his inflection.

"Your servant, Alexandre Litard."

Unconsciously Hal had envisioned Litard in the dumpy corpulence and silk hat of the cartoonists' magnate. The man confronting him was tall and straight. The towering physique of a majestic natural endowment had been improved by discipline and exercise. A thick mane of dark hair had traces of silver at the temples to dignify a broad brow. The nose was firm and long with a suggestion of predator in its small hook; the jaw was bold. His skin showed the rich red of good living; the vein tracery could mean either the first signs of excess or continuing ones of a choleric disposition.

From the shadows Francois Monet now appeared diffidently, carrying two glasses and a bottle on a tray.

"A glass for yourself before you leave us," said Litard.

Francois took a third glass from the cupboard obediently. It was Litard who pulled the cork and poured with seigneurial composure.

"To Allied victory," he proposed.

Francois drained his with a nervous gulp, muttered an inaudible phrase and vanished, closing the inner door behind him. Litard nodded with absent-minded approval.

"We shall converse more easily alone. Please have a chair and tell me more of your mission for the press, Major."

The irony on "for the press" was almost derisive. Hal settled to his cover story with the near certainty that Litard knew he was lying. If so, the manufacturer was not ready for direct disclosure of his advantage. He listened with careful concentration, and when Hal stopped a blandness replaced the mockery.

"The power of your press is known to us."

"Our politicians fear it."

"One hears that it sometimes prints truth?"

"Sometimes."

"It must make for difficulties." Litard shook a sympathetic head. Whether he had forgotten his skepticism or was simply preserving a diplomatic complicity in Hal's statement was impossible to tell.

"They're not my problem. I just have to get a story."

"Surely zeal like yours is addressed to more than the gratification of press readers?"

"My zeal is to do what I'm told, M. Litard."

"Commendable, Major. But one follows even capricious orders the better for some cognizance of their purpose."

"Are you asking me what this story is for?"

"It is indispensable to confidence between us."

"We'll have Germany beaten soon," said Hal. "After that there's still Japan. My guess is that our Air Forces want the best case they can make for continuance of high priority. We know what we hurt when we bombed Renault motors or Michelin tires or ball bearings at Annecy. If we can prove that bombing your plant hurt them too, deep in Germany, it strengthens the case."

"You make a persuasive conjecture, Major."

"That's all it is." Hal grinned and took his notebook from the chair by the door and spread it open on the table. "How about some help on it?"

Litard glanced at the blank sheet and back at Hal. "The proof you desire would have a high value."

"Are you talking about money, M. Litard?"

"I am talking of survival," said Litard. "When one is alive and free, money takes care of itself. You have examined my plant. Before I give you my confidence you must understand my personal position."

"I wish to." He extended cigarettes and Litard took one with evident relish.

"Ah, America: even the small amenities. I regret that at the moment I cannot return you a better wine for this treasure."

He refilled their glasses, puffed contentedly and then began a considered instruction.

"There have been Litards in Alsace since the Roman days. My people fought with Charlemagne. We endured the German periods with unwavering faith in ultimate reunion to France. Now, as the latest of these dark periods lifts, you behold a Litard of Strasbourg seeking asylum in Germany, sneaking back to his homeland by dark in the canoe of a mechanic.

"Why is this so? I reply with one word: Communism. France did not lose this war, Major. France did not fight it. We were sabotaged, first in our factories and then betrayed in battle. I shall not bore you with the names of parties and unions. Under many guises, they had a solitary determination: to rob and to destroy their betters. Those of us whose forebears had known tumbrels and guillotines were as powerless as our poor nation was to become.

"We who tried to arm France were denounced as profiteers. When the time came to accept reality and seek salvage, the hatreds did not change; only the words. Then we became collaborators.

"When England still had its channel and you your oceans and Russia its spaces, we had to beg German permission to work for our bread. At first the firebrands who crippled my factory and a thousand others were very brave: 'We shall never work for Germans' they said.

"For whom *were* they to work? Where was I to get steel, where even coal and coke and pig iron, not to speak of chrome or molybdenum? There was only one place.

"One was tempted to let our treasonable scum absorb a little German discipline, to let them taste the joys of working for the state instead of benevolent employers. But behind the Service Travail Obligatoire, as behind everything German, was political purpose too. Remove our labor to Germany and what becomes of a French birth rate already declining? Where to find the workmen and soldiers of the future? I had to think a generation ahead for a rabble who could not foresee dinner time. When those delegations came to me next, the tune was very different: 'Open the factory! Get us work here or we shall be deported!'

"I got it. I groveled to Germans with hypocrisies about a Europe unified, under the Reich. I kept my people with their families and kept their families fed. Were they grateful? For ten minutes: until their bellies were full again and the S.T.O. lists made up of others!

"Very soon they were reviling me for intimacy with those Germans. Could one tell them that to dine with Schacht or Speer was to sniff the wine, not for bouquet but for cyanide. To go partridge shooting with Milch or Goering was to remember other guests who had not returned from German hunting parties.

"I had to do these things to get our contracts, to feed my people. It was our only future. None of us knew then that Britain would hold out; no one anticipated the attacks on Russia and Pearl Harbor. The dawn of those new hopes intensified our own troubles. With Russia and then America in the war it was evident that Germany would be beaten. Now my people became brave. Moral scruples reinforced their malevolence! To work for Germany was to work against our blood sisters of revolutionary origin. A blow at the Litard plant, at me, was a blow for the Allies.

"The Germans could no longer laugh at the decadent, inefficient French. As your bombing took hold they needed us the more. And the Germans know how to make workers work. In my plant alone we soon had Abwehr, Geheim Feld Polizei, Gestapo, Schupo, and S.D. as well as our own Deuxième Bureau and the milice of Vichy. Deportations for sabotage gave way to summary executions. I tried to protect the innocent but the Germans know how to make suspects talk. What does one plead against confessions?

"I did save some. Were the others grateful? Never! They said I was selecting victims, conspiring with the Germans to exterminate the dissidents and strengthen my postwar control. Others said I dreaded Allied victory and was already working against the universal Communism that would follow Russian triumph. They said Americans would chase the Germans across the Rhine and then tire of the game and go home again, leaving

France to join a classless Europe — after suitable blood baths!

"To you, Major, I shall confide an answer that would have been suicide then. From the moment when Allied victory became possible, I worked for it, not with the senseless sabotaging of French machinery, but by furnishing Allied Intelligence the names of German aircraft production targets. When you return to London ask your authorities if they had not a valuable source in Strasbourg."

Involuntarily Hal had started and he was sure Litard had observed it. He tried to cover by toying, with the appearance of impatience, over his unmarked notebook.

"Not sure this affects my story, M. Litard. All right to use your name if I check on it?"

"I did not dare to use my name," Litard shrugged. "I was known only to my contact as Number Eighty-three."

This time Hal was ready: he made a note, ostentatiously, and then shook his head.

"I'll check; but aren't we getting away from the story?"

"We are coming to the heart of it!" The asperity revived a shaken hope. Perhaps, after all, Litard did believe that he was only talking to a single-minded and rather stupid newsman. He was continuing vehemently.

"I, Alexandre Litard, directed your bombardment to Kassel, to Regensburg, to Leipzig, to Stuttgart, to Oschersleben, to Marienbad, to a dozen more. No doubt your Intelligence had other sources, too, but my leading part in this is of record in London, Major.

"Finally, when the progress of your Armies was inexorable, when I knew that my people would soon be protected by our allies, I advised London that my own factory here was making parts for the new Messerschmitt 262 jet plane. I told them this, knowing that I invited the bombing of my own plant. Was this collaboration, was this inhuman profiteering?"

The problem now was not to overdo it. Hal could feel himself straining for a foolish, approving grin.

"Gee, M. Litard, I'd say that was real patriotic of you. Did the bombing here really affect jets?"

"We shall come to that" – Litard was the tart master of a backward pupil now – "when you understand how it affected me. The destruction of my plant confronted the Germans with the choice of rebuilding in the path of your advancing Armies or of moving. They chose to move. The moment I could no longer employ or feed my people I became again a collaborator, tyrant, profiteer. I had to take asylum in Kehl. Do you see why I came to you?"

"Well, selfishly." Hal grinned. "I sure hope you came to help me."

"Another corpse at Natzweiler cannot help you. I must have protection."

"I'm afraid I don't get that; what kind of protection?"

"You saw what these anarchists would have done to Francois Monet. Soon these same people will be begging me for jobs again. Until then your occupying forces and the French divisions under them must guarantee my safety and the arrest of those who plot my murder."

He stopped. Hal feigned thought before chuckling ruefully.

"No press officer could promise you that, M. Litard."

Litard reached into his jacket and produced the copy of Hal's orders.

"The man who signed this can."

"For a press story?" Hal tried to look incredulous.

"For valuable information about new German targets, Major. That is why I told you of my work as Number Eighty-three."

His eyes were probing Hal's face now, probing that foolish grin behind which his mind was racing. The list of targets for which Litard had claimed personal responsibility was preposterous. Litard could have memorized them all from public news stories. Most of them had been bombed before the Eighty-three gen first appeared. But a press officer would not know that. And Litard would not be foolish enough to claim them before a man he believed to be an Intelligence officer.

"I don't mean to sound skeptical," he smiled, "but if you're such hot stuff, why aren't our Intelligence people already protecting you?"

"When I had to go to Germany it broke my connection with them. He is no longer alive. I was wondering how to restore contact when you came. Even if you do not understand the value of what I offer, your Intelligence authorities will."

Hal nodded. "I can certainly see where we might want new targets." He flipped the notebook to another blank page and tapped the pencil on the table slowly. "Anyway, I'll be glad to send 'em along to London."

"Unfortunately, Major, once this information is given, I should have no recourse against neglect or ingratitude."

"That's up to you, M. Litard." Hal flipped the notebook page again. "But I sure hope you don't mind giving me some dope for my news story."

"Before helping you in any way I must insist on protection."

It was deadlock. He had to decide, fast, whether this was empty opportunism, an enticing deception plan or jackpot. It was out of the question to promise Litard power of arrest over real or imaginary French enemies. Otherwise, the price of good targets was immaterial except as it betrayed intentions. They would be cheap at the cost of sufficient guard to allow Litard to resume life in Strasbourg. The question was how to convey this without exposing his own hand. He was pondering it when they both heard the clear knock at the door. For all his size Litard moved like a cat. By the second quick knock Hal was looking into the muzzle of that pistol.

"Is this a trap, Major?"

"No."

Gustav's heavy voice came through the door clearly.

"Major, it is Antoine; are you safe?"

"Perfectly," Hal replied. "Is Mademoiselle with you?"

"No. Only my friends."

Litard's face twitched: the pistol did not waver.

"What do you want, Antoine?"

"We want M. Litard. Can you open the door or shall we?"

"I'll open it." He spoke quietly to Litard, "Put that gun back on the mantel before someone gets hurt."

"This could be a trap!"

"If it's a trap, killing me won't help you. These are my friends. If you obey me I'll protect you."

Litard hesitated and then made himself smile.

"I have always trusted Americans."

Stepping to the mantel he placed the pistol on it.

3

Hal unlocked the door for Antoine. Exultant eyes animated the unshaven whiskers and deep fatigue lines in the hotelman's face. The fog had lifted. The morning outside the blackout curtains made Hal blink. Gustav swung the door wide, admitting the whole day before he entered to confront Litard stonily.

"The house is surrounded," he said.

"I am under the protection of Major Brett."

"Antoine, what the hell is all this about?"

"It was evident," said Gustav, "that you desired a meeting with M. Litard. So did we. You have done France a favor. I only interrupted because I was fearful of your safety. That one is without remorse."

"How long have you been outside?"

"The house has been observed since Monet canoed into Germany."

"What do you want Litard for?"

"Betraying French workmen to German slave labor. He will also be charged with advising the Allies to bomb his own factory."

"He says that was to help us, Antoine."

"A noble excuse! He offered the lives of this neighborhood to insure himself a war damage claim for a new factory! His plant was never bombed until the Germans were preparing to move it."

Litard snorted.

"Do you see why I required your promise of protection?"

"You are under the protection of France," said Gustav. "Are you done with your business, Major?"

Hal could feel Litard's eyes as he hesitated.

"Not yet, Antoine; we have much to discuss."

"You have been long enough to write a book." There was sadness in Antoine's skepticism. "Is he unresponsive?'

"He has much to remember."

"We should enjoy stimulating his memory."

"No. He wishes to offer information of strategic value."

"Let him get on with it; we shall wait."

"It may require several days to verify, Antoine."

"We shall keep him safe for you – at Natzweiler."

Litard's voice remained firm: "Major Brett, remind this anarchist that I am in the custody of the American Army."

"You are in my custody," said Antoine. "Come here."

Turning a contemptuous back on both of them, Gustav walked to the doorway. The natural force in his voice drew them after him. One piercing whistle lifted a blue-jeaned workman with a thin scarred face and a Sten gun cradled in his arm, from behind Hal's jeep. Marcel stepped forward cautiously from one side of the house, Alphonse from another. Both were covering the door with pistols. Antoine checked them where they stood with a gesture.

"The Allies will win this war without M. Litard, Major. We have to think of France.

"The German labor drafts were only in part for labor. They wished to destroy us in our seed, to leave our women barren and our cradles empty. My conscription class of 1914 called up six hundred thousand men. For the class of 1940, one war later, France could summon less than one fifth of that. What shall we have in 1965? We understand that his policy was in accordance with the German nature. M. Litard and other Frenchmen assisted them.

"Do you know why Gervais is an orphan, why he will never have brothers or sisters? His father – my son, Robert – was an engineer at the Litard factory . . ."

"He was a Communist criminal!" exclaimed Litard.

"A Catholic Communist?" Antoine snorted. "Robert was a graduate of the Institute here with honors, a valuable scientist . . ."

"He used his education to inflame workmen!"

"He used it to defend them from you . . . until you put him on a German list. Our daughter-in-law, Celeste, died of grief. They called it pneumonia but it was more. She had lost the will to live in the world of M. Litard. It is no longer his world. I regret opposing you, Major, but he is ours."

He waited, polite and implacable.

"He confirms everything I told you, Major Brett. I remind you that you agreed to protect me."

"I did, Antoine."

"He bargains cunningly, that one. In this, however, you are blameless because you are not able to protect him."

"Antoine, you have seen my orders. I speak for your allies."

"I have seen the orders, Major. With all respect I do not see the Allies. I see you and a criminal traitor in clandestine meetings. From just such meetings M. Litard always emerges with new power."

Turning, he whistled again and made an arm signal. The blue-jeaned Sten gunner stepped forward a little for clearer coverage of the doorway. Alphonse and Marcel waited until he was placed and then began a measured approach from the sides.

"Walk out alone and you will not be hurt, Major."

"No, Antoine. I have promised to protect . . ."

He stopped and the armed men before him looked quickly back over their shoulders. A jeep turned into the lane, bounced up to the gate and stopped. Swanson jumped out of it with the tommy gun in his arm.

He looked younger this morning than Hal had remembered. There were traces of adolescent fat in the rounded face under the helmet rim. Now his blue eyes surveyed the field with one panoramic sweep. They stopped on the Sten gunner. Swanson jerked a left forefinger sharply toward the ground; his right hand slowly raising the tommy gun. The Sten gunner stooped and put his Sten gun at his feet.

"Okay, Colonel," said Swanson, "the rest is just popguns."

Graves was already helping Elsie out of the jeep. Behind them the driver finished barking into a radio telephone, jumped from his side and ranged himself about ten feet from Swanson, covering the other half of the circle with an M–1. Hal could hear a long sigh from Litard.

"What's all the fire power about?" asked Graves.

"They want to arrest a man I'm interviewing," said Hal.

"Ain't that the goddamned Frog of it . . . Pardon me, Miss Vane . . ."

"Don't be absurd," snapped Elsie.

"You don't want this Frog arrested?"

"No."

Graves turned calmly to Elsie. "Tell 'em in Frog the arrest is over and everyone puts down those guns before Swanson gets nervous."

"I ain't nervous," said Swanson indignantly. "You just say which ones you want alive, sir."

"All of 'em," said Graves, "unless they act mean."

Elsie had already begun to speak in quick conciliatory tones. She was addressing herself to Antoine who continued to glare defiantly; Marcel and Alphonse slowly returned their pistols to their pathetic, homemade holsters.

"This man belongs to France, Colonel," protested Antoine.

"Not till Major Brett's done with him, he don't," said Graves. "You still want him, Brett?"

"Yes."

"Exactly my own wish." Litard moved out of the doorway confidently now. "We were discussing my hope of meeting the Colonel . . ."

"You met me," said Graves. "Shut up and do like Major Brett tells you."

Unexpectedly he turned to the apoplectic Antoine: his voice was gentle.

"Frenchy, you ain't got the cards; you better cool off."

Elsie moved quickly to Antoine with another flood of pacificatory French. Graves beckoned Hal and led him out of earshot of the others.

"Flyboy," said he, "you must have been living right. I was coming for you with handcuffs this morning when we got a signal from London. Army and Corps and Division had all three held it for query 'cause they couldn't believe it."

"What couldn't they believe?"

"Don't let it strain your hat, Air Corps; but the amount of it is we got to do what you say."

"I'll try not to bother you too much." Hal grinned.

"Orders don't never bother me, once I got 'em. Far as I'm concerned, you're the new king of France. What do you want?"

He had to struggle against lightheaded laughter before he could reorient his mind. His first request was immunity for Francois Monet. No one could guarantee this. Hal asked that the French liaison officer assigned to Graves's division should explain it as a firm Allied order to the market camp, to Gelan of Natzweiler and to whoever might be in charge of the local committee of cells.

"Just write his name," said Graves. "They'll know they get clobbered for touching him. What else?"

"The same for Antoine Gustav and his gang. He's been a good friend to us, Colonel."

"The little lady said so," agreed Graves. "All I need is their names, too. Go on."

"Gustav wants to kill Litard and I'm not sure I blame him. But I've got to interrogate him some more. Can you spare me a couple of guards for him?"

"A battalion if you want 'em."

"Two's enough. I should be done with him very soon."

A final problem would remain after he and Elsie had completed their work and departed. Antoine Gustav and his men had served them loyally, right up to the surprise of this morning. They might be subject to reprisals when they were left alone. In addition to substantial presents of rations and gasoline, Hal wanted to leave the hotel-keeper and his men some modern weapons.

Graves scowled. Gas and rations were easy. Army ordnance regulations had teeth. He thought Hal's orders would bend them but not before lengthy paper fights with the red tape at Division, Corps and perhaps even Army levels.

"How about Kraut weapons for them, Brett?"

"You got any?"

"I got a weapons carrier full of side arms and light automatic stuff. We just use 'em to trade chair-borne heroes out of the dope on rear echelon whorehouses. Your one-armed chief of staff can have all he wants."

"He lost that other arm at Verdun, Colonel."

"The hell he did." Graves scrutinized Antoine with new respect. "That was a good battle. I read about it."

He led Graves over to where Elsie was still trying to placate the stony Antoine and made a formal introduction, as much for the benefit of the others as to appease Gustav. The hotelman received it with an icy dignity.

"Colonel Graves wishes to make you a present of weapons, Antoine."

The severity began to soften.

"The Colonel is very kind."

"The present is Major Brett's idea," said Graves easily. "I'd kind of like to know one thing, though, Mr. Gustav."

"I have nothing to conceal from you, Colonel."

"What do you and your friends want with weapons?"

Gustav considered. "It is our experience, Colonel, that allies come and allies go. Germans are always near."

"You don't expect 'em back with *me* here do you?"

"From Germans one expects only the worst."

"Well I'll be dawg," said Colonel Graves. "I'll make a deal with you, Mr. Gustav. You get them Krauts back on this side of the river where I can get at 'em and I'll give you a battery of 155s."

Hal outlined the steps that would be taken to protect Francois Monet and explained that they would be extended to enjoin a similar immunity from local persecution for Antoine and the men he chose to list.

"You are thoughtful, Major. I cannot pretend to condone this interference in French affairs. One tries to remember that you did, after all, liberate us. Mademoiselle has told me that you consider Litard's life of value. It will be safe from me. I should advise a close guard over him."

"May I have your permission to take him to the hotel?"

"You do not need my permission."

"I should not take him there without it."

"Forgive me." The face melted now. "Permission is yours."

"You come with me, Frenchy," said Graves. "Dawg if I don't give you enough fire power to take Berlin."

An incongruous accord was already astir between Graves and Antoine. Litard was watching it with anger and with envy. He was not used to being excluded from councils. Now he came forward again with bold confidence.

"May I thank the Colonel for saving my life?"

Hal had no way of knowing how much Elsie might have told Graves on the way out. It didn't matter. There was intuition under that placid exterior. Graves regarded Litard calmly.

"It's too soon, Mr. Litard. You just obey Major Brett."

Turning pointedly from the manufacturer's angry flush, Graves addressed himself to details. His jeep would follow Hal's to town. He would radio for guards to be awaiting Hal's instructions there. Then he clapped Antoine familiarly on the shoulder.

"You come with me, Frenchy."

Wondering faces had begun to show in the neighboring windows and through the gaps in the hedge. Monet came forward to Hal diffidently.

"If the Major would shake hands with me so my enemies can see it before he goes . . ."

Hal did it warmly and told him of the precautions that would be taken for his safety. Then, measuring his words, he turned to the now uneasy Litard:

"Have you anything further to say to me?"

"I have *everything* to say!" That aplomb was shaken.

"Get in my jeep" – he indicated it – "we'll talk in town."

A backward glance showed Hal that the first turn of their wheels had broken a dam of restraint. Now from every door and gate in the neighborhood people thronged to the yard in which Francois Monet was holding court.

6

LITARD's presence in the jeep precluded conversation between Hal and Elsie on the drive into town. Graves had hurried past them once they entered the city. They drove into the courtyard to find that his radio had done its work. Two stalwart privates with carbines and grenades clipped to their jackets came to smart attention as Hal alighted.

"Good ol' boys," said Graves. "Jim Hogg."

"Not me, sir, rightly," said the taller. "That was just my mother's kin. I'm really Webb."

"Webb's a good county," said Graves. "You boys just do like the Major tells you, hear?"

"Yes, *sir*!" They were eying Litard hopefully.

Antoine emerged from the hotel to inform Hal that Madame would give him the key to a room for their new guest. He had given orders that Litard was not to be disturbed under his roof. He himself would be absent for a little while.

"The Colonel desires my help for the selection of our weapons."

With the guards flanking Litard casually, Hal walked him past the desk and received a key among clucks of angry disapproval from Madame. The room reserved for Litard was on the same floor as their suite, and it amused

Hal to observe that the Gustavs had chosen the meanest quarters in their place. The narrow little cubicle was severe enough for a cell. Its solitary window gave on a blank wall. Four by Four with a dust cap on her head and an unused rag in her hand squeezed herself out the door to glare at them.

"Are we now a jail, Major?"

"Yes. You are not to trouble M. Litard or even speak to him, Gabrielle."

"Alors! Who in all Strasbourg would speak to that one? As for trouble . . ." She paused for a long and speculative look at the broad shouldered guards: "Do those little ones speak French?"

"I'm sure they don't."

"How uncivilized! And such brave lads! Pray tell them I have never been afraid of soldiers, Major."

She laughed and sauntered down the hall with a hopeful jiggle of her vast rump.

He ushered Litard ahead of him into the room and reclaimed the wandering attention of the guards with a strict order. M. Litard was neither to receive guests nor to leave the room without explicit permission from himself.

"Does he savvy this or do we learn him, sir?"

"He'll savvy it before I leave," said Hal.

Inside he found Litard glaring indignantly at the meagerness of his surroundings. Hal repeated the orders that had been issued for his protection.

"You are not a prisoner, M. Litard. It's for your own safety."

"I thank you, Major. But are we not to talk?"

"I'll be back soon."

A drawn Elsie was waiting at the door of their parlor.

"I *am* sorry. You were right this morning."

"Luck." He shook a rueful head. "Anyway, now we know what Antoine wanted out of us. How blind can I be?"

"Me too; it *was* right in our faces. I didn't have a clue about his wanting Litard. When Graves came I took him out there just because I was worried about you."

"That's progress." He smiled. "But you've a long way to go. A good wife would have had breakfast ready. I'm starved."

She flushed and her eyes were soft. "Success *does* make you cheeky." Then, swiftly: "We're not done yet."

"We're close. Feed me and I'll tell you about it."

Over coffee and K ration he told her the morning's disclosure and watched her inner elation fade.

"Do you believe it, about Antoine's son?"

"Yes. Don't you?"

"I do. How can you credit anything Litard says?"

"That's the crux of it. I want your judgment on this."

Taking their notebooks and extra chairs they went down the hall to Litard's room. His eyebrows raised at the sight of Elsie. Hal had not bothered to introduce them at the Monets'. Now he explained that she was a colleague from the Ministry of Information. Litard bowed a tacit acceptance.

"May I ask what you propose to do with me?"

"That will depend on how much you help us. I'm after a news story and we'll do that first."

"What do you wish to know, Major?"

"Begin with what your plant did for the Germans, from the first."

"My first contract," said Litard, "was for rebabbitting main bearings on Gnome Rhone engines . . ."

Elsie's pencil was moving as briskly as his own. He had let himself in for the old cold trail of the past deliberately. It sustained their cover. It would excuse any subsequent slip up of his own knowledge of Strasbourg-Litard and it gave him check points on the veracity of this account.

For an hour the manufacturer wove an ingenious fabric of truth and insinuation. The truth was credible technical information; it carried a persistent intimation that Number Eighty-three had determined the policies of Allied bombardment. Litard's knowledge of targets, dates and attacks was accurate. Any student of the press could have duplicated it. Every manufacturer of aircraft in Europe must have had that list burned into his memory as he awaited his turn.

The insinuation encouraged Hal. If Litard suspected his connection with Intelligence he would scarcely have risked such effrontery. His fingers tightened on his pencil as they came to the subject of jets.

". . . a newsman must understand German industrial planning, Major. Your bombing had almost extinguished piston plane manufacture on the eve of the Allied invasion and the Russian summer offensive. Speer's countermeasures for jet production had the highest priority of men, materiel and security in the Reich.

"Unmarked boxes were loaded into unmarked trucks in our yard. Security officers rode with every shipment. Drivers were changed, sometimes twice, in the same Luftgau. Returning trucks had had their speedometers disconnected.

"When I began making jet exhausts, I was allowed to see blueprints and prototype only to facilitate retooling. I was told a transparent lie about their being parts for the new V weapons. Only by acquiescence could I hope to learn, and report, the crucial new targets. Do Americans use the expression: 'to kill the goose that lays the golden egg'?"

"Sure," said Hal. "We use that one."

"For this I did not risk premature report or sabotage. In the Messerschmitt company I knew very well a certain engineer named Hermann Loeder . . ."

"Would you spell that please?" asked Elsie calmly.

Hal did not dare look at her. She might have been covering some inadvertent reaction to the name. Litard's quick compliance gave no indication of noticing anything amiss.

"Loeder," he resumed, "was never a Nazi. He realized that Germany was losing the war and he was terrified of the inevitable reprisals. His wife and children lived near Breslau, in the path of the Russian advance.

"He had pulled every string at his disposal to have them moved but of course every bigwig in the Reich was playing that game. When he was assigned to my plant, Loeder soon intimated that he would pay a high price to have his family placed in France. The word was only a hint; both of us knew what the postwar mark would be worth. Gradually he disclosed to me that his hope was to trade strategic information for Allied gratitude.

"Either of us could have been shot for such conversations. Each of us had to wonder if the other might be a provocateur. Nevertheless we were reaching accord when, without notice, another engineer replaced Loeder at my factory, overnight. Under the pretext of sending him some wine we had bought together, I tried to get his new address. I was told that the less I spoke of Loeder, the better it would be for me.

"You may imagine my fright. If he had been arrested

and broken he would almost certainly have implicated me. It was already too late to protect myself by denouncing him first. I could hope for nothing more from Loeder. I had to think of my own life, of earning the Allied gratitude I would need. I went straight to my Intelligence contact and confirmed to him that my plant was making jet components. I was promised that I would be gratefully remembered and your bombing followed very promptly on my report.

"Within hours of it, I myself was arrested. A guard at the plant had heard a workman as deluded as that anarchist of a hotel-keeper say that I instigated the bombing for postwar reparations.

"I had a hard time to make the Germans believe such talk was Communist lies. It exposed my insecurity here, and they demanded harsh terms to give me sanctuary in Kehl when they decided to abandon Strasbourg. They knew the Allies would soon be at the Rhine. I had to agree to recross the river when they wished and bring back information on the occupying forces."

"Are you telling me you spy for the Germans?" Hal thought he made it a convincing exclamation. Elsie, quick on cue, lifted her head from the notebook to stare at Litard.

"I tell you" – Litard chuckled – "because that is what I tell them."

"Oh."

Hal made a quick note and was rewarded by a knowing smirk. Litard had not escaped the magnate's occupational hazard of complacency. He was right: he was invincible, he had prevailed over the stupid Germans.

"Well" – Hal yawned and jiggled his notebook as if restless – "did our bombing cut into their jet production?"

"Delayed it, Major. Jet production has the highest priority over there. You can assume only a brief delay."

Hal scribbled again. "At least we set 'em back. I guess there's part of a story in this."

"You sound less than satisfied."

"Good stories have to be specific, M. Litard. This one ought to say exactly where and how we hurt production in Germany. But if you don't know that, I guess it can't."

He smiled forgivingly, closed his notebook and was shuffling his feet to rise. Litard bit, angrily.

"Do you imagine I crossed that river, under machine guns, to make you a good story?"

"That's what you said."

"What I have been saying," Litard repressed his anger, "is merely prelude, to assist your comprehension. Since taking refuge in Kehl I have been able to renew contact with Hermann Loeder. I can offer your Intelligence the entire target system of jet production, as soon as we understand each other."

Elsie was still writing steadily. Hal reopened his notebook to a fresh page and, when he judged that his voice was under control, raised his eyes to Litard again.

"What is there to understand?"

"My future and that of Hermann Loeder."

"Oh, of course. You want protection for him, too?"

He was rewarded by a deepening of Litard's angry flush.

"Major Brett, your concentration on your own duties is blinding you. Your Intelligence people will understand the value of what I offer. I must insist upon being taken to them at once."

He was back to naked instinct now. The simple solution was to acquiesce, to pack Litard off at once to Shaef Forward or London and get the rest of his story there. He could see color stirring along the back of Elsie's neck and he knew that she, too, was feeling the same temptation. The strength of the desire generated its own resistance. Litard was still holding out; there was still more to learn right here. He made himself smile a little.

"M. Litard, you must think I'm crazy."

"Not at all." Litard strained for patience. "I confess I think you are excessively engrossed in your own concerns . . ."

"You're asking me to go to our Intelligence folks with a man who admits he's a German spy . . ."

"I did *not* admit it. I *told* you . . . to prove my sincerity, to secure your protection . . ."

"You have my protection, right now."

"I appreciate this. You could have let those anarchists murder me this morning. Your treatment of Francois Monet showed humanity as well as zeal. But between you and the levels that can appreciate my offer I could encounter more zeal than humanity."

"I'd be sticking my neck out." Hal smiled apologetically. "Intelligence doesn't like press officers butting in. First thing they'd ask me, is for proof. You haven't given me any . . ." He smiled again and then touched the gold leaf on his jacket. "I know a major doesn't look like much to people like you, but I worked hard to make major. I could be busted, demoted back to captain for this."

Litard's eyes quickened; he was making an effort now to keep the scorn out of them, out of his voice.

"I assure you, my proofs will be incontestable. Instead of being blamed for this you will be promoted."

Hal reopened his notebook slowly.

"I hope you're right," he said. "I'm gonna take a chance on you, M. Litard. You give me the names of those places and I'll send 'em in. The rest of it will be up to Intelligence."

Litard scrutinized him through a long silence.

"At the moment, I do not have the names."

"*What?*"

Chagrin had exploded out of his mouth before he could check it. Through the silence that followed he could have bitten off his tongue. That single outburst had destroyed his pretense of indifference, perhaps their whole cover. If Litard had been goading him to it on purpose he could not have been more successful. He was pretending not to have noticed it now.

"Herr Loeder has to protect himself, too. He is assembling our proofs. I was to have seen him today. We agreed by phone that it was more important to begin understanding with you . . ."

Hal snapped his notebook shut and rose to his feet. His guts were churning with chagrin now.

"M. Litard; how do I get rid of you?"

"Rid of me?" This consternation was genuine.

Hal continued briskly. It was out of the question for him to bother Intelligence for such empty assurances. He was grateful for Litard's help on the press story. He would guarantee his safety at the hotel through the afternoon and would ask Colonel Graves for permission to launch him from the French shore after dark without danger from the American patrols.

"Unless you prefer to stay in Strasbourg on your own," he concluded.

"No, no. Major, we must talk . . ."

"We have talked," said Hal, "and I've got a story to write. Any further questions, Elsie?"

"None; this covers it, I think." She arose, and Litard spoke from a face that was now chalky.

"Miss Vane, if the Royal Air Force Intelligence . . ."

"So sorry, M. Litard." Her voice was frosty. "Major Brett and I are in total agreement."

From the door Hal smiled at the gaping face again. "Shall I have some lunch sent up for you?"

"I shouldn't dare eat in this hotel."

"I'll send you some sealed American Army rations."

2

He took K rations and wine from Graves's present down to the guards with instructions to offer some to M. Litard and then walked back to their parlor chafing. Elsie was no longer drawn and tense. She had been re-examining her notes and as he reentered the parlor she quoted from them with crackling rage:

" '. . . it was already too late to protect myself by denouncing him first . . .' the swine!"

"Artful swine. I'm afraid I ripped our cover, Elsie."

"Who cares? You couldn't trust that man if he led you to the targets by the hand."

"We don't have to trust him."

She looked at him intently, quickly now and he could see anxiety dissipating her rage. Her voice was a little forced.

"Of course we don't. Do you realize we're through here? You won't even have to take him back to the river."

"That will depend on Graves," he evaded, and he knew that he was not deceiving her.

"He has to do whatever you say."

He went over to her and took one of her hands gently: it was limp until she caught herself for a quick responsive squeeze.

"I gave you a bad scare this morning, didn't I?"

"It was worth it. I *am* alive again, Hal. I'm going to show you . . . in London. Can we start back this afternoon?"

"We've got to wait for Loeder's proof."

"Hal! You told Litard you weren't playing."

"I'm letting him figure out how to make me. It has to be his idea."

She checked her dismay now for a good imitation of calm reason.

"Could you believe *anything* he says?"

"Most of it." He nodded. "It's pure self-interest. He's made Strasbourg too hot to hold him. Germany's a sinking ship, and he's probably worn his welcome very thin, even there. The Russians may break in before we do. He's got good reasons to help us."

"The whole thing could be a deception plan."

"Always; you can't judge that till you hear the whole thing."

"There's one very sore spot in his story."

"The discrepancy about when Loeder left here?"

"Yes. The postal clerk was definite that he came to her *after* the bombing. I didn't bother to mention it because . . . Hal, are we really going to stay on here?"

"If he plays — and I think he's going to."

"I'm afraid you did rip our cover with him."

"So am I, but what of it? We're not going into Germany. They're not going to recross the Rhine here with the whole Seventh Army praying for them to."

Her face set. Her voice was brisk now:

"Stay we do. Back in a minute."

She was halfway through the door to her room when he saw the convulsive sob shake her whole body. He hurried to the door. She pushed it shut. He forced it and entered to find her leaning against the wall, shaking soundlessly and dabbing at her eyes with a handkerchief.

"Elsie!"

"Can't a girl cry in peace?"

"My girl can't."

He took her in his arms and held her until the resistance and the tears subsided together. Slowly her head came to rest on his shoulder and her breathing became even.

"Tell me."

"I'm ashamed to; that man frightens me, Hal."

"Nothing can happen to you here."

"*Me!* Oh, you can be so obtuse!" Clenched fists struck at his shoulders and then stopped. "That's it, don't you see? You're shrewd about some things but it's not the same. You're good, inside, and he isn't. That's why the bad ones always do win; to play at all you have to be like them and – you're not."

She disengaged herself from his arms, took a step away and made herself smile.

"There! Now, do get out of here before we're both . . . silly."

He went back into the parlor and in five minutes she reentered it, composed and brisk.

"You're trying him again, soon?"

"Very. Either way I've got to arrange to get him across the river after dark."

"You'd have a better chance with him alone. The presence of a female demeans him. He's used to dominating."

"You're probably right; take it easy in here."

She shook her head. Since Hal would not need her for another interview with Litard, or for the arrangements with Graves, she wanted to check the post office again on the date of Loeder's departure. After that she intended to maneuver herself into a tête-à-tête with Cassandra.

"It's odious, planning in cold blood to probe about their son. It could be relevant, though. If we're going on with Litard we should know all we can."

"We should. Take Antoine or one of the boys though, and be home before dark."

Her face softened.

"I'll be home; I'll be waiting for you here."

Litard challenged him sharply by name before unlocking the door. Hal went in smiling and put a bottle of Graves's brandy on the table.

"Souvenir," he said. "I know you took a lot of trouble to come over here and I really do appreciate it."

He continued casually while the dark eyes searched his face. He was off now to see Graves and arrange for the safe launching of Litard as soon as it was dark. He would return in good time and go over the final plans. He was turning toward the door with a sense of failure when Litard stopped him.

"I've had another thought about all this."

"Well?"

"I have had time to consider your natural fear of losing your very impressive rank, Major . . ."

It had been an improvisation to speak of that, a hunch attuned to the man before him. Litard was just the man to understand a mean motive, to know how to exploit pettiness. He was also up to penetrating tricks. At the moment he seemed to be taking this one at face value.

". . . when the value of my information is understood, I shall be able to recommend at the very highest levels your deserved promotion to Colonel."

Hal managed a half smile and then shook his head. "They wouldn't believe either of us without proof."

"With one trip to Loeder I can bring proof."

"Tonight?"

"Impossible. It would take at least two days. I could hope to return the third night."

"What's Loeder going to want for this?"

"Protection, as I told you. I will take this copy of your orders. He will realize that I come and go under your safeguard. While I am gone you could ascertain, in principle at least, whether your superiors are interested. In two days they could have a qualified Intelligence expert here to meet us."

"I hadn't thought of that," said Hal slowly.

"You have nothing to lose, Major."

"I'd be sticking my neck out," said Hal, "and I got those two days to lose."

"You could be writing your story here. I should be bringing precisely those specific details you desire for it."

Hal counted five silently, pretending to mouth the bait, and then he nodded.

"Okay, I'll take a chance for a couple of days."

"And you will notify your Intelligence people?"

"I'll tell 'em what you claim you're offering."

"Agreed; now to planning!" M. Litard had taken charge of his backward pupil again.

Hal would return to the Monets' at once and instruct Francois to set the ladder by the afternoon light. It was a warning to the German sentry system as well as communication to Litard and was the only way to insure their holding their fire for river craft tonight.

The return trip, as Monet had told Hal, was the more dangerous one. With suitable orders from Graves to his shore patrols however that hazard could be obviated. Litard instructed Hal in his wishes for simple light signals to announce his approach two nights hence. He still refused to consider coming to the Hotel Gustav on his own. He wished to be met at the shore by Hal. When Hal demurred that this might not be feasible at the time, Litard agreed to go as before to the Monet house and send Francois to the hotel.

"If they capture him again, I could still send his wife. They have those children to think of." He smiled.

The return of Litard's arrogance was encouraging. Once again he was Alexandre Litard, managing his inferiors. It was still possible that he was simply masking his own penetration of Hal's cover. If so he was doing a good job. His manner was that of a man trying, imperfectly, to conceal his satisfaction at having the best of another one. Hal attempted to match the new cordiality and tried to look gratified at a final condescension.

"I know a wise man when I see one," said Litard.

Downstairs he encountered a more welcome change of manner. Antoine had departed with Graves in the glacial remoteness that had closed over his chagrin at the loss of Litard. Now, in the lobby, he was all warmth and deference. Mademoiselle had gone out for some errands under the protection of Marcel. The mason had sworn not to leave her side. Antoine insisted on escorting Hal to the garage for the jeep. He led the way through the back rooms with excitement animating his ponderous steps.

At the end of the passageway he tapped ceremoniously. There was an answering knock before a bolt clicked inside and the door swung open to revelation.

The garage had become an arsenal. The entire workbench was covered with the dismantled parts of German pistols and automatic weapons. Alphonse and the lean Sten gunner of the morning had put on mechanics' aprons to dignify their task. Two other members of Antoine's cell were up to their shabby white cuffs in grease and solvents, strip-cleaning each weapon. At Antoine's entrance they whipped up completed ones; clicking triggers, snapping springs and chattering simulation of rapid fire as they brandished tommy guns like small boys playing gangsters.

"This is your generosity, Major."

"You forget; they're from Colonel Graves."

"We do not forget. He is a soldier, that one; but this munificence is from you."

The others exploded into thanks, wiped their greasy hands and insisted on wringing his. Antoine sent a man out to search the alley before opening the doors for the jeep. Its front bumper had not cleared them an inch before they were slammed shut. Alone with him in the alley Antoine reiterated his thanks and then spoke evenly.

"We still harbor M. Litard, Major?"

"Upstairs, under American guard until dark. I regret offending you; he may be of great value to us."

"I regret my own petulance this morning," said Gustav. "You need not fear my intrusion again. You should realize, though, that even with your generous presents mine is not the strongest band of friends in Strasbourg. M. Litard is deeply hated here. You are wise to keep the American guards with him at all times."

"I didn't realize why you hate him so until this morning. May I express my sympathy for your loss?"

"It is war." Antoine shrugged and then brightened. "Colonel Graves has consented to dine with us, Major. We beg that you and Mademoiselle will do us the same honor."

"The honor will be ours, Antoine."

Francois Monet readily agreed to bicycle to the factory and set the ladder by full afternoon light. At Hal's offer of a ride in the jeep he shook his head.

"Field glasses could see me in a jeep. Those pigs are used to the normal way. And any Frenchman who sees me alone will assume I am simply stealing broken glass to recut for private sale."

Change awaited him at the gate to Graves's headquarters. The sentry with the tommy guns saluted him over a broad smile. At the porte cochere he was greeted by name. It was the reply from London. The best of message centers always leaked a little. This was why Joe Collet had been so insistent about the preservation of the cover. The boys who saluted him so respectfully now would be spending their off duty hours with lighthearted girls who knew the value of information.

Today the big windows in Graves's office framed a dazzling vista. The metropolitan mass of city roofs and blank dormers obscuring the narrow streets was still oppressive and faintly sinister. Above them the towering spire of the cathedral reached proudly to a benign sun sparkling alike upon French and Germans as if to admonish them that Black Forest and Vosges were only political symbols for the same mountain range.

If so, Colonel Graves was indifferent to its silent sermon. He sat as usual with his back to the view, his boots on the inlaid desk and *Guns Along the Pecos* nearly hidden in his huge hands. At Hal's entrance he put it down reluctantly.

"Improving your mind, Colonel?"

Graves eyed the paperback wistfully. "If Ike won't let me fight I can still read about guys who do." He tapped the book with his knuckles. "This ol' boy does, too. He comes back to this town where everyone hates him 'cause they think he murdered his daddy to get the ranch. Truth is, it was the foreman, dry-gulched the ol' man so he could get the boy hung for it and get the ranch for his own self. Wants to marry this ol' boy's stepsister, too. So the foreman's in a dark house with three windows at the end of the street, an' this ol' boy has to let him shoot first so he can see where the flash is . . ."

Graves sighed again and put the book firmly on the desk.

"Innythang I can do for you, flyboy?"

"Send this to London in the clear."

Hal took out the message he had already prepared. Within the framework of a few paragraphs of routine bomb damage report its code requested Joe Collet to lay on immediate photo reconnaissance of Gustel.

"Too easy." One shout from Graves produced the message center clerk. As the door closed behind him the signal was on its way. "What else?"

"Litard tells me he's a part-time German spy."

"Want him shot?" Graves brightened. "Or can we use him?"

"I want you to let him cross the river tonight."

Graves's eyes narrowed attentively. Still confining

himself to the limits of the cover story Hal told Graves enough about Litard to explain why the manufacturer had to return to Germany to complete the information Hal required for his bomb damage report.

"How does he get by them Kraut shore patrols?"

"I told you; they think he's spying on us, for them."

He had expected argument. Graves was only thoughtful.

"You reckon the Krauts sure enough trust him?"

"They don't know what trust is – and neither does he."

"Someways, flyboy, you could make a soldier." It was praise.

"Thanks just the same. I've heard it's dangerous."

"Not here." Graves's grimace was rueful. "You reckon if I gave this bastard the real McCoy on who we are and where we are he could get me up a fight?"

"He says the Krauts won't recross the Rhine."

"He's a spy all right," Graves nodded. "That's the trademark: mouth full of Top Secret information everybody already knows and can't show you the way to the local whorehouse."

"I didn't ask him that. All I want is to get him over tonight and back Tuesday night, alive."

Graves had forgotten *Guns Along the Pecos.* He was staring at the ceiling with a faint smile that made Hal think of poker tables.

"Brett, I got orders to help you. Can a country boy ask what you're giving Litard, to stick his neck out like this?"

"He wants to be king of France, when I retire."

"With me providing the fire power?"

"Unless I give him Bradley or Patton or Montgomery."

The poker table smile widened; the voice was innocent.

"Pretty big tip for a news story, isn't it?"

"Too big," Hal agreed. "He's offering to find out where jet planes are produced, so we can bomb 'em."

"You branching into Intelligence, flyboy?"

"If he really offers targets, I'll pass them on to Intelligence. Then it's their baby."

Graves nodded easily; his voice very casual now.

"Myself, I never set much store by G–2. When I'm Chief of Staff I'm gonna put all G–2 back to work and run my Intelligence on just one word: 'Advance.' That's all there is to it. You keep moving forward and you'll get all the Intelligence you'll ever need. If Ike'd let me cross the river, even in company strength, I bet I'd flush that goddamned battery right now . . ."

He sighed, scratched his head and became brisk again.

"Well, he won't. All I got to do is sit on my ass here and help you. How do you figure to work this crossing?"

Hal outlined the scheme of lights Litard had proposed while Graves listened with narrow-eyed attention.

"This light stunt was all his idea?"

"It's the way he works it with the Krauts."

"Okay. But the difference is that *I* place the lights. He isn't about to make clay pigeons out of *my* shore patrols."

"As you like. I want to see him launched."

"Why?"

"Every word he's spoken could be a lie. It won't prove everything but I want to see him take off in that canoe."

"Brett, in some ways you're not as dumb as you look."

Rising, he led Hal into the next room. There on a

paneled wall were thumb-tacked General Staff Geographical Survey maps, photo-reconnaissance and artillery grids of the city, river front, Rhine, city of Kehl and stretches of Germany beyond. Hal completed a personal orientation that included factory and Monet's house while Graves pondered his domain in thoughtful silence. Presently a heavy finger came to rest on marsh symbols at the confluence of canals and river near the factory.

"Either of these guts will handle a canoe. The fact is we been letting single Frogs in canoes and skiffs come and go as if they're fooling us. If the Krauts open up we get flash sightings out of it, and I've always kind of hoped that some of these jokers would bring their friends back and get us up a real fight. You sure enough expect this Litard back Tuesday night?"

Hal repeated the obvious considerations of self-interest for Litard. Graves listened in enigmatic silence, scratching his high bald dome.

"Plausible, but you got no real check on him."

"I wish I had."

"Would it be worth a little risk?"

"If we don't spook him."

"Litard is spooked already," said Graves. "That one-armed chief of staff of yours claims he's done told Litard cold turkey that he's goin' to kill him, and dawg if I don't believe him."

"He's welcome, after I'm through with him."

"Could be he wouldn't wait that long."

"That's why I borrowed your guards; this is the only thing I wouldn't trust Antoine about. He told you a lot, didn't he?"

"I an' him are buddies," said Graves. "After I give him that hardware we punished some brandy and won the battle of Verdun all over again. Then he told me how your friend, Litard, sent his son and a lot of other boys here off to Kraut labor camps and got his own factory bombed, just to give him a war damage claim."

"He's told you more than I've got out of him in four days."

"You ought to paid more attention to Verdun," said Graves. "It wasn't Cold Harbor but it was a right smart battle for Europe."

In his own office again Graves picked up *Guns Along the Pecos*, folded a dozen pages back to the spine with a heavy crease and shouted for his message center clerk again.

"Take this to Captain Bennet and tell him I said to read this part before his chow, hear?"

The man hurried out. Graves stretched his heavy arms through a long look at the eastward vista beyond his big window. Abruptly he nodded to himself and arose.

"Set easy while I make some phone calls, Brett."

Ignoring the waiting instrument on his desk he went out, leaving Hal alone in the office.

3

After several minutes the Colonel returned in beaming good humor. He had exchanged his boots for well shined shoes. His battle jacket had been replaced by a tailored blouse with Silver Star and Purple Heart ribbons.

"It ain't every night a dogface like me dines out."

They went out together. At the porte cochere he ordered his driver and Swanson to follow with his jeep. He would ride with Major Brett. They drove to town through the lengthening shadows of the early winter dusk with Graves slapping his knee in happy accompaniment as he whistled "Deep in the Heart of Texas." In the lobby a proud Antoine made a ceremony of introducing the Colonel to Madame and the excited Gervais.

"In more abundant times I ask my guests if their dinner flies, swims or walks. Tonight Gervais insists that it flies to you – from the trap of the good Major."

"It has caught seven in two days and once two with the same drop!" exulted Gervais.

"I'll talk to Frenchy while you get Litard," said Graves. "But don't you take him out of this lobby without me."

Conversation and laughter echoed from above while Hal was still ascending the stairs. In the hallway he found the two guards and Gabrielle engaged in a happy exchange of French and English lessons. At the sight of Hal she left the soldiers and strutted down the hall smiling to herself. They reported that Litard's door had not been opened in his absence. Webb County took a long look at the receding Gabrielle.

"Excuse me, Major: we on duty all night?"

"No; you'll be off very soon."

"Thank you, sir." They looked at each other hopefully.

"I think you ought to know, though, that the Colonel just gave her husband a lot of Kraut tommy guns."

"Oh, thanks again, Major." Webb County's head shook regretfully. Jim Hogg took a long last look down the corridor.

"Boy howdy! Wouldn't she keep a man off the floor!"

He left them to guard the door while he went down to his own parlor. Elsie's face lighted up at the news that they were taking Litard to the river at once.

"Pity you can't just drown him."

Her visit to the post office had been inconclusive. The clerk thought she might have been mistaken about the date of Loeder's appearance. She associated it with the bombing: she could not be positive whether it had been just before or just after.

With Madame Cassandra she had had better luck. Finding her alone in the lobby Elsie had asked her up to their suite for a cup of coffee and over that a question or two had opened the flood gates.

"So easy I was a little ashamed, Hal. I'm afraid I shirked it, about their boy. It's not really our affair but I picked up a lot that may be."

Elsie had apologized for the presence of Litard in the hotel and then reiterated their thanks for finding such a welcome haven after their shock at the sight of the Hotel Pourvalle.

The coupling of the names had been enough. Madame's morbidity had enjoyed confiding everything she and Antoine knew about that catastrophe. Edouard Pourvalle had come to Gustav, deeply troubled, a short time before the Litard bombing to confront his old friend with a moral problem. If one had credible information that the factory was of significance to German aircraft production should the matter be reported to the Allies?"

He had phrased it as a hypothetical question. Both men knew that a bombing would cost French lives. Both had served in the First World War and understood the immemorial equation of lives for results.

Antoine knew that Edouard Pourvalle, like himself, had harbored fugitive Allied air crew. He assumed that the information would go out with one of them. He had foreborne any question about either that or the source of Pourvalle's knowledge.

Reluctantly, Antoine had said that he thought serious injury to the Reich was worth some French life. The air crews they harbored had been risking their lives to effect, among other purposes, the liberation of France. Antoine was glad the decision was not his; if it were he thought it should be for bombing.

A few days afterward he had been astounded to see M. Litard leaving the Hotel Pourvalle one evening after dusk. There had never been any intimacy between Litard and Pourvalle. He had been pondering it, uneasily, when the first bombing occurred. Edouard had offered no further confidence. Very soon after the second bombing he had closed his hotel and gone with his wife to visit relatives in Nancy. Within a week after they had returned and opened their doors the Gestapo had struck.

"It's still circumstantial," said Hal slowly, "but it fits perfectly except for one thing."

"It fits everything," retorted Elsie. "Litard used him, for the reparations claim, as Antoine says, and then informed and had him killed so it would never come out."

"Wouldn't Imrie have told you Pourvalle was feeding us?"

"Imrie wouldn't tell his mother it was raining," said Elsie. "He might not even have known Pourvalle by name."

"It's certainly all possible," said Hal.

"And we're setting him free!"

"To use him."

"I know. Before you take him out, could you say that when you give his offer to Intelligence they might ask you for the name of his contact here?"

He thought hard and shook his head.

"Revenge isn't our purpose, Elsie; we're after a target."

"Right you are." She nodded, and then he could see anxiety under her control. "You will be careful tonight?"

"We'll have Graves himself and that converted gangster of his covering us with a tommy gun."

"Of course." She made herself smile. "Do go now and get it done."

He entered the manufacturer's room to find Litard tense with apprehension. He listened closely as Hal explained that Graves himself would accompany them to the launching to make sure the American patrols held their fire.

"Excellent! May I ask one other thing?"

"Anything."

"You yourself will be with me, to the river."

"All the way."

"Good. I am not safe under this anarchist's roof." He donned his heavy jacket, picked up the unopened bottle of brandy and pointed to the Wehrmacht stamp on it with a contempt equal to Antoine's.

"I appreciate your intentions but . . . this is quite good enough for German sentries." He slipped it into his pocket.

With Webb and Jim Hogg counties flanking them, they walked down the stairs to a deserted lobby. It occurred to Hal that Madame Cassandra had purposely relinquished her throne behind the iron grille cage to spare herself another sight of Litard upon their premises. In the dining room off the lobby Gabrielle and Josette were quarreling happily over the setting of places at a long festive table. At the sight of Litard they closed their mouths and vanished into the kitchen.

Litard pressed forward to the door. Remembering Graves's injunction Hal stopped him, despite his obvious fear of ambush, and sent Webb County to the kitchen for Graves. The Colonel appeared almost at once to confront Litard with a long, cold scrutiny.

"We're doing what the Major wants, Mr. Litard. If you start any trouble, you won't finish it."

"I have no such thought, Colonel."

"Let's go," said Graves curtly.

They had reached the door to the courtyard when Hal heard pounding steps behind them and whirled. Instead of an ambush it was Antoine Gustav, looking so benign in a white chef's jacket and hat that his effort to glare at Litard was ludicrous.

"Colonel, if the generals arrive before you return?"

"Colonel Hastings will be here to help you get the party started."

"Do I wait dinner for you and Major Brett?"

"No. We'll try to be back by seven thirty, but you start promptly then. The generals have to leave at nine."

"Accord, Colonel."

4

Outside the hotel Graves took charge with curt commands. Hal's guard would take him and Litard in Hal's jeep. Graves, Swanson and their driver would follow it. With the dim blue lights of the other jeep bobbing behind them they pulled up at the rough lane outside the Monet house. There the frightened Francois confirmed that the canoe was where they had left it that morning. Reluctantly he agreed to receive his employer again upon his return and bring word of it to the hotel.

At this point Graves changed the order of progress. Now his jeep led them through the labyrinth of old roads, canals and wooden bridges until they reached a turning close to the factory. There a bearded sentry in helmet stopped them with his tommy gun. Swanson got out to confer with him. Then he waved, and from a dark spur of lane a weapons carrier with twin fifty machine guns mounted drew up behind them. A captain with grenades clipped to his jacket spoke briefly with Graves who then climbed into Hal's jeep.

"Direct us as close as we can get to your canoe, Mr. Litard. My boys are right behind us."

Litard guided the driver eastward over a deteriorating dirt lane, wet and slippery with proximity to the perpetual moisture near the river. The mucky trail was paralleling an old canal. Vegetation along this was thinning into open water before Litard craned into the darkness and checked the driver.

"There, by that shack."

They pulled up, and in the dim starlight Hal could see men with tommy guns jump from the weapons carrier and vanish into the darkness.

"Sit tight," said Graves.

It was the front line, albeit a river's width from the German positions. Hal could feel his hackles rising and his nerve ends tingle with quickening of perceptions. The wet, oily Rhine was strong in their nostrils here and through the silence he could hear its sibilation at the mouth of the canal. The Captain materialized out of the gloom with a note of disappointment.

"Negative, sir."

"Captain Richards, this is Mr. Litard. He'll be coming back here Tuesday night or Wednesday morning. Tell him how to get here alive."

"Yes, sir. First, get your canoe, Mr. Litard."

The manufacturer unlocked the little shack to reveal

the outlines of a fifteen foot aluminum canoe, now painted black. Bending over he checked the paddles tied under the thwarts and then swung the whole load up over his head with practiced ease. Burdened as he was, he walked down the sloping bank of the canal more easily than the others could follow and lowered the canoe into the water without a splash.

"I make the river itself fifty-three yards, right?" asked Captain Richards.

"In kilometers it is . . . yes, fifty American yards."

"Then you come right abreast of this shack on your return."

"Abreast of this shack," Litard repeated.

"Will you be alone?"

"I hope for one companion."

"Okay. Right here you turn crossways to the canal. Put your flashlight down under the gunwale, on the west side, so it's masked from the river and blink it into the water exactly three times. Like this." Richards demonstrated with his own light.

"Very good, Captain. And after that?"

"Sit still in the canoe. Don't try to get out till someone speaks to you. It may be five minutes; it may be an hour. Just don't move till you're told and you won't get hurt."

"You are very clear, Captain. May I speak to Major Brett?"

"Fast," Graves was showing tension, "or we'll be late for dinner."

"I merely wish to thank him!"

"Thank him Tuesday – and get paddling!" snapped Graves.

Litard stepped into the canoe with a long stride that gave it impetus. Before it was out of sight his paddle was biting silently. As the canoe vanished into the gloom Graves was already speaking tersely to Richards.

"One false move on Tuesday and you plow him right back into the water, hear?"

"Too easy," said Captain Richards. "The boys were hoping for some fun, Colonel."

"You'll get your fun in Germany," said Graves.

Taking Hal by the arm he half dragged him up to the bank and shoved him into his own jeep.

"Follow us!" he yelled to Hal's driver.

Swanson swung easily into the front seat, and Graves barked at his own driver.

"Back the way we came . . . fast!"

"Hold your hat, Colonel," said the boy.

The jeep leaped forward so hard that Hal could feel his neck recoil with the motion. He hit the roof three times in the first hundred yards and then simply concentrated on holding on. Once in motion, the tension in Graves began to ease. He rode the jeep easily, seeming to post with the jolts, and then snapped a thumb back toward Captain Richards.

"Hardin boy," he said. "East Texas is all right if you like Tabasco."

In front of them Swanson nursed his tommy gun and torso as one unit in easy swaying equilibrium, humming softly to himself. At the intersection of the better road well back from the river Graves tapped the driver on the shoulder.

"Pull over, son."

The boy stopped the jeep. Graves jumped out, craning his neck and straining his eyes back toward the darkness. Swanson had vanished into the faint star shadow of higher underbrush along the road. Hal alighted to see him covering the approach ahead of them, tommy gun muzzle a little higher. Graves stopped peering, extended cigarettes and cupped his hands around his lighter for both of them.

"Let it rain, let it pour, flyboy."

"What the hell got into you, Colonel?"

"Orders to help you, don't mean help you into a booby trap."

"What were you expecting?"

"In this business," said Graves patiently, "you keep your mind on what you don't expect."

His voice, as if taking assurance in inverse ratio to the distance from the river, carried the old undertone of amused indulgence. He kept his cigarette hidden in one hand and began walking back and forth behind the jeep, stamping on the harder surface that marked their slight elevation from the swamp, peering at the dial of his wristwatch and turning every few seconds to peer back into the impenetrable darkness over the river.

"I thought you were spoiling for dinner."

"I'm fixin' to show you one more thing first, flyboy."

He looked at his wristwatch again and swore angrily. Then before he could swear again the darkness to the east of them was suddenly patterned with the fiery stripe trails of rising mortars. Hal counted five of them lobbing gently up through the black along a line covering about half a mile of river front. At the pinnacle of their short ascent they burst almost simultaneously above the center of the Rhine.

The first flashes of the star shells were blinding. Then as Hal's eyes adjusted to incandescence brighter than sunlight he could see flights of starlings bursting in terror from their roosts on the little islands. The Litard factory was bathed in light that showed even the pocks of bomb fragments in the masonry walls. The signal ladder was in place; the shadows of its rungs were bold on the gaping window frames behind it. The shore on the German side was illuminated with a brilliance that opened the bare willow clumps along it.

Graves jumped to the hood of the jeep, pulled Hal up after him and extended binoculars. Hal didn't need them. He had already picked out the canoe with its single figure making the water boil behind his paddle. Litard was almost at the far shore now. Before the light began to fade the bow of his canoe rose, his feet splashed into the water, he dragged the canoe a few yards into one of the willow clumps and continued into them himself until they hid him. Despite the perfect lighting not a single shot had broken the silence.

"That much is true, anyway," said Graves.

"You might have got him killed."

"You said a check was worth some risk." Graves shrugged.

Hal was beginning to revive from the paralysis of that sudden explosion of light.

"He may never come back!" he exclaimed angrily.

Now in the fading glow Graves turned to face him, suddenly taut with concern.

"We can win the war without him, flyboy. I want you to remember that. He ain't worth the sorriest dog-face alive or you either, you hear me?"

"I hear."

The light died rapidly. Before they were settled in the jeep a stygian darkness closed over their dilated eyes. The driver slowed his pace, aware that the emergency was over. Graves reclined against the back seat humming "Lili Marlene" contentedly. They were almost at the hotel before Hal's mind completed the review of the evening.

"What was that crack about generals dining with us?"

"Just building you up for Litard." Graves chuckled.

"Why?"

"All these top Frogs are rank happy," said Graves. "You seen how he tried to ditch you and move in on me, even this morning. All big shots figure only other big shots are fit to deal with 'em. If he thinks you pal around with the high brass he's likelier to keep after you."

"So, no generals?"

"Hell, no," Graves snorted. "Frenchy asked me if I wanted to bring the Old Man. He knows Army, that Frog does. I told him I was fixin' to enjoy this dinner."

7

ELSIE was waiting in the lobby with the Gustavs. She had put on the white shirtwaist, skirt and sweater, and fluffed out her hair until the candlelight scintillated from its curls. Only the tension knot along her jaw belied her composure. It began to ease as Graves reported cheerfully to Gustav.

"You're shut of him, Frenchy: he's over the river."

"Alive, Colonel?"

"When he hit the shore." Graves shrugged and told them all how he had verified the actual landing with star shells. The Gustavs listened with strained politeness. It was Elsie who snorted.

"You don't approve, Miss Vane?"

"I wish you'd killed him!"

"I offered to. Flyboy here still claims he can use him."

Elsie turned apologetically to the Gustavs.

"I hope we shan't have to impose him on you again."

"And I am sorry for my anger this morning. In the long run such things attend to themselves, Mademoiselle."

"Antoine," wailed Cassandra, "if you kill him the Gendarmes . . ."

"Peace, woman!" He flicked his empty white sleeve suggestively and then turned with deference to Elsie.

"Mademoiselle has consented to select the wine."

"Frenchy claims my liberated Kraut wine is poison," Graves chuckled. "I told him he ought to let our rich uncle put up the chow if he's cookin' it, but he claims the kid caught them pigeons just for us."

"Where is Gervais?" Hal suddenly realized he was absent.

"He leaves you his regrets, Major," said Antoine quickly. "It was necessary for him to dine with his cousins tonight. Shall we watch Mademoiselle perform her duty?"

His quick glance had gone to Graves and at the Colonel's nod he ushered them out through the kitchen. Graves had been as liberal with the supplies of his rich uncle as with those of the Wehrmacht. One of the anterooms was stacked with quartermaster's cases of butter, sugar, flour, cheese and coffee as well as tinned rations. A half beef hung from a meat hook. And to one side of the laundry room in isolated disgrace sat unopened cases of Wehrmacht wine and brandy.

"With peace we shall have German tourists some day." Antoine pointed to them with a chuckle.

Taking a multiple candleholder in his one hand, Antoine preceded them down stairs as steep as a ship's gangway and kicked open the latch on a massive oak door. The cellar was a large room built in the classic rectangular pattern with a long center aisle dividing racked bottles on one side from tiers of casks and jugs on the other. Most of the bottles were crusted over with dust. At the far end of the aisle a litter of discarded casks, cases and straw sleeves rotted out their final rest in peace, perfuming the air with a heady vinous smell.

"Now, if Mademoiselle will honor us . . ." Gustav

raised the light above her head as she began a diffident scrutiny of dim labels.

Graves watched her with a widening grin as she proceeded from section to section, obviously trying to merit Antoine's generosity with commensurate care in selection. After several long looks she shook her head.

"I'm sure they're all delectable, but . . . you choose for us."

"Mademoiselle does not see what she desires?"

"I'd really prefer to have you do it, Antoine."

Gustav grinned triumphantly.

"Mademoiselle has both tact and judgment!" He shrugged a contemptuous shoulder at the whole array. "What you see here is the dregs of Alsace . . . or that part of them which survived the thieving of four different gauleiters. Now if the Colonel will help me . . ."

"You and me, Frenchy!"

Graves sprang at the debris covering the end of the aisle. With a few motions he kicked, lifted and shoved a free opening among the litter. Antoine approached and kicked the end of the wall. A trap door covered with mortared stone to match the floor sprang open on interior springs.

"Now we shall look at wine."

This time they descended another flight of stairs of equal steepness to enter a vault cut from solid rock, chill with depth. Here were orderly tiers in many times the volume of the upper cellar with clean, dustless bottles slumbering in immaculate eight foot racks. Only a ventilation shaft broke the symmetry of whitewashed walls. Not a splinter of wood or straw, not a speck of dust marred the scrubbed stone floor.

"Ain't this something?" Graves exulted. "That whole damned rig above this is just Kraut bait."

"Perhaps Mademoiselle would honor us here?" Gustav held the light again.

She stepped forward with eager curiosity now, scrutinized the labels of the bottles in the first bins and then stepped back in awe. Her voice echoed from the rock walls.

"Antoine! My father himself never saw such treasures."

"In what year was your father born?"

"Seventy-nine."

Gustav elbowed Graves toward another rack. The Colonel, after prodding, lifted out a bottle and scowled at the label.

"Dawg if that ain't eighteen seventy-nine, Frenchy."

"And your father's year, Colonel?"

Graves's mouth opened and then shut fast. Hal could see his eyes go back to Elsie's reverent scrutiny of the bins. Suddenly he clapped Antoine on the shoulder; his voice was a littly shy.

"Frenchy, my old man didn't know there was wine. I can't tell red from white on a cloudy day. You save the rest of this here for folks that savvy it. I just wanted to show these two how you fooled the Krauts."

"We were badly robbed in '70," said Gustav. "My grandfather planned this long before he dared begin it. My father began the excavation when we were restored to France in '18."

He designated two more bottles and insisted that Hal carry them upstairs. As they regained the level of the upper cellar Graves studied the light pouring down into it from the floor above. His humility vanished in a curt order.

"Leave them candles burning, right here, Frenchy."

"I had intended to, Colonel," said Gustav.

In the dining room the Colonel's normal ebullience returned. He had dispatched his tensions across the Rhine and left his momentary diffidence in the lower cellar. He confided happily to Hal that the vintages bored him. His delight was in the guile of Gustav.

"This ol' Frog's got it! I bet I slept over fifty caches like that, crossing France, and never even suspicioned they was there. First thing I'm fixin' to do when we hit Germany is have my boys liberate a couple of double jacks and bust the bottom out of every cellar they show us."

He glanced at his wristwatch, as if to reaffirm the verities by which he lived.

"Eight o'clock on the nose, flyboy. Cost us half an hour to do that but I figured it was worth it. Time for everything if you plan right."

The Gustavs had planned on their own account. Sherry, brandy and champagne waited on the sideboard beside a massive tray of Baccarat crystal laden with foie gras and truffles. Gabrielle puffed in with another tray of the thinnest toasted wafers Hal had ever seen. Her glance at Graves was approving.

"For American flour it does very well," she conceded.

Graves was unexpectedly abstemious, limiting himself to a thimbleful of brandy.

"I'm not about to spoil my taste for bourbon an' branch," he explained. "Dogfaces don't always live high on the hog like this."

For the women, including Josette and Gabrielle, he poured lavishly from the liberated champagne.

"If this would hurt you my whole outfit would be dead." He grinned at Elsie. "Take it while you can, Lieutenant. In wartime tomorrow can be hungry."

"Americans learn quickly, don't they, Colonel?"

He gaped at her dry smile and then burst into happy, spontaneous laughter.

"Dawg if I didn't ask for that. Will you excuse my big mouth, Miss Vane?"

"If you'll call me Elsie."

"You got a deal; I'm Earl. Before I shoot my mouth off again I'm gonna ask the only other person here who *does* know about war. Tell us about Verdun, Frenchy."

Gustav looked at them all affectionately.

"Verdun spoke for itself . . . and for the France that will live again, by your help."

He raised his glass and they responded in silence.

"Now that was real graceful," said Graves. "But I wasn't askin' you to brag on yourself. I wanted you to tell us more about your tactics."

"Our tactics" – Antoine shrugged – "were the same as yours: we killed Germans."

"That's the whole deal, ain't it, Frenchy?"

"I believe so." Gustav was suddenly somber. "In war it is easy to become beguiled with the inanimates, the concrete, the guns, the ships, the tanks, the planes. To speak of only one of them is to recall our disastrous confidence in the Maginot Line. War is older than all of these toys. In the end it always comes back to men killing men."

"Put that in your bomb story, flyboy," said Graves. "They'll boot you out of the Air Corps, and then you can come back here and I'll make a soldier out of you."

Gabrielle appeared in the door straining with the burden of a soup tureen half the size of her own blocky bust. Antoine ushered them ceremoniously to the table. As they moved toward it Graves turned back to put down his unfinished thimbleful of brandy on the sideboard. Over Elsie's shoulder Hal saw the Colonel take a surreptitious glance at his wristwatch. The top of Hal's mind was dismissing it as normal military obsession with punctuality, before a deeper instinct felt the warning stir of curiosity. He was looking at a simple thing that was not as simple as it looked.

Graves had no appointment, no reason for such preoccupation with the time. Their work was done; he was manifestly enjoying himself where he was. And yet he had left most of his brandy untouched on the sideboard. As he came to the table he shook his head at the wine bottle in Antoine's hand.

"Just a sample, Frenchy; that stuff's wasted on a country boy. Hey, Air Corps! Your soup is freezing over."

He had seen Hal observing his quick glance at the wristwatch and he was deflecting comment on it. Hal took his place at the right of Madame who had already begun to ladle out the most delicious soup he had ever tasted. For a while he was able to relegate the stirring unease in his head to the subconscious by focusing attention on his hostess.

"You must not fear our soup, Major. Antoine and I have experience with the mushroom. We regard it with especial vigilance since the error of my nieces in Baccarat."

"Madame has nieces in Baccarat?"

"*Had*," she corrected him with lugubrious satisfaction. "In the dark times, my aunt so far forgot herself as to marry a German there. No doubt his deficiency of comprehension was transmitted to them by heredity. In any case Philomèle and Greta, though sweet little girls in some ways, could not remember the characteristics of the toadstool and one day . . . Pouf!

"It was a double funeral, and stingy as that Boche was, he did have the finest hearse in Strasbourg sent up.

It intensified local feeling in Baccarat where he was not loved. But I assure you that you may drink *our* soup without trepidation."

He was drinking it with delight, and the mention of Baccarat eclipsed his unease with remembrances of his folly and Elsie's fury there. He found himself wondering if he had already loved her then and he warmed himself with the thought as he prodded Madame to prolong those memories.

"But everyone knows Philippe Daivren! We stayed with him at the time of the funeral, and while one must admit that compassion for our bereavement was not reflected in his charges he is a good man. Since *this* war one hears that he has, perhaps, too many friends, but of whom in Alsace could that not be said? He may be quite loyal."

Elsie had thought so. She had breached their cover to save his life while they were still almost strangers, while she still had to weigh the breach against her memories of the fate of Robin. He wondered, greedily, whether she too might have been responding unconsciously to the combustion already alight between them.

He stole a glance at her and saw that she was apparently relishing her dinner with female instinct alert to divide her attention between Graves and the glowing Gustav. While he watched them Graves lowered an arm below the table: his eyes went down to the wristwatch on it.

If there was tension in anyone but himself and Graves, Antoine seemed unaware of it. With napkin tucked high under his collar and his happy face reddening to the color of the wine, his single hand dismembered his casseroled pigeon by filigree tracery of his razor-sharp knife. He looked a symbol of contentment with hearth, table and guests, a man who could preserve faith and felicity alike in a world that had already demanded of him an arm and a son.

And yet he had sent the focal point of his life away from this table. Gervais had expected to come to dinner with them; he had wanted to come. Gustav doted on him. He had understood the boy's pride in providing these pigeons: he had wanted him to bask in the gratitude of their guests. When had he changed his mind: why? If there was something seriously askew, Madame seemed unaware of it. She had launched into another happy reminiscence of local history.

". . . so when the francs were subscribed and the contract signed and notarized and the deliveries marching every day, what did they find in that herd? Tuberculosis in every cow, Major! Three of their customers were dead in a week and our friends were ruined. Now! One cannot *prove* that it was those Germans who also wished to sell their milk from Kehl, but nevertheless . . ."

Perhaps it was her use of the word, "Kehl," perhaps only the pace of the process in his subconsciousness. His mind seemed to explode like one of Graves's star shells. The first burst of it was as blinding. Then his brain adjusted as his eyes had to the white incandescence above the Rhine, and by the new light the scattered fragments of his unease fused.

He could feel the blood leave his face and he looked first to see Elsie chatting cheerfully with Graves and Gustav. He took a sip of wine without tasting it, and when he was sure he could do it casually he looked at his own wristwatch. It was seventeen minutes to nine. He gulped and spoke across the table.

"Earl, you said those generals were leaving at nine?"

"Yes." Graves was suddenly guarded.

"Is what I'm thinking right?"

Graves hesitated; his guard relaxed into a grin.

"You're slow but you get there, flyboy." He glanced openly at his own watch now. "We won't know for sixteen minutes."

"You might have told me!"

"No use spoiling a good dinner for you, too."

"What about the others?"

"Cool off," said Graves. "I been chasing that battery for two hundred and fourteen miles and they never hit anything yet with a searching round. We can have everyone in Frenchy's cellar before they range in. My boys are ready, Brett. If they get off more than three rounds I'm goin' to chop my battery commander down to size and shoot him back at 'em."

"May we share your riddle?" asked Elsie.

He was wondering what to reply and he did not have to. As if on the cue of her question they all heard the approaching rumble, muted and high and unmistakable. Graves was on his feet with the sound. One hand on Elsie's wrist and the other on Madame's he barked to Hal.

"You bring the maids."

Antoine, calm and purposeful, helped Hal to herd the protesting Gabrielle and Josette out of the kitchen and down to the candlelight waiting in the first cellar. They had pushed the women past it into the second cellar and forced Antoine after them by the time they heard the second high rumble. Graves checked Hal at the top of the lower stairs, his eyes gleaming now.

"These aren't for us; let's go see the fun."

He raced up the first stairs and out through the kitchen toward the street. Hal followed with Elsie's anxious call still echoing in his ears. On the stoop outside the front door, facing the open sky above the little park, Graves had stopped, peering anxiously toward the darkness to the west of them, glancing at his wristwatch and muttering angrily.

"Slowest son of a bitch in uniform! If he wasn't so good when he does shoot . . . Oh! There!"

The western sky split with light. The detonations and the rumble reached them almost simultaneously. The rumble passed into an arcing, high screech. Graves looked at his watch again and rose on his toes craning his neck toward the dark eastern horizon.

"Three minutes and ten seconds! He'd better be right."

The noise became a brief, continuous thunder as other shells screamed eastward now, until they began to hear the distant detonations far across the Rhine. The eastern darkness blossomed with fainter explosions of light. As the first ones faded others replaced them. Slowly they became a constant, dancing fire that grew, even through intermittent eclipse by brighter flashes.

"Tankers! Fuel tankers and caissons too, by God," muttered Graves. "Elmer *was* right! Let's go check!"

Hal was not entirely in the jeep seat before it slammed his back, and with a screech of rubber they careened madly through the narrow streets. At the Hotel Command Post, Graves pushed the duty officer aside, grabbed the phone and barked a staccato burst of unintelligible artillery language. He waited through a short silence, and then Hal could read the answer in his face before he heard the words:

"Tell Elmer I said that's better!"

He hung up and turned to Hal, grinning broadly. "War's over, flyboy – at least for those bastards. They never got off a third round before my boy clobbered 'em. Their whole damned battery's burning."

"How can you tell?"

Graves's grin became a little defiant.

"I got spotters up in the cathedral tonight. And don't talk to me about international law or religion. The Lord helps those that help themselves. That pile of rocks has been here eight hundred years, to hear 'em brag on it, and it never kept the Krauts out of Strasbourg yet! But the ones it helped us with tonight won't be coming back this way."

He drove back to the hotel slowly, savoring his triumph aloud. The idea had come to him with Hal's first declaration that Litard was a spy. Graves had reasoned that if the manufacturer was a petty opportunist he would have been glad to give his German contacts an Allied generals' dinner party for a target.

"I sent my gunner that book I was readin' an' told him I was fixin' to get him first flash tonight."

He was sure now that the German flashes had been only the routine exercise rounds with which he had played hide and go seek all the way across France. They had not been trying to hit the hotel and that told its own story. Either Litard had been too smart to fall for the bait or too intent on his own purposes to compromise them with a target of opportunity. It was at least negative evidence that Litard was after the larger game of his deal with Hal.

"So we both win, flyboy."

He drew up before the hotel and they stood together, looking at the faint, flickering glow in the eastern horizon. It was too dark for them to see the gutted Hotel Pourvalle across the square. Hal did not have to see it: he could remember its empty interior and gaping windows vividly. The Hotel Gustav would have been just as inflammable.

"Earl, did the women have to be here?"

"I offered to move the whole party when I first worked it out with Frenchy. That was when he showed me those cellars. He said they were better than he'd had at Verdun and safe enough for anyone."

"But not safe enough for Gervais."

"First thing he thought about." Graves nodded. "He said he'd better get him out, just in case. He figures France is gonna need that boy, for the next war."

"You should have got the women out, too."

"She wouldn't have gone." Graves chuckled. "She's fixin' to marry you, flyboy."

"I wish I thought so. Why do you?"

"The way she looks at you," said Graves. "That's a good woman, if you want a good woman. I studied right hard before I let her set down to dinner in the bull's-eye. The more I studied the more I figured that was the way she'd want it. If you're hurting for luck, you got to be willing to work at it."

"You have put us back in the war," Antoine exulted to Graves.

He had apprised the others of the strategem while they sat in the lower wine cellar. Hal and Graves reentered to an atmosphere of exuberant pride. It became exhilaration at Graves's report on the end of the German battery. Only Madame's habituated reflex to the general sense of accomplishment was half hearted.

"Yet Germans spare what is their own. Perhaps one only reads here their true intentions for Strasbourg."

"I wish I knew how to make 'em try," said Graves.

"It is *not* like M. Litard to spare us either" — Antoine's eyes narrowed now and he looked speculatively at Hal — "unless he fries larger fish."

Elsie had been miffed at her relegation to the safety of the cellar with the noncombatants. She let Hal feel her pique obliquely by warm gratitude to Graves.

"You made us good for something," she said.

"You did fine," Graves assured her. "If I could keep you for bait, I could force that Siegfried Line while Ike sets up there waitin' for Groundhog Day to bring 'em out."

For the interruption of the dinner party Graves had already planned amends. Hal, Elsie and the entire hotel staff were to dine with him at his mess the following night.

"Trying for an air raid?" inquired Elsie.

"I could use one." Graves grinned. "But a man doesn't get luck like this every night. Tomorrow you're goin' to have to settle for Spam an' beans with liberated Kraut booze. The fireworks around here are over."

In the privacy of their parlor she challenged his silence.

"What's wrong, Hal?"

"That monomaniac might have got you killed."

"All of us. He's a good type, Graves."

"I don't like him using you for bait."

Instead of flaring she looked at him fondly. "It's good for you. Once upon a time men could leave us in safety and march off to their fun with good conscience. Now you get a taste of the worry, too. If enough of *us* get killed maybe men would think up a new game."

"It wouldn't be using you for bait."

"We're the original bait." She looked into the mirror with a flash of pride. "We're nature's own booby trap, luring mankind into perpetuity in spite of your obsession with war."

"Show me!" He reached for her and saw her responsive move toward him. Then she checked it.

"Not till we're done with your game."

2

He awoke to dazzling sunlight and lay still, absorbing the unfamiliar brightness until his mind caught up to it. He had gone to sleep with his blackout curtains in place. Elsie must have come into the room and removed them to make him a present of this radiance.

He jumped out of bed and went to the window, savoring the tingle of chill through the shorts and T shirt in which he had slept. The entire eastern horizon sparkled. The river that could reflect brown despair to fog, or sinister black to Graves's star shells, was a deep blue flecked with tiny whitecaps. The protruberant fragments of bridge tops, framed in laughing eddies, looked as innocent as broken toys.

Kehl was the foreground of a Christmas card, snug and serene among the little fences, farms and roads. Beyond it a backdrop of snow patches and evergreens rose to the distant blur of the Black Forest. He strained his eyes half expecting to see foresters' huts and reindeer pulling sled loads of yule logs, topped by dancing elves and kobolds. Instead he saw a single plume of smoke, rising from behind an intermediate hill. It was not the traditional blue of happy hearth fires. It was the oily black epitaph of the fuel tankers Graves had clobbered in the darkness.

He heard a gentle knock and called. The door creaked,

and he smelled coffee and turned to see Elsie, scrubbed and glowing in the white shirt, extending a tray.

"I heard you stir. Like coffee in bed?"

"I'd rather have you in bed."

"Hal! Stop it!"

He had reached for her. She maneuvered the tray between them and then, when his hands were filled with cup and pot, moved warily closer.

"Thanks for pulling my curtains."

"I wanted you to see this; maybe it's a portent."

"For us?"

"For everyone. I know what that fire is, but there has to be a last one, an end to all this. I can't even remember what peace was like. Tell me it will always be clean and bright like this."

"It will be better."

"How could it?"

"When we're married we'll let the coffee stand around waiting till we cool off."

"I'd better get out of here." But the laughter and her color were happy now. "Make yourself decent. I left you hot water and I've got a famous start on breakfast in the parlor."

They toasted rolls and hard tack on the hearth through a leisurely meal, and then she vanished to reappear swathed in wool and battle dress. They went out together into the frosty effervescence of the morning. For the first time since Henderson had told him about the Strasbourg-Litard imprint on the exhaust he had nothing to do. It was all up to Litard now.

The cessation of urgency and purpose would have been an intolerable vacuum without Elsie. With her it was, as she had said, a portent. In the cold air and bright sunlight he could forget the promptings of passion that always vibrated, however faintly, through the seclusion of their quarters, for contentment in companionship itself.

Her spirits were as buoyant as his own, gay and eager with a hint of mischief in her merriment as if their aimless indolence shared the happy secret guilt of a truancy. He hurried her past the Hotel Pourvalle and then over to the street of the Fishers and Tanners and on to where fresh ice had closed the more tranquil reaches of the canal ring. They made a slow circuit of the inner city, descending the stone steps now and then to run and slide on the ice, laughing and clutching each other's arms.

When they had done the ring he led her casually through the streets to one he had marked in memory, and then pushed her through the door into a jeweler's. Only as he asked the man to see engagement rings did she suddenly flame and shake her head. The merchant was appraising them in alternations of doubt and hope. He had at first insisted that he had no rings. As he studied them he volunteered that it might, after all, be possible for him to send for some if they would wait.

"He's got 'em: he's just playing it safe."

"No, please, Hal. Not yet. It's bad luck."

"Please, kind sir." Hope was winning in the merchant. "It is possible to find them very soon. It was only that with the Germans here . . ."

"You're quite right; keep them hidden," said Elsie. Her eyes on Hal were warm, though. "We can all wait a little."

They left him in anguish over the loss of a safe sale and sauntered slowly, arm in arm, through the strengthening warmth of the sun. As they came to the square of the cathedral Hal slackened his pace.

"Like to see it?"

"Go ahead. The glass has all been removed for safety anyhow. I'll wait out here in the sunlight."

"We've never even talked about religion."

"Talk is pointless; you either believe or you don't."

"You wouldn't say that if you did believe."

"I did once; maybe it's the war." She shook her head. "The stonework is still worth seeing. I'm glad to wait."

"I'd rather be with you."

"Good. Then if it is true it puts us in the same hell. Did you ever believe, Hal?"

"I was taught to." He shrugged. "I haven't the war to blame; it's never touched me but . . . remember *King Lear*?"

"No special part."

" 'As flies to wanton boys, are we to the Gods. They kill us for their sport.' Do you suppose it would surprise Earl Graves to know that he's one of the Gods?"

"It would alarm him." She laughed. "He'd have you shot for blasphemy and then go back to his headquarters and order his chaplain to pray for that German counter-attack."

They strolled with an aimless languor of perfect accord until the muted tinkle of cheap pianos, a sudden redolence of wine and Mirabelle, and a sharp turn in one of the narrow alleys brought them face to face with the garish chalk legend of Gonorrhea Gardens over a dark and busy door. Soldiers with girls were passing in and out under the envious eyes of the military police.

There was still none of the open drunkenness of Nancy. The rare sunlight had simply brought some of the festivity out of doors. Most of the soldiers carried bottles. The girls on their arms were chewing G.I. candy bars. And the eyes of the arm-banded Fifi bustling around among them were livid with jealousy. They passed a young American rifleman with two German Iron Crosses dangling from ribbons around his neck and a girl on each arm grinning with possessive pride.

"Envy him?" asked Elsie slyly.

"Stop fishing. I don't envy any man alive."

"Even unlimited combat and a different girl every time?"

"I want unlimited time with you for the same combat."

They came out on the canal again to a clear strong sheet of ice on which clamorous urchins were knocking C ration tins around with sticks. At the sight of Hal the more aggressive ones quit their game to storm up the towpath with strident demands for cigarettes and "Choon gum, Yank!" Elsie rifled the pockets of his jacket and produced some candy and gum. Tossing them high over the heads of the nearest, she laughed with him at the melee and then her eyes sobered.

"Biological booby trap or not . . . they're sweet."

"Did the sweetest one get that candy, or the toughest?"

"Yours will be both: they'll have everything. Do you know when I first felt . . . as you do?"

"I didn't know you did."

"I do. It was when you were helping Gervais with the traps. It was perfectly melting. And then yesterday again when you said: 'Be home before dark.' I've been selfish."

He closed a hand over hers. "It's all right. I can wait."

"It isn't all right," she said, "but it's going to be. Take me home, Hal: now."

3

The telephone in the parlor jangled faintly and then its long, insistent screech bit like a dentist's drill. He looked at his watch. It was four o'clock and the light outside Elsie's window was showing the first shadows of winter dusk. He kissed her again, got up and hurried into the parlor. Swanson's voice on the phone was firm.

"The Colonel wants you, sir."

"Is he here?"

"No, sir. I'm taking you out."

"We're dining there; didn't he mention the others?"

"He wants you alone, pronto, sir."

"I'll be right down."

He went back and told Elsie while he tried to get into his clothes without taking his eyes off her.

"This is a hell of a way to spend a honeymoon."

"It's a wonderful way." She laughed. "I want to be alone awhile, to think about it. Then I'm going to get ready for dinner and send for Gabrielle to tidy up so she can tell everyone in Strasbourg that you love me and I'm proud of it."

He kissed her again and hurried downstairs with her faint fragrance lingering on his lips. Swanson and Antoine were at the desk, engrossed in a painstaking comparison of army and municipal maps.

"The Colonel claims he trusts that ol' Frog," Swanson scowled as the jeep started. "Do you, sir?"

"Yes. Why?"

"Either he's lying," the scowl darkened, "or I've missed two whorehouses here. Makes a man wonder about all them other towns we come through."

The rare sunlight that had filled the city that morning was gone. A voluntary curfew seemed to have emptied the streets before the official dusk. They passed not a single soldier. The few civilians they saw were hurrying purposefully with eyes averted from the jeep.

Today Graves's feet were not on the inlay. He was standing by the big windows training binoculars toward the far hill from which Hal had seen the smoke rising that morning.

"Did you see my battery burning?"

"We saw the smoke from the hotel."

"Elmer got the works," said Graves. "I took a run over in a grasshopper this morning. If I was Air Corps, I'd put myself in for a D.F.C. Come to think of it, I ought to recommend you for one."

"I'll settle for an extra drink at dinner."

"Dinner's off," said Graves. "We're moving out."

"Moving out . . . when?"

"My recon patrols go with the dark. I'll roll all night." He grinned now. "Somebody must have made Ike and Patton face the facts, so they sent for me."

"How long have you known this, Earl?"

"It wasn't official till an hour ago. Army! It's like when your wife is cheating or knocked up! The guy himself is always the last to know."

"Who's relieving you?"

"Nobody. Some say Shaef and the Frogs are feuding again. Some claim they're fixin' to pull the cob out up north. We don't need Strasbourg either way. My guess is they'd like to suck the Krauts back across the river down here to mop 'em up after I take Berlin."

"Who else knows this?"

"It's Top Secret," said Graves, "so probably everyone in France has known it a week. Oh, London knows it too."

He went back to his desk and handed Hal a teleprinter flimsy, time-stamped fifteen thirty-one. Hal picked his own name and Joe Collet's out of the welter of higher ranks at address and signature, and then read the text: "Strategic changes make advisable abandonment your mission and immediate return you and Vane under protection local troop movements."

He sat very still, staring at the letters.

"Sorry about Frenchy and his harem," said Graves. "You and the little lady can chow with me here just before we take off, and I'll drop you somewhere up by Nancy."

"I'll bring her out while I'm deciding."

Graves's smile congealed into the poker face. He tapped the flimsy.

"Those are orders, Brett: 'you and Vane.' "

"They don't order. They say it's advisable. I can be done here tomorrow night."

"You could be floating in the Rhine face down ten minutes after I leave here. I got squads of M.P.'s pulling my boys off the whores downtown right now. You saw Litard cross that river. Do you think others can't, with me gone? All dynamiting those bridges did was save the Kraut-half of Strasbourg paying tolls. They got spotters over there with field glasses strong enough to read that message in this room.

"We can't keep a Division movement secret. I know the Wehrmacht doesn't want this town. No private on either side would give you two cigarettes for Strasbourg. But that crazy corporal might. Remember the Ardennes? You can't play Hitler by the book, Hal. You fixin' to sit here like Horatius at a busted bridge, fightin' off Panzer grenadiers with one hand while you stick your neck out for a goddamned bomb report?"

"They can't put a Division across in one day."

"They don't have to. When their first patrol hits this shore every Fifi arm band in town will be turned inside out to the swastika. My orders are to move the outfit, Hal. I can't leave you a guard here to be chewed up piecemeal."

"I could go into civvies for one day."

"You'd just double your price, as a spy. The talk is sweet while we're here, flyboy, but inside, these Frogs hate us. They hate us 'cause they lost the war and we're winning it. They hate us 'cause your people bombed 'em. They're gonna hate us most of all for pulling out of here and giving the Krauts one last romp. You got clear orders." He tapped the flimsy again. "Go pack."

"Earl, when you're given a mission, don't you try?"

Graves studied him and then sat down on the top of the desk.

"Brett, I can talk about your mission, if you can't. Your story wouldn't fool a farm boy at a state fair. I once paid thirty-five cents cash money in Austin to see the aboriginal girl from Zulu with three tits, and your story didn't even fool me.

"I figured it was security cover for something. I didn't tumble till you told me about Litard and the bombing targets. But these Frogs aren't as slow as I am. They know the Krauts would pay a good price for you. And for that matter you don't have to cross that river for trouble. They hate your guts at the market camp and at Natzweiler. They'd love catching you here, alone. Now go get the little lady."

"She'll be here, either way."

Graves choked back an angry exclamation; there was affection as well as conviction in his voice now.

"You can't complete your mission; it depends on Litard. He'll know we've pulled out of here before we go. You reckon he's gonna come back and let Frenchy pat him in the face with a shovel for you?"

It was so true that there was nothing to reply. It was past the point of talk. It had passed that point when Graves said he was pulling out, and they had talked because it was a convention. Ecclesiastes had listed a time for talk and a time for silence. There also came a time when the talk ended and you had to act.

"Will Swanson take me back for my jeep?"

"He's waiting," said Graves, "with two very eager Val Verde boys to ride shotgun for you. I was wrong about one thing last night, Hal. The fireworks in Strasbourg will be starting very soon. Go get the little lady out of there and come back with her, you hear?"

It was almost dark when they left the headquarters with Swanson driving and the eager boys from Val Verde nursing carbines on the seat behind him. As they approached town he could remember the premature emptiness of the streets they had left by daylight. They were totally deserted now. He felt a premonitory unease and told himself angrily it was sheer nerves. The streets had always been empty after dark. The windows had always been blank with blackout curtains. Tonight clear starlight twinkled down on roofs and gables. He had not even the excuse of fog to feel oppression in the air.

He directed Swanson to drive through the alley before Gonorrhea Gardens and nodded a reluctant head at its confirmation of Graves's warning. There was not an M.P. in sight, not a single streetwalker lurking in the shadows, not a piano note from behind the closed door.

A closer confirmation marked his brief interview at the desk with Gustav. The secrecy of Graves's orders precluded truthful explanation of the change. They had agreed that Hal could say to Antoine only that it was impossible for Colonel Graves to entertain civilians to-night. He sent his apologies and hopes for another time. As Hal finished the best effort he could make over this transparent fabrication, Antoine's knowing eyes seemed to penetrate his skull. His tolerant acceptance was more embarrassing than ridicule.

"Accord, Major. Please give the good Colonel our regrets."

"I shall, Antoine. I'll be taking my jeep from the garage and returning early."

"As you say." Antoine could make open disbelief polite.

"We'll wait in the lobby, sir," said Swanson. "I got a bet with these two guys this ol' Frog can settle, if they'll believe him."

Antoine turned to the soldiers as courteously as if he could not understand English. Hal climbed the stairs with feet that felt like bricks.

She must have been waiting right behind the door. The inner bolt clicked before his second knock. He had scarcely time to realize that she was wearing only a blue wrapper, before she was in his arms and he was kissing her and trying to kick the door shut behind him.

"Oh, I was *so* wrong. It isn't more fun to think about it. I could have been with you. I could have been looking at you while you drove and hearing your voice and touching your hand when I wanted to. I'm a fool; it was time wasted."

He kissed her again to postpone it, to hide from it, and even as he did he knew it was no good. There was no deception with Elsie. She drew back, a little guarded and trying to conceal her own tension now.

"What's wrong?"

Pure cowardice compounded his mistake. Instead of

blurting it out, he reached in his pocket and handed her the teleprinter flimsy. She took it slowly, eying him, and then hitched the cord of her wrapper a little more tightly about her narrow waist. The color drained from her face as she read it. She managed a forced smile, and it stabbed him to see her pretend.

"I don't get it . . . we're through? We're going home?"

"You are, tonight. I'll be along later."

The muscle knot in her jaw tightened, her color began to return, the new tone of her voice rejected further evasion.

"You're going to wait for Litard, here?"

"Yes."

" 'Strategic changes' and 'troop movements' mean Graves?"

"Yes."

"Are other American troops replacing him here?"

"He doesn't know."

"I know. And so do you, or that's the first thing you would have told me."

"He's going very soon. You'd better be packing."

She examined the flimsy again, reading slowly.

"This says you, too. You don't have to stay here."

" 'Have to' is inside you, Elsie. It's only a day or two."

She choked back the outburst on her lips and hurried across the parlor. He followed fast. She reached the door to her bedroom and tried to slam it. He forced it and held her in his arms through her first uncontrollable tears. Her outburst was brief. She looked up suddenly and realized that he was staring over her shoulder, surveying the room that was unchanged since he had left it.

"I didn't call Gabrielle," she said. "I wanted to leave everything exactly as it was. I didn't want to change anything, ever . . . I just wanted you to come back." Another spasm of tears shook her and then she forced herself out of his arms.

"We've got to talk rationally."

Point by point, straining for logic, she went through every detail of the arguments Graves had already pressed on him. He listened with only occasional brief responses. She had to say it, as he had to hear it all over again. There was a time for talk and a time to act, and he wanted to give her all the respite he could. Talk was release as well as refuge for as long as you could afford it. He thought it would end with reiteration of Graves's objections. It did not.

"Do you know why Whitehall opposed your coming here?"

"That security rule."

She nodded. "You know too much to be here at all. But there was something else. We've known these French longer than you. Sooner or later they always get intractable. We knew they'd make themselves so troublesome that Shaef would have to act. This is the action. Imrie warned me to get you out of here the minute your troops pulled out."

"I had no such orders, Elsie."

"I told Imrie he was warning the wrong person. He said you can't tell Americans anything; you're too confident and impetuous because you've never seen things go really wrong. I've hated acting like a Nanny but . . . they sent me to."

"I'm grateful, for more reasons than one," he smiled. "I never would have thought of that post office inquiry. It may be all we need. But I want a final check on it, if I can get one. After that you'll have the rest of our lives to play Nanny."

"Not if you send me back now!"

"You offered to go back two days ago."

"You were safe then, with Graves here."

The word stung. It took an effort to keep his voice level. "I've been safe behind a Graves of one kind or another all my life . . ."

"I know," she flared."You spelled it out that day up in the Vosges when you told me men fight to prove something to themselves. That's why I tried so hard to resist . . . loving you. You're going to get yourself killed for some damned fulfillment you won't even let me share. If I could at least be with you . . ."

"I'm not going to be killed! I'll be back in London this week . . ."

The window exploded glass all over them. He heard the bullet thud into the ceiling on the echo of the report from the street below. He looked at her numbly, comprehending slowly that she was unhurt. She had begun, mechanically, to comb the glass out of her hair. He looked at the shattered window again. They had forgotten to put up the blackout curtain.

He blew out the candle and closed the door to the parlor and then adjusted inner shutters and curtain. After they were secure he went back to the parlor for another candle and a flashlight.

"Pack up, Elsie, fast!"

She was staring at him silently when they both heard the stutter of automatic fire, muted by shutters and curtains now. It was more distant than the solitary shot that had crashed in on them. He was certain that it was on the French side of the Rhine.

He hurried into the bathroom and saw that only his

own things were there. She had never left so much as a toothbrush in it. From the parlor he phoned down to Antoine, reporting briefly that they had been careless about blackout curtains. They were uninjured and he would pay for the broken glass. In his own room he checked the curtain and shutters. For the first time since they had shared the suite, the door between the two bedrooms was closed.

He returned to the parlor to find the door from it to her bedroom also firmly closed. With an effort he made himself wait by the fire until she emerged, fully dressed, carrying her little kit bag and typewriter. He reached to take them and she eluded him, her voice curt:

"Thank you, Major, I manage nicely."

Dodging past him she hurried into the hall and after a minute's reflection he followed slowly. Anger would help her tonight. In the lobby personal speech was impossible. Graves's eager boys and Swanson, with their carbines unslung now, were happily advising Antoine as he experimented with the placing of one of the little German automatic rifles under the steel mesh cashier's cage, covering the door.

"Right like that," said one of the Val Verde boys. "Just leave your hand right there an' wait till the first Kraut swings that door an' let him step in till it clears his body. Then you just say, 'Welcome back, my friend,' an' turn on the heat."

He stopped, and in the second of silence they all heard another burst of small-arms fire somewhere in the city.

"Ain't them Frogs having a time?" grinned Swanson.

"Where was that, Antoine?"

"I judge at the market, Major. Your soldiers are being withdrawn."

"Scuttlebutt claims we're goin' up to learn Patton how to fight." The other Val Verde boy was grinning, too.

"Mademoiselle is leaving us?" Antoine eyed bag and typewriter.

"Orders. I am sorry." She kept her eyes away from Hal.

"And I am relieved," replied Antoine.

"May I say good-bye to Madame?"

"I am sorry" — the kind face clouded — "she has gone to the cathedral to pray."

"Then give her this for me," said Elsie.

She kissed him on the cheek without relinquishing her grip on her gear and then hurried toward the front door. Swanson passed her and cut in front, blocking her progress as he indicated his own tommy gun.

"Little Nell goes out the door first, Miss."

"I'm taking Miss Vane in my jeep from the garage," said Hal.

"Sir, the Colonel said if you did, these boys ride shotgun on you." He turned now, glowering at the eager boys. "You get them out there alive too, you hear?"

The Val Verde boys looked amusedly at his truculence.

"Cool off, hero; you and little Nell can fight all Germany next week."

Hal had been relying on the drive out, on the reaction that must follow her first fear and rage, on the return of her own discipline to reconcile her to the change of plan. Her discipline had returned, but the presence of the Val Verde boys precluded conversation. She sat, frozen and distant across the divided front passenger's seat. When he tried to steal a glance at her through the darkness, the muzzle of one of the carbines thrust forward from the rear concealed half her face.

"Hot time here tonight," said one Val Verde wistfully.

"They can have it," said the other. "Myself I'm ready for real Fräuleins."

"Elsie, have you talked sense into him?" Graves's inquiry was as bland as his smile. His eyes had gone straight to the single musette bag and typewriter Hal had carried into his office.

"I'm afraid that wants more than talk, Earl." She had gained an icy, official self-control. Hal could see him measure the frost in it and see the half head shake as Graves accepted it.

"I reckon he likes this Frogpop better than we do. Sorry about our dinner party but we got hot beans and cold brandy."

He looked at his wristwatch, and as he did a tall lieutenant colonel in a field jacket with faint stains of dried blood on one arm began to lead a file of officers into the room.

"Well! For once, you're on time, Shorty."

A staff, like a family, developed and cherished indigenous jokes. You could measure the antiquity of this one by the burst of conditioned guffaws it provoked. Graves had already moved with ceremonious formality to Elsie's side.

"Brandy at the table 'cause we roll in fifteen minutes. Now, if you gents will step up, I want to make you acquainted with the flyboy and the little lady from the R.A.F."

Hal was sure now that Graves understood the tension between them. He was already assuming full responsibility for Elsie. When the introductions were completed he took her arm and maneuvered her through the door so that Hal had to walk behind them down the long hall to the dining room.

Inner shutters and blackout curtains hid the windows. Fires blazed from two different hearths at the end and one side of the room. Overhead dishpan lights with lanky black wires leading out the doors to the distant hum of a G.I. generator flooded the bare trestle table and elegant wood paneling alike with a harsh glare.

The instant Graves entered the room mess boys with trim white jackets over their brown wool began to place steaming metal trays of beans, stew and hardtack at each place. A gallon pot of coffee was already on the table. There was a cut-open can of condensed milk before every other seat and a pair of tin cups at each one.

"Get the brandy started, Shorty," said Graves.

It went around by the tin cupful. Many declined. Those who took it either gulped without ceremony or poured it in coffee. The conversation might have been prescribed by a Field Manual: Senior Officers' Entertainments for Guests. In the order of their rank every officer present volunteered to Elsie that he either had or had not been in London. Those who had, spoke of the weather during their stay. When the last lieutenant had exhausted the last rain Graves himself had to cope with the silence.

"Where'll we make tonight, Red?"

"Sir, I got in mind a real high grade Milwaukee-type rathskeller about nine miles east of Berlin . . . unless Shaef stops us again."

Graves led the laughter and let it echo into another silence before consulting his wristwatch.

"Any of you gents who want to linger over coffee and brandy got fifteen seconds."

Their heels hit the floor with the crashing unison of a

drill maneuver. Hal found himself squeezed against the corridor wall on Elsie's left. Graves was holding her firmly by the right arm and, as before, she kept her eyes upon him. At the porte cochere the Colonel's jeep was pluming a faint stream of exhaust. Swanson had just finished putting Elsie's little blue bag and typewriter into it. Graves seemed to notice Hal's presence for the first time.

"She'll be safe with us."

"Thanks, Earl."

"I do hope I shan't be a burden." She was keeping her face averted from Hal.

"Burden, hell!" Graves grinned. "First roadblock I'm gonna stake you out for 88 bait. You brought me luck last night."

"Nice to have been of some use," her voice bit.

"Brett, you want cover back to town?"

"No."

"Then get moving." He indicated Hal's jeep waiting behind his own. "We'll need this whole road in ninety seconds."

Hal had to take Elsie by the arms to turn her frozen face toward him.

"I'll see you in London, very soon."

"Not likely. This was a temporary assignment, Major."

He moved to kiss her and she eluded him, climbing into Graves's jeep. He hurried back to his own and got her blanket, and reached for her again as he tried to wrap it around her feet. She took it from his hands and moved farther away. Graves looked at his watch again.

"We'll take care of her. Good luck, flyboy."

"Thanks, Earl, for everything."

He had a last look at the dim whiteness of her face

and called again: "See you in London." There was no reply. As he started his own jeep he could hear the whirr of other starters and then the explosive catch of a dozen motors, shredding the darkness around him.

8

FOR perhaps half a mile the chugging of the other motors and the purposeful, confident rumble of tank treads hung about him like a protective armor, enveloping him in its own surging unity. Then imperceptibly it began to fade, softening as it receded into a distant murmur that died.

Silence brought returning consciousness of his closer surroundings. Fog creeping inland from the river swallowed the twinkling stars one by one until vision was limited to the low blue half moons of his headlights. It was protection for a solitary jeep. It would also be cover for troops crossing the Rhine toward the undefended French shore.

He slowed down, dreading return to their suite. It had been more than sanctuary, more than refuge from the forbidding oppression in which they had first entered the canal ring as aliens together. It had vibrated with the progressive intoxication of love. Now she would not be there.

His desolation of spirit quickened with ignoble prickles of pure fear. He no longer had to maintain assurance before her. He had to face things as they were. He was an unwelcome alien here, skulking in anarchy, under the shadow of invasion. German troops could be crossing the river right now. There could be a patrol, already billeted in the Hotel Gustav.

He cursed and gripped the wheel harder. He made himself drive by the last turn into the Place Egalité for a slow circuit of the town, aware that his bravado was evasion, conscious stalling from the first showdown.

Tonight curfew was absolute. There was not a sound, not a shadow in the main streets and squares. The exterior of Gonorrhea Gardens was dark and mute, the piano music only a memory. No M.P. stood at ease before the hotel where the Command Post had been.

The Place Egalité as he turned into it was as bare and soundless as the rest of Strasbourg. Fog was down to the level of the upper storey windows here. The chugging of his jeep reverberated from the broken walls of the Hotel Pourvalle. He pulled the key with his left hand in Antoine's courtyard. His right was on the automatic at his hip.

Graves's patrol should be passing Schirmeck by now. His main column would be grinding up the mountain road and the noise would carry to Natzweiler. If Gelan did not already know of the American withdrawal he soon would. It occurred to Hal that he might have been in the center of that column now, on his way back to London with Elsie. It was a long time since he had wondered whether it was lucky to be safe.

He had to wait through several knocks before the little peephole showed him a fragment of Madame's face, strained and white. Relief flooded through her recognition of him. The door opened swiftly and he entered it to blinding light. A new arrangement of candles isolated entrants in impenetrable glare. He had to step past it to see that Antoine had been covering the door, with his hand under the counter while Madame opened it.

The hotelman was obviously as surprised as his wife at Hal's return. He'd had time to recover while she opened the door. Now without wasting a second on amenities he made the familiar waving gesture.

"I'll unlock the garage."

The doors were swinging open into the alley as he drove up to them. He slowed to clear them and, through the lower pulse of his motor, heard again the brief rattle of automatic weapons from the direction of the market. The wooden doors, banging shut behind him, smothered it. The bolt slammed, a match flared to a candle. Gustav's heavy voice was surcharged with more than the puffing of exertion.

"One did not expect you so soon."

"Did you expect me at all?"

"I hoped that Mademoiselle Vane and Colonel Graves would take you with them. We have had to prepare for other guests."

He raised the candle to reveal a transformation in the garage. The improvised arsenal had disappeared. The workbench was completely concealed under an artful camouflage of rusted screens, garden tools, vineyard wire and stakes, a half-rotted wooden door, and the crowning touch of an outmoded baby carriage with horsehair bursting from its torn upholstery.

"Your petrol is safe," Antoine assured him.

"You do expect invasion, don't you?"

"Many here would welcome it. Even without it, one must expect other disturbances."

His somber eyes came to rest on the jeep. Belatedly, Hal began to realize that obsession with his own purposes had obscured the other potential consequences of his presence.

"Is my being here a danger to you, Antoine?"

"Everything is a danger now." It was evasion.

"If you like I'll go to another hotel." He suddenly remembered the dark front of the old Command Post.

Gustav had thought of the same thing, sooner. His cogitation was brief, his slow head shake final.

"None of us could defend you against invasion. Even the honest hotels would not resist their neighbors for you. Thanks to your weapons we may hope to oppose local swine here. May I ask you some questions that may be asked of me?"

"Anything."

"Is your mission so urgent you could not return, later?"

"It is."

"I may be asked how soon you hope to complete it."

"I hope that two days will suffice."

It was out before he had fathomed the depth of the simple inquiries. The same questions might indeed be asked of Antoine. Hal's answers had already informed him that he hoped for another rendezvous with Litard in the next forty-eight hours. The candlelight was too dim for Hal to be certain he had seen a quiver of the nostrils, an intensification of gleam in the blue eyes. Gustav spoke blandly.

"We have hidden air crews longer; one can hope."

As if anxious to terminate the conversation, he led Hal through the back rooms to the kitchen. There, instead of proceeding to the dining room and lobby he opened the door in the other direction and descended the steep stairs to the first wine cellar. It had already been converted to a new kind of storage. The petrol, jerricans and ration boxes were neatly stacked. On top of them were Hal's musette bag and typewriter.

"Your room would not be safe," said Antoine.

It was reprieve. Upstairs every wall, chair and curtain would have evoked her fragrance and her laughter. This was a clean break.

Gustav went on to explain that a mattress and bedding would be arranged for Hal in the lower cellar. The bulk of his supplies and petrol would go down there. A few cans and boxes would be left upstairs to satisfy irresistable search parties. The concealment of the debris pile would be replaced over the trapdoor while he slept. The jeep could not be hidden. In extremity Gustav would have to relinquish it, explaining that the haste of the departing troops had left it behind.

The opening of the trapdoor to the lower cellar stirred claustrophobic protest. There was no other exit from this hole. A sudden vision of the fire-blackened Hotel Pourvalle assailed him. He would be entombed down here, with enough gasoline to lift the hotel off its foundations. On the verge of insisting that he would take his chances upstairs he stopped. The chances were not exclusively his. The Gustavs were accepting conscious risk of torture and death to harbor him at all. Antoine seemed to read his misgivings.

"We have safely concealed fourteen air crew men here."

"We'll do it your way."

"Grandpapa can always fool those pigs!" Gervais had appeared on the upper stairs, arms full of bedding for Hal, face aglow with the honor of participation. Always before, the sight of the boy had lifted Hal's spirits. Tonight he found himself eying the little hands that clutched the blanket roll and remembering the knotted stump on the wrist of Ambroise's nephew in Baccarat.

When they had made him a bed and shifted the gasoline and prepared the camouflage for the trapdoor, he persuaded Antoine to let him share the preliminary vigil on the lobby. For his promise to retreat without heroics at the first alarm, the hotelman allowed Hal a chair near the path of exit through dining room and kitchen. Taking his own place by the cashier's cage from which he could cover the front door, Antoine accepted a cigarette from Hal and lifted the phone with that grimace of distrust he always accorded it. He spoke with a low-voiced velocity Hal could not follow and hung up, shrugging.

"No invasion yet, Major."

The Council of cells had improvised a volunteer sentry system along the river to replace the withdrawn Americans. Its purpose was the opposite of defense. If German troops came in force efforts would be made to prevent irresponsible French fire upon them in order to save the town from their artillery. Impromptu resistance would be suppressed, if possible, by the cells while their leaders sought terms for peaceful submission. All who disliked this plan were at liberty to leave the town. Antoine thought there would be a major evacuation.

"What about yourself?"

"I stayed in '40." He seemed to be reassuring himself and then, with Gallic candor, he shrugged. "Of course this time it is different."

The difference, he added quickly, was the activity of himself and his friends in the air crew escape work. No degree of discretion could entirely blind neighbors. It was possible that the exuberant Gabrielle had boasted of the Germans they had killed. He offered no further reasons, and Hal did not press him. The discipline of

Marcel, Alphonse and the others spoke for itself. Exemplary as their security was, it was patent that this cell had been up to its collective neck in other resistance work. Now it was known through the town that the Hotel Gustav had housed Allied officers this week.

"Many fractions covet my place. If the Boche do return, one denouncer could put me in Natzweiler."

"Has Francois Monet been returned to Natzweiler?"

He had caught his host off his guard as he intended. The eyes flashed reflexively to the phone.

"He hasn't yet . . ." Antoine caught himself and tried to cover. "At least one does not hear of it."

It was only negative proof. It seemed to confirm the purport of those innocent questions in the garage. Antoine knew that he would be staying only for another meeting with Litard. That look at the phone suggested that he already had the Monet house under surveillance again.

There was a soft footstep behind him, and he whipped around and then slumped in momentary relief at the sight of Madame Cassandra. She was carrying by their hanger wires the two freshly pressed German uniforms Gustav had removed from their closet on the night of their arrival. Elsie's words echoed suddenly in his ears: "I hope you don't mind ghosts." They had laughed over it then. Madame mounted the stairs silently and Gustav spoke dryly.

"We must be prepared for what happens, Major."

"I say it's an ill wind," laughed Gabrielle. She had followed Madame with an armful of linen and was chuckling at the way the men had looked at the uniforms.

"You will remember our rule!" snapped Gustav.

"Pouf!" The broad face defied him. "There are more

places than this little hotel to give those pigs a true French welcome. With petrol for Marcel's truck we could take bodies back into the Vosges like cordwood."

"Shut your mouth and do your work!" said Antoine.

She ascended the stairs, smiling.

"Is Monet likely to be taken back to Natzweiler?"

This time the hotelman was on guard. He merely shrugged.

"He might return as commandant. It would not be the first time guards and prisoners have changed places there."

Sooner or later Hal would have to deal with this. Later might be too late. He tried for an easy, factual tone.

"I shall have to see him tomorrow."

Antoine replied with an identical innocence.

"We will be glad to take a message for you, Major."

A simple message would accomplish his need. The question now was what else it might accomplish. Litard would surely be aware of the withdrawal of the Americans. If he assumed, as he well might, that Hal had gone with them, he would not risk a return tomorrow night. The only way to reassure him would be to have Francois or Valéry raise the ladder again. A message ordering that would invite Antoine and his cell to the rendezvous.

"Thanks, Antoine, I'll go myself."

"It might be dangerous for you to go about in daylight."

"You have just told me everything is dangerous."

Antoine regarded him through a cogitation in which Hal thought he could discern solicitude struggling with guile. His voice was troubled.

"Major, we owe you our freedom and we have not forgotten the grace that allowed our divisions to reenter our city ahead of the forces that made their return possible. Now freedom itself confronts us with the older problems that put us into German power. Litard and Natzweiler are examples.

"It is known here that you have been intriguing with Litard. Do you imagine Commandant Gelan released Monet to you out of fear? He did not. He released him because I confided to him my surmise that your purposes might bring M. Litard within our reach. They did, and then you took him from us and set him free. Would you expect Gelan to trust me again? Colonel Graves is no longer behind you, Major. I beg you to let us carry your messages or, if you prefer, bring Monet here to you."

It was more than fair warning. It was a reminder that other lives beside his own were involved in whatever he did here. He could no longer remember the words of the oath he had taken at March Field. They had committed him, by implication at least, to death itself if necessary in the line of duty. They had not stipulated obligation to have Gervais's fingers squeezed off in a vise, or Antoine and Madame incinerated in their own hotel. The earnest eyes that reminded him of these hazards had already accepted potential commitment to them in his behalf. Antoine could have refused Hal readmission to the hotel. He could have disposed of his own danger with a word to either the market camp or Gelan.

"Let's see how things look tomorrow, Antoine."

"Accord." Antoine knew he had made his point. "Will you sleep?"

"Not until you do."

"I shall watch all night."

"I shall watch with you."

He continued firmly. He intended to share the hazards to which his presence contributed. German invasion would terminate all hope of fulfilling his mission here. At the first valid warning of this he would drive the Gustavs and Gervais to safety in his jeep. Local disturbances were another matter. If his presence provoked action against the hotel he would assist its defense.

"I'm only a paper soldier, Antoine. But if you'll check me out on one of those Kraut carbines, I'll do my best."

He was rewarded by warmth in those troubled eyes.

"Madame and I should be grateful. Marcel and Alphonse are on the river watch tonight."

He shuffled toward the back room, leaving Hal to reconsider that impression of warmth. It was fatuous to think Gustav could be acting from personal affection. Generous and kind as he had been from the first, the magnet had always been Litard. Marcel and Alphonse might very well be on the river watch. If so they would be looking as eagerly for Litard's canoe as for German landing craft. Gustav returned carrying a little drum-fed German automatic rifle.

"One appreciates your offer to evacuate us, Major. Thanks to your petrol, Marcel's truck and Alphonse's motorbike are also available if it comes to that. The pigs have not come yet, however, and the fractions will move me out of here dead or not at all! Now, regard this little one."

He gave Hal expert instruction in the rifle and then nodded approval of his pupil.

"Colonel Graves said you were wasted with your paper work. This is a dainty thing even if made by pigs. Remember only that in long bursts the muzzle climbs. It is well to begin about the navel."

Madame fluttered back presently, a musical comedy witch now in billowing nightdress and cap. She paused for a long whispered colloquy with Antoine, at the end of which he grunted and indicated Hal.

"My rear is defended! Sleep and cease bothering us!"

She retired, cackling lamentations. Together he and Antoine rearranged his chair to insure a clear field of fire at both front and kitchen doors and dimmed the parlor candles to a single flicker of light. Toward the end of their dispositions they heard again the muted rattle of automatic fire. After listening carefully Antoine grunted satisfaction.

"Market again. Those fractions have had time to be here if they are coming. Sleep, and I shall call you in an hour."

He slumped in the chair, more fatigued than he had known, and tried to force his thoughts through analysis of the problem. It was useless. It all turned upon the enigma of Antoine, if it was an enigma. So far he could think of no possible way to meet Litard without leading Antoine to him. When he finally dozed it was to be haunted by remembrance of Elsie's set white face and final words:

"Not likely. This was a temporary assignment, Major."

A touch on his sleeve rescued him. Five minutes later Antoine was snoring unambiguously in the chair. For the first time since Graves had said he was moving out, Hal felt a brief renewal of self-confidence. So far, at least, Antoine trusted him.

At five they made coffee which Antoine laced heavily with his own brandy. At a little after six Hal was galvanized by a single faint tap at the door followed by a rhythmic pattern. Antoine had been asleep. His carbine muzzle was up before the last tap. He lowered it, blinking and smiling.

"Marcel: that one cuts marble as gently. Poor Alphonse shakes the building to hang a picture."

The mason entered shivering from cold and went straight for the coffeepot on the fire. He seemed to take Hal's presence for granted. It might mean nothing. It might mean that Antoine had found a way to let him know of it. The hotelman was interrogating him in unintelligible idiom and his final head shake seemed satisfied.

"No invasion yet, Major."

"What was all the shooting about?"

Marcel had not been near it. Hearsay was circulating reports of attempts to deliver or assist the breakout of prisoners in the market camp. So far all had been frustrated and a firm control retained by the cells in charge. It was impossible to tell whether the abortive efforts had been coordinated with expectation of invasion.

"Fog still obscures the river. One would have hoped to hear the mounting of a major effort by now."

Fog would also obscure the signal ladder. Antoine spoke as if reading his thoughts.

"Marcel will deliver any message you wish, Major."

"Let us see how things march," he stalled. "They might be awaiting better light to move in strength."

"They do not need to move in strength," said Marcel. "If one platoon raises the swastika in the Place Kléber we are theirs."

Reluctant winter dawn lurked late in the fog that morning. Marcel sprawled in one of the lobby chairs with a familiarity he had never previously permitted himself. When Antoine cooked breakfast the mason joined them at the table. It might mean nothing; it might be undeclared imprisonment. They lingered over coffee and Hal's cigarettes until a removal of the black-out curtains disclosed enough outer light to see across the square to the Hotel Pourvalle. Hal yawned and stretched.

"I shall be going out for a while."

Instantly the hotelman's eyes went to Marcel's.

"It is not something we could do for you?"

"Thank you. I wish to see things for myself."

This time Antoine avoided Marcel's eyes. Without further comment he led Hal through the kitchen to the garage. There he stalled, changing and rearranging the camouflage over the workbench, scrutinizing it from the angle of the door, returning to change it again. He used up five minutes before the brief opening of the wooden doors.

Emerging from the alley into the street leading toward the Quai, Hal could hear the muttering of a motorcycle behind him. He drove a rough circle for a few minutes, retracing his tracks through the labyrinth of little streets converging on the canal. Approaching it again, he turned away from the normal course to Monet's house, crossed the bridge and entered one of the main streets to the Place de la Gare. A block along it he slowed, until a backward glance showed him Marcel turning into it on his motorcycle. A moment later he lost sight of the mason in the steadily increasing traffic.

This was composed of pedestrians carrying bundles under their arms or strapped to their backs, trundling them in wheelbarrows, children's carts and baby carriages. Bread, bottles and bedding showed in every one. Some were alone, some in couples, some in family groups. The adults plodded along inertly; the faces they lifted to brief scrutiny of the jeep were sullen.

The immense square before the station was so jammed that he would have turned back except for the pressure of the crowd around him. Thousands of people milled and chattered and churned, surging toward the station building itself and then recoiling from the compression of the throngs ahead of them.

The men were bearded and red eyed from all night vigil. The women were drawn of face with unkempt hair showing under scarves and ancient hats. Some gnawed on long loaves of bread; many drank from nearly empty wine bottles. Every eye on the Place kept returning eagerly to a vast new bulletin board on which there was so far no message. Children cried and squabbled and relieved themselves over the gutters. Their parents scolded and cuffed them without removing stony gazes from the blank board. The seething talk was all questions, answered with questions. No one knew whether trains would run at all that day.

Their fixed preoccupation with the board and with every minute chance to squeeze themselves forward in the crowd let Hal inch the jeep through them. It took him half an hour to go about four blocks.

From the far side of the square egress into the Boulevard President Wilson was easier. He was now breasting an equal spate of pedestrians coming toward the station, and their anxiety to reach it worked for him. They dodged and squirmed past the jeep nimbly to avoid losing position in the stream around them, augmented by every converging alley.

As he progressed, traffic thinned noticeably to his

right. The people approaching kept their eyes to the right and ran a little as they passed an intersection ahead of him. He was abreast of it before he recognized the deserted street as the one that ran between the market and the internment camp.

He stopped, staring with incredulity. The four motionless figures sprawled along the paving were corpses. The wall of the camp was manned in double strength by hard-faced guards, brandishing weapons. For the first time that morning he was seeing men who still dared to wear the tricolored arm band. These sentries were flaunting them. The internees beyond walked the same weary circuit of wires and walls in the same vain effort to keep warm.

He was still staring with disbelief from guards to corpses when a gate opened in the wall and an ancient black Renault chugged out toward him. He let it approach without thought until he could see the armbanded driver and guard on the front seat. Behind them rode the Commandant of the market camp and Gelan of Natzweiler.

They gaped at recognition of each other. Then Gelan bent to his driver, pointing and exhorting him toward Hal. He put the jeep into gear and let it jump forward, almost decimating a family of oncoming fugitives in his first wild surge of flight. He swerved past them on two wheels and careened down the Boulevard, blowing his horn to warn the stream of people he breasted.

On open streets Hal might have dodged or run away from the Renault. Here the density of pedestrians forbade full speed. The Renault, with the advantage of the path he was clearing, closed steadily on him. Driver and guard were shouting and the guard was waving a pistol, not quite willing to shoot into the throng. They were within fifty yards of the jeep when Marcel overtook the Renault on his motorbike, swerved crazily in front of it and then began to gesticulate wildly. His motor spluttered out and he lost momentum. The Renault squealed its brakes. Marcel wobbled to a stop and fell over in its path, and the driver of the Renault, with an angry wave at Hal, stopped before he hit the motorbike.

With a kneading stomach, Hal sped on. Marcel had risked his life to let him escape. To return was to be captured. He could not free Marcel if they wished to hold him. He could only hope the mason was up to a story as plausible as his accident had seemed. Gelan had no reason to associate Hal with Marcel so far. Now he did know that Hal was still in Strasbourg, and he had known from the first that Hal was living with Antoine.

He drove on wondering whether Marcel had acted to save his life out of good will or out of determination to preserve their chance at Litard. Traffic and fog obliterated the group behind him quickly. As soon as he was out of their sight he turned off the Boulevard and criss-crossed his own trail a dozen times in aimless circuit of the back streets. Sure at last that he was no longer followed, he zigzagged a careful checkerboard through the outskirts of the town to the house of Francois Monet.

Proximity to the river brought the fog down, accentuating the desolation of the district. The nearest red tile roofs were dim, the thatched huts hazy, the lanes shrouded. He had to slow down to a pace that would have permitted easy ambush. He drew up to the Monet house with a sense of respite that did not outlast his first glimpse of Madame Monet's face straining through the window. Its normal ruddy hue was ashen.

He had to wait through an uneasy interval at the door until Monet himself opened it and almost pulled Hal inside in his eagerness to shut and bolt it again. The six-year-old girl slipped from the room with feline stealth.

Madame Monet set a bottle and glasses on the table through greetings and commonplaces. Today instead of withdrawing from masculine meetings as was her custom she took up a firm position before them. Her back was to the wall, her bare arms crossed, her dark eyes hovered protectively over the agitated Francois.

"Major, will the American soldiers return?"

It was the universal anxiety of all Strasbourg. Remembering the position in which he had first met Monet, Hal was torn with compassion. It took effort to remember that he had not been sent here to sympathize with pitiable family groups. Jet planes might be killing Fortress crews while they talked.

"I'm here," he said. "Will you raise the ladder today, Francois?"

Monet hesitated; his wife did not. It would be impossible for Francois to leave the house. He was in great peril. He would go out only over her dead body. The Monets could risk nothing more to do with those who had endangered him. Even if he dared to try, it would be impossible to accomplish Hal's request.

"The bad ones watch at all hours," she concluded.

"The bad ones who took you to Natzweiler?"

"No. The bad ones of Antoine Gustav."

It was so final, so unequivocal that he had to force himself to concentrate on the corroborative detail. Little Hilda Monet had taken three eggs to the house of a friendly neighbor the previous afternoon. A schoolmate there had just returned from the house of the closer neighbor who coveted the Monets' asparagus patch. She told Hilda that Marcel had arrived there at dusk and been taken at once to a bedroom from which a window looked on the Monet house.

By starlight Monet himself had made a reconnaissance. That particular window, though dark, was not shrouded by the customary blackout curtain. The Monets had mounted a reciprocal watch. Francois had seen Alphonse enter the house between five and six. A few minutes later Marcel had emerged and pushed the motorbike well down the lane before they heard it splutter and depart. As far as Francois knew Alphonse was still watching them.

Confirmation that Antoine was still using him as a stalking horse brought Hal a paradoxical relief. It mitigated the guilt inherent in the jeopardy his presence forced upon the Gustavs. It pacified a conscience already troubled about deceiving his host, even as it complicated further deception. He had relied upon the assistance of Monet. Now he would not have it. Certainty of the new obstacles suggested a new chance. The surveillance that immobilized Monet also immobilized Alphonse.

Sympathetically, he told the Monets that he understood their dilemma and regretted his part in responsibility for it. He withdrew his request for further help. He had hoped for a final meeting with Litard. If the manufacturer should return he would still reward Monet handsomely for tidings of it. He might be at the hotel a day or two more. After that he would probably be leaving Strasbourg.

Over a fresh tirade of apologies and regrets he lingered in their doorway long enough for a persuasive pantomime of final farewell. In full view of the neighboring window, he brought from the jeep candy for the children and a final box of K ration for their parents. Then after kisses and handshakes, he got into the jeep and set out on the normal course for town.

As soon as the fog had enclosed him again he zigzagged through the lanes of the wretched suburb until he was very sure of no pursuit and then drove straight to the factory. Patches of light were opening the overcast with a promise of early visibility across the river.

This time Valéry shuffled from his cinder-block house as soon as Hal drew up to the gate. The watchman was still sullen and resentful. It was problematical whether he would obey at all, without the stimulus of Antoine's severity. Hal might have driven into the plant itself through one of the blast holes in the wall. Access was not enough. He had to have continuing subservience and he had to test it before he relied on it.

After an inquisitive scrutiny of the empty jeep, the watchman nodded agreement to Hal's instructions and opened the gate. Once in the inner yard Hal drove around to the rear and into the concealment of the building itself. Valéry limped in presently from the front. Hal gave him a carton of cigarettes and asked him to raise the ladder on the upper east balcony at once. Valéry tucked the cigarettes into his jacket, stepped back and refused categorically.

He regretted disobliging the American soldier. It was no longer safe to appear on that balcony. The fog was breaking up and would be gone any minute. The whole balcony would then be exposed to German snipers. Previously they had never shot at the factory for fear of provoking return fire from the American soldiers on the French shore. Now the Americans were gone.

"They would shoot me for sport," said Valéry.

Antoine would have had the old man up on that balcony with two words. Neither Hal's uniform nor the automatic on his leg would stir the crafty peasant. Generations of servility had sharpened his judgment. The American would not shoot him. Hal went to an opening in the wall and took a long look out toward the river. The fog certainly was lifting.

"Show me where the ladder is."

Valéry turned without comment and preceded Hal up the relatively undamaged back stairs to the first filing room they had ransacked so fruitlessly. From it a second flight, scarred with bomb fragments, led upward to a high interior catwalk that had evidently served for cleaning and repair of one of the long new banks of saw-toothed upper roof and windows.

On the whole eastward expanse only a dozen isolated panes remained intact. The catwalk was a litter of glass fragments along which Valéry led him to a little door. Unlocking this, he stepped back and indicated to Hal an outer balcony running parallel to the catwalk. Hal stepped through it and felt his heart turn over as the door slammed behind him.

Panic put his hand back on the knob. Returning self-control stopped him from trying it. If he was locked out, he was locked out. He had come up here to set the ladder. It awaited him lying at length behind the knee-high outer screening of the balcony, in a litter of glass similar to the one inside. He stepped to it quickly and then paused for an orienting look. Open patches in the fog showed the river itself now. He could see dim vistas of the little islands.

Closer, on the French side, he got a valuable perspective of the maze of canals, ditches and lanes between factory and river. Working from his memory of Graves's maps and the brief configurations revealed by the star shells he traced out the lanes until he identified the shack from which Litard had taken his canoe. By daylight it was closer to the factory than he had thought. As he craned forward to imprint it more clearly on his mind a change of light brightened the river and began to expose the willow banks on the far shore.

He grabbed the ladder, thrust its upper runners through the cavities of two empty panes and tested its base. It was firmly planted. Done, he hurried back toward the little door, glass crunching under his frightened feet. Even above its crackle he could hear the echo of the words Elsie had spoken in the yard below: "It's elementary that someone should know where one is."

No one knew where he was. Valéry was capable of locking him out, of leaving him to the snipers. He didn't even have to depend on snipers. A single shot or blow as Hal reentered that door would do it. No one along the Rhine for hundreds of miles would look up to see another dead soldier float past.

The door opened readily. He was inside and halfway down the stairs before reaction made him grasp the rail until his knees stiffened again. The sight of Valéry waiting stolidly by the jeep helped. With five minutes more of partial fog he could be out of the place. Concealing his haste he gave Valéry a bottle of the Wehrmacht brandy and then whirled into the clearing day. This time, instead of waiting for the gate, he drove a rough path to one of the gaping bomb holes in the wall and satisfied himself that, with care, it was passable. From the road a backward glance showed him the ladder still in place.

3

There was no certain way to obviate the chance of being trapped by Gelan at the hotel. As far as Hal was aware Antoine knew nothing of the ladder signal. Alphonse had seen Hal go into the Monet house and leave it, however. If he failed to return to the hotel in a reasonable time it would not take Gustav and his friends long to find out everything that Monet knew.

He gambled another hour on a reconnaissance of the town, traversing the main streets and the open squares of the Kléber, Broglie and Gutenberg. Their testimony was uniform. Only a few scurrying civilians and bicycles were to be seen.

The corpses had been removed from the paving before the market camp. New sunlight glinted bravely on the arm bands and guns of the guards. The Place de la Gare seemed even more crowded. If a single train had departed, its load had not decreased the sea of faces still straining toward the bulletin board. Some of those waiting had already made the other choice. There was a steady trickle of carts and feet moving against the incoming tide along the Boulevard of Metz. The line of exodus stretched toward the open country roads to the foothills.

The Place Egalité seemed as deserted as the other squares. He made a first fast run through it and verified that at least no car or Fifi arm bands guarded the hotel entrance. The alley was equally empty. The second time around, he turned into the courtyard, pulled up to the stoop, and with hammering pulse knocked on the door. Antoine responded to the first sight of him with a hurried wave toward the garage. There the new camouflage was undisturbed, and with the doors locked Antoine's voice was as bland as ever.

"Did you have a good morning, Major?"

He might have been asking about a sightseer's tour of the cathedral. Hal kept his eyes locked on the blue ones before him.

"Commandant Gelan pursued and nearly caught me."

"One hears of that." Antoine chuckled.

One hears, but one does not speak until the subject is broached, he reflected. At any rate it was in the open now.

"Marcel saved me," he continued.

"You were most fortunate," replied Antoine.

As if aware that he had not spoken at once of so significant an incident, the hotelman amplified suavely now. Marcel had decided to have a look at the internment camp after Hal left. He wished to verify the rumors of the night. He had been astounded to see Hal, and then the pursuing official car. Once he understood the predicament, he had acted boldly.

"Our Vosges grouse feign broken wings to draw pursuit from their chicks," chuckled Antoine. "Marcel improves upon nature with a broken petrol line. You were most fortunate, Major," he repeated more soberly.

"I wish to thank him."

"You may thank yourself. Only your petrol put him where he so conveniently was." The simulated levity vanished. "I have to tell you that Commandant Gelan came here to ask for you."

"What did he ask?"

"He said he merely wished to pay his respects."

"What did you tell him?"

"Happily Marcel had returned to inform me of the

encounter so it was pointless to lie. I told him you had spent the night and gone out early and I had no knowledge of your plans."

"It's time you had, Antoine."

To his surprise the hotelman shook his head.

"I do not wish to force your confidence. It is idle to deny that Commandant Gelan might."

"I went to see Francois Monet," said Hal. "I had hoped for another meeting with M. Litard. He says Litard will not return now that our soldiers have gone."

"That is easy to believe," Antoine nodded.

"Therefore," Hal continued, "I shall depart this afternoon."

He continued easily under Gustav's unflickering scrutiny. Since there was no hope of seeing Litard to confirm the last details of his story it was pointless to remain here. With Antoine's permission, he would nap at the hotel through the early afternoon and then set out for Schirmeck, Baccarat and Nancy in the dusk, trusting to the cover of the night for a safe passage through the mountains.

"I am relieved," said Antoine. "This is wise of you."

The evident sincerity of it stabbed him.

"Anything further on the invasion?"

"I was going to ask you. I have not been out."

Marcel had learned that the corpses in the street before the market were consequences of the shooting they had heard during the night.

"The greediest pigs are first to slaughter." Antoine spat on the floor. "They were Volksdeutsche hoping for favors from their returning friends. They now share the heaven of all swine."

He spat again and looked at Hal with relief.

"We shall miss you. I cannot deny that we hoped you might lead us again to M. Litard. But time itself will do that, and we shall enjoy thinking of you in London with Mademoiselle."

He wanted to believe it. He wanted to believe that the hotelman reciprocated the respect and affection he had stirred in Hal from their first meeting. You could admire resolves that opposed your own without deluding yourself. If Antoine suspected Hal's true purposes his first concern would be to maintain the appearance of being deceived by them.

It was a relief to turn to tangibilities. They would fill the jeep now. Hal would need only enough additional gas and rations to reach Nancy. The rest of his stock were for Antoine and his friends.

"I should like to say good-bye to Marcel and Alphonse."

"Name the hour and they will be here."

He set it at four o'clock and sat in the kitchen over a drink while Antoine brushed the women out disdainfully and cooked them an omelet with his own hand. Hal was going to miss this place more than he would have suspected. The forced cheer and inner melancholy of all partings had to be suppressed in vigilance now. It was impossible to be natural with people you were deceiving, or hoped you would be deceiving. He couldn't help wondering if Antoine was having the same difficulty.

He asked the hotelman to call him at four o'clock and then retired to the imprisonment of the lower wine cellar. Fatigue underlay his tension. Excitement ruled out any hope of sleep. He had secluded himself to reduce the strain of continuing deception, to avoid the chance of a careless remark. Now he could only toss and turn on the improvised bed, trying to anticipate things he could not control.

Antoine knocked gently at three fifty. Hal lit the candle, stripped to shorts and T shirt, and pulled on long wool underwear from his musette bag. Over that he put a sweater before donning shirt and trousers, and then carried his lightened bag out to the jeep.

"You must drive with vigilance," said Madame. "The automobile is a monster of treachery."

Incongruously, the words evoked another echo of Elsie's voice: ". . . they don't even trust each other. That's the alphabet of Alsace: distrust."

It intensified the poignancy of this parting. No matter who started it, deception spread like contagion from perpetrator to victim. He shook the hands of Marcel and Alphonse with genuine affection, even as he wondered whether Alphonse had abandoned his watch on the Monet house or simply been replaced. When he thanked Marcel for his timely assistance of the morning they laughed together at the discomfiture of Gelan. Both of them preserved the pretense that Marcel's presence at the scene had been an accident.

The mason had brought the latest news from the center of town. There was no invasion yet, and hope had risen with the lifting of the fog. The German shore was clearly visible and no preparations were in sight. Hal's hopes rose too. Litard could see that ladder, if he was watching. If not, his mistress would tell him.

Parting with Gervais was hardest of all. Those warm young eyes at least were concealing nothing.

"If you will return with peace, Major, we can fish

and trap grouse in the Vosges until the year of my conscription."

He promised to do so and drove down the alley, waving back with emotion. It did not blind him to careful count for as far as he could see them. The little group was intact. Perhaps he had fooled them. Perhaps the experience of the morning had prompted them to assign some member unknown to tail him.

No motorcycle followed as he crossed the canal bridge and angled off toward the road for Schirmeck. Long before he reached it he was engulfed again in heavy traffic. Hand carts, dog carts, baby carriages and an occasional farm wagon drawn by cow or bullock thickened the stream of weary pedestrians.

Old people were sitting by roadside ditches to rest, exhausted before they had entirely cleared the town. Some helped each other to rise and stagger on. Some evidently would go no farther. Remembering the ascent, even to the hamlet of Schirmeck, he shuddered for these fugitives. There were not enough farms along the way to shelter a fraction of them, not enough roofs in Schirmeck itself to cover them. Hope against invasion had been rising as he left town. The Germans might not return at all. Thousands of people who remembered them preferred a winter night in the open to the chance that they would.

To stop or even to slow the jeep was to be mobbed with pleas for a ride. Hal drove as fast as he dared, honking imperiously, shaking a stony face at all appeals and keeping a hand visibly close to the automatic on his hip. From time to time he slowed a little for a long look back. The throng made it impossible to tell whether one of Antoine's tireless men might still be tailing him. Lowering dusk brought the moment when he had to use the last of the light, whether he was being followed or not.

Forking south and then eastward along the back lanes he now breasted their lesser traffic on a circuitous return course. Starlight was pinpricking the darkness over the familiar road leading toward the Monets. He had timed it with care, and his eyes had adjusted enough so that he was able to maintain a slow speed without using his dim headlights.

No light showed at either the Monet house or that of the neighbors as he slipped by in the shadow of the hedge. There was no light in Valéry's watch house. Instead of stopping at the gate he turned sharply along the steel mesh fence and, craning his eyes for craters, retraced the exit course of the morning, through the bomb hole in the stone wall and around to the rear of the factory. He drove through the open doors into the building itself with his heart hammering. This was unavoidable risk. A patrol in here would have him before he cut the motor. It was the only alternative to leaving the jeep outside for any passers to see.

He turned the switch off and heard his heart pounding through the welcome silence. There were only muted echoes of his own movements as he pulled the key, took out the distributor rotor and then with his hand on his pistol made his way to the cinder-block shack.

Valéry opened the door to his peremptory knock with angry fear. Hal explained curtly that he was expecting a rendezvous with M. Litard. He had left his jeep in the factory. Injury to it would imperil M. Litard. Furthermore it would be punished as an act of sabotage against the American Army. The old man nodded, spat, and slammed the door. Hal could hear him testing the lock within.

Avoiding the gate, he slipped through the darkness to the blast hole in the wall and then made his way along the gravel road to the intersection with the dirt trail paralleling the canal. In all the plain around him there was no sound except, as he approached it, the faint sibilation of the river itself. The western skyline that should have sparkled with the lights of a quarter of a million inhabitants added not a candle's flicker to the last perceptible glow of sunset. Well down the dirt trail he cupped his hands closely over his flashlight and verified from moisture patterns that no tire had traversed it that day.

Litard's shack materialized out of the gloom like an old friend. He risked another glimmer of cupped light to ascertain that its padlock was undisturbed and then circled the shack slowly, pausing often to strain his ears. A battalion could have been hidden in the nearby underbrush. If it was, they were keeping security as tight as his own.

Leaving the shack, he walked the dirt lane along the canal past the point of the canoe's launching until he came to the margin where flood action had scoured bare the banks of the river itself. Darkness shrouded the far shore. By starlight its dim blur was quiescent.

His spirits rose. Patrols, if there were any about, would have stopped him by now. He had gambled that Fifi sentries would be concentrated along the firmer landing shores by the broken bridge abutments. So far it appeared a good gamble.

He made his way back to the precise point Captain Richards had designated for the return signal. Snaking into the underbrush he found the best compromise of view along the trail, canal mouth and river, and dropped his blanket to the wet ground.

The temperature was falling. Tonight increasing chill seemed to be preventing the normal generation of evening fog. With eyes oriented to the new horizons he could see the dark blur of the far shore line. It was a bad portent. Crossing by canoe in such visibility would be rash. Litard would know as well as he did that the alerted American sentries had been replaced by trigger-happy Fifi, expecting invasion.

The sharpening edge of the cold was cumulative. Every hour, after straining his ears to the utmost, he risked bends and push-ups until he could feel the sweat on his back. Twice after the exercises he allowed himself a carefully shielded cigarette. At midnight and again at four he could hear the distant rumble of a truck from the direction of the destroyed bridge approaches. It was brief and it came no closer to where he was. He could only surmise that sentries were being changed.

After his five o'clock exercises he was sure the air was warmer. A perceptible thickening of the atmosphere began to confirm belated formation of the normal shroud of fog. It became steadily denser.

At ten minutes of six he was galvanized by the rhythmic chunking and splashing of oars. They approached from downstream in the river, and for a few minutes he thought they would turn into the mouth of the canal. Instead the noise stopped well beyond the bank. Whether the boat had drifted back downstream or proceeded out of earshot on an eastward crossing he could not tell.

Tension increased with the ticking away of the night and the impenetrability of the thickening fog. When he finally had to admit to himself that its dark mass was lightening to gray, his spirit slumped. He did another set of exercises and was settling without conviction to a last hour on the damp blanket. Then, from the canal mouth, he distinctly heard the whish of a paddle.

9

THE canoe magnified itself gliding silently into focus through the fog. He could identify Litard before the man rose to his knees, scanning the bank for his landmark. He checked hard with a silent thrust that brought the little craft to a motionless right angle with the shallow ditch. His hand slid over the western thwart and a flashlight blinked three times into the water.

Hal preserved an equal silence, ears aquiver for other sound. None was audible. Litard shifted back to the seat and composed himself to wait in meticulous conformity with his instructions. After ten minutes had revealed no indication of intruders Hal arose from his concealment, engaged Litard's attention with a flick of his arm and put a hand over his lips. Litard nodded. Hal beckoned him ashore. Litard landed expertly and waited beside the canoe. As Hal came down to him, the manufacturer's hand went into his pocket.

"Are you alone, Major?"

"For the moment."

"We heard your troops have left Strasbourg."

"You can hear anything in a war."

"I am relying on their protection." The eyes narrowed.

"You have mine, if you do as I say."

Litard swept the short horizon from the canal with a suspicious scrutiny. The bare hand came slowly out of his pocket and fumbled with a glove on the thwart. He was manifestly dissatisfied.

"At your service, Major."

"Did you bring the information?"

"For the proper authorities."

"Let's hide that canoe."

"You promise to take me to your authorities?"

"If I believe you. If not you'll need the canoe."

Litard grunted and extended the paddle to Hal, almost contemptuously. His long torso bent over the little craft. He lifted it clear of the water and over his head with a rhythm that carried into momentum for a long stride up the bank. After it was locked in the shed again he turned to Hal with expectation.

"I am in your hands, Major."

"We'll go to your factory."

Litard searched the empty lane with quick eyes, nodded as if to himself and set off with a swinging pace Hal found it hard to match. They were almost at the gravel road before he spoke again.

"Why did you fire those star shells?"

"To see if you really did go into Germany."

"So I reasoned. It was clever."

Fog was thinner along the gravel road. Hal judged visibility at about a hundred yards and was conscious of the quickening of his heartbeat. Maximum hazard of interception would occur between the intersection and the plant. He had to risk it and he had to dissemble his anxiety. Conscious as he was of this, he botched it.

The first touch of his feet on that gravel turned his head irresistibly for quick right and left search. In the next instant he realized that the sharp eyes beside him had seen the reflex and understood. He might as well have told the man that they were alone and he was afraid. It was the more ominous that Litard's superior self-control had not betrayed his quick comprehension. His face remained expressionless.

"We'll go through that hole in the wall," said Hal.

They pounded along the gravel, turned without a word on the shortest line to the hole, passed through it and entered the factory from the rear. This time Hal was able to suppress a sigh of relief to see the jeep exactly where he had left it. Litard saw the effect and understood. His stride toward it was lengthening. Hal checked him.

"First we talk."

He led the man across the main gallery, past the board room and, swinging the door, ushered him into his own office. It was dank with the night air and lit only dimly by gaps in the upper part of the plywood window cover. Litard swept it with a glance. His hand went back into his pocket. He opened doors for a long look into the board room and another at the main gallery of the plant. Then he closed the doors quietly.

"You have answered my question."

"I brought you here to answer mine," said Hal.

"I relied upon the protection of your Army."

"My instructions are to hear your statement and then decide whether it is worth taking you to them."

"I am entirely dependent upon your judgment?"

"Entirely."

"I have no proof that you will do what you say."

"I am here to consider your proofs of what you say. If you don't like it you are quite free to go back to Germany."

"Once you have my confidence you could deliver me to that anarchist."

"If I had intended that, he would be here."

Litard cogitated for so long that Hal was beginning to wonder how he would cope with refusal. Abruptly, his face set.

"Draw up a chair, please."

Authority spoke again in manner as well as in his voice, now revived perhaps by familiar surroundings, perhaps by the very act of formulating final intentions. Litard was burning his bridges. It occurred to Hal that no matter what his revelations might be, he would have to pretend to accept them. Risky as it was to take Litard out through Strasbourg, it would be suicide to turn his back on him here. The manufacturer was already speaking with a strained formality that did not conceal acute disappointment.

"I went straight, that very night, to Dr. Loeder who is temporarily in Stuttgart. I told him that despite your personal good will we must have proofs to be certain of your Army's gratitude. He was naturally frightened at the risk and uncertainties. Fortunately for us there is no uncertainty about the advance of the Russian Armies. They are very close to his family.

"I warned him that the opportunity you offer would never come again. He vacillated about his accursed family and the danger of getting them across the Rhine, but finally he got me the proofs.

"If you had had an expert here as you promised" — Litard was cross with his backward pupil now — "I could explain it all in two minutes. Since I am dependent upon your judgment you will pay close attention.

"Your bombing last winter brought German aircraft production almost to a standstill. Fortunately there was already in the office of Reichsminister Speer a master plan for new production. The realities of both engineering and war determined its location.

"It had to be as nearly as feasible equidistant from the workers and salvageable machinery of Leipzig, Regensburg, Augsburg, Dessau and Wiener-Neustadt. It had to make the best compromise of railroads and trucking roads; it had to be close to synthetic petrol extraction and to hydroelectric power. It had to lie in the Procrustes bed between your bombing and the Russian Armies. It had to be in the most politically stable sector of Germany . . ."

Hal was missing details now in his concentration on covering his excitement. He no longer needed details. Every word of this rang true. He bit his lip as Litard swept on.

". . . an equation that by itself answered: Bavaria. Now below Regensburg in the valley of the Danube there was already a large sanitaria of connecting hospitals . . ."

"At Gustel?"

It was fatigue; the question had exploded out of his eagerness before caution could guard it. Too late he saw Litard's eyes narrow, saw suspicion darken that arrogance.

"You know about Gustel, Major?"

"Everyone knows of the sanitaria there." He tried to look skeptical. Litard's suspicion became impatience again.

"That was the very point," he scolded, "the final protection. The wounded were moved out and the machinery moved in under the Red Crosses of those very hospitals. My exhausts were sent to Gustel. Jets are being assembled there today."

Hal sat very still choking back an insane exultation that wanted to shout: JACKPOT! and run for the jeep. Elation was compounding his loss of sleep. He was light-headed at the very moment when he needed all the judgment he had. He got a grip on himself: deception plans always told you what you wanted to believe.

"This sounds reasonable, M. Litard," he said slowly, "but it still isn't proof. You can't expect our people to waste bombs on a hospital just because you say so."

"I have brought you proof," said Litard.

He unbuttoned his heavy jacket and then the wool shirt under it, and produced a cardboard envelope of letter size, bulging with an inch of papers. Untying the string he took out the file and began stripping samples from it.

"Here is Loeder's copy of the original activating order of Dr. Speer. Here are priority orders to the Reichsminister of Transport, Reichsminister of Power, Reichsminister of Metal Allocation, copies of confirmatory orders to the Luftgauen . . ."

He didn't have to read the snaky black Germanic script of the text as the papers fluttered by. The letterheads and the heavy "Most Secret" overstamping, the seals and the signatures were enough for now.

"That'll do."

He took the envelope from Litard's surprised hand, replaced the whole file in it and then, unbuttoning his own jacket and shirt, secreted it next to his sweater and buttoned up again. Litard had made only a half gesture of protest. His hand had gone back into his pocket and he was concentrating on Hal's face.

"What about Loeder?"

He had caught Litard off guard and fleetingly it showed.

"My offer to him was contingent upon the assistance of your troops. They are not here, are they?"

"No." It was out before he could check it. He amended quickly and, he knew, lamely. "I'm to take you to them."

"We must go at once, Major. When everything else is arranged we can think of Loeder. It is not safe now."

It was callous betrayal and Hal was going to abet it. For the first time since he had put on uniform he had more than a personal concern for his safety. Up to now he had done what was required of him competently. Most of it had been useful. If he had not been available someone else would have been sent to the Hole and done the same work, perhaps better.

The papers in his shirt were a potential reprieve for hundreds, perhaps thousands of men who would never even know what had saved them. By now Joe Collet should have fresh reconnaissance of Gustel to weigh in judgment. There was no further way to obviate the hazard of a deception plan here. You couldn't have everything, and what he had was the next best thing to certainty.

"Let's get out of here," he said.

Relief showed at once through Litard's face. Up to that moment the manufacturer too must have been wondering how he would cope with dismissal from Hal. It was evident that he was glad to have the problem behind him, too. He hurried to the office door for a cautious look and then led the way to the jeep with long strides. Hal had raised the hood to replace the rotor when they both heard the guttural:

"Halten!"

A German in field uniform had arisen from behind the nearest pile of rubble about twenty feet away and was covering them with a drum-fed automatic rifle. Either flight or attack was hopeless; the man could have cut them in half with two bursts. The German barked again and Hal raised his hands slowly. Litard's were already up above a face as white as salt.

The German spoke again and a second one, similarly armed, appeared from another rubble pile. They had had the door to the office triangulated for perfect cross fire. Now the second man hurried forward, moving with experienced care not to mask the covering gun of his comrade. Hal felt a hand slide around his waist from behind, unlock his web belt and swing it and its automatic deftly away. Out of the corner of his eye he saw the man remove a pistol from Litard's pocket.

The soldier covering them now indicated the door to the office with a peremptory jerk of his gun muzzle. The second stepped briskly away to regain a safe angle of fire. Hal began to walk and Litard's whisper reached him.

"Let me talk for us."

An angry exclamation from behind silenced him. At the door to Litard's office they were halted again. This time a short spate of German behind them ended in rapid, approaching strides. A German Captain of infantry had been watching the whole capture from a nearby corner. He was thirty odd with an alert, weathered face and an outward composure somewhat contradicted by the pistol in his hand. Despite the overwhelming success of his ambush and the margin of two automatic rifles against bare upraised hands the Captain was alert for further trouble.

A single command detached one of the guards for a search of the office Hal and Litard had just left. A second command marched them and the other guard into it. The enlisted men disposed themselves for cross fire from different corners of the room. The Captain closed the door they had entered and stood very still, listening intently.

Hal's stupefied wits were reviving. It was manifest that this whole operation was surreptitious. In extremity the men would undoubtedly shoot. All three of them however were acting with the caution of intruders rather than the confidence of invaders.

Remembering the oars he had heard, Hal was the surer of his surmise. This might be nothing more than a reconnaissance patrol that had found the jeep in the factory. It was probably limited to a single small boat load, perhaps to the three men they had already seen, though routine procedure and the Captain's confidence indicated another sentry somewhere outside the office. Their purpose was probably tactical information, prisoners, or both. Until five minutes ago Hal might have hoped for the relative safety of just another anonymous prisoner of war. The papers under his shirt had suddenly become the warrant for a painful death.

After half a minute of concentrated listening the Captain studied the dim light from the exposed upper part of the windows and then, going over to one, eased the plywood covering back for a long scrutiny of the fog. Hal's eyes followed his. Then something drew them down. Just as the Captain replaced the plywood Hal had a glimpse of Valéry's body, face down on the road beside the open gate. No shot had been fired. Valéry must have been knifed or clubbed. It was further evidence of secrecy, haste and caution.

The Captain moved with authority now to the chair behind Litard's desk, seated himself deliberately and then motioned Hal and Litard to chairs before him. The guards in the corners eased their backs to the walls, their guns still covering their captives. The Captain spoke in French with a heavy German accent.

"You are Herr Litard."

It was a statement of fact. Hal heard the intake of the manufacturer's breath and felt his own stomach turn over. Then Litard gathered himself and replied to the Captain in a long burst of fluent, idiomatic German. Hal could read German proficiently. Try as he would, he could only comprehend isolated phrases of Litard's first statement or of the extensive cross-questioning that followed it. At the third interchange the Captain introduced the name, Loeder. It recurred in Litard's reply and in the conversation that followed.

A perceptible mixture of deference and perplexity modified the Captain's firm authority. After his first shock, Litard's confidence had begun to return. He showed a bold assurance that increased with the uncertainty before them. In response to a final question Litard got a grunting affirmative. He composed himself for a second of frowning concentration and then addressed Hal in English.

"Unfortunately, Dr. Loeder has fallen under suspicion . . ."

"The way Edouard Pourvalle fell under suspicion after you had used *him?*"

It had burst out of Hal's unthinking anger. Too late, he saw Litard blink. With an effort the man controlled himself.

"This is no time for sentimentalities, Major. Loeder has been arrested and the coward has compromised me. Nevertheless, I hope to be able to save your life."

"How?"

"It has been necessary to persuade the Captain that you are worth more alive than dead."

"In short, you're selling me?"

"His instructions were to capture or to kill. You have the advantage of a uniform. It should be possible for you to demand the treatment of a normal prisoner of war."

"With these papers on me?"

Litard hesitated and then continued quickly.

"When I can reach my friends, I shall explain that these were simply part of a deception plan."

"If they were, they wouldn't be chasing us. They'd want us to have them."

His stomach had stopped kneading. Fury was replacing his fear. His last doubt about the information under his shirt was resolved. It was authentic. Possession of it was automatic sentence to whatever was done with the bodies after a German Counterintelligence interrogation.

"I shall try to protect you," said Litard. "He demands an answer."

"To what?"

The German Captain was frowning at them impatiently.

"Your word, as an officer, to go quietly to their boat. He wants to return before this fog burns off."

Hal tried to keep his voice in conversational vein.

"They're scared to make a noise. Let's refuse and fight when they close in."

"They won't close in," said Litard. "There's another man outside with another automatic rifle. If we could fight off all three of these, he'd kill us."

"It beats what they'll do to us over there."

"Major! This is our only chance!"

"It might be yours. It's no chance for me."

He turned from Litard to face the Captain.

"Nein!" he said.

The Captain regarded him intently and Hal could imagine a trace of regret in his half head shake. Abruptly he went to the window and moved the plywood again for another long scrutiny of the sky. Then he replaced the plywood and barked a short sentence to his guards.

Their backs came off the wall instantly. One of them twitched the muzzle of his gun to demonstrate readiness. The other one put his gun down on the floor, reached under his jacket and produced a trench knife. He was a thick, powerful man with a square, unshaven face that unexpectedly showed reluctance. He shot a quick glance of appeal to the Captain and waited. The reply snapped at him angrily. Cautiously, deliberately with one eye on the other guard covering his movement, his immense frame lifted on the balls of his feet, and he stepped toward Hal, moving springily, like a prize fighter. Hal was nerving himself for a counter-rush and kick when they all heard the rumble of a truck outside the factory.

The Captain barked a command. The soldier whipped his knife back into his jacket and picked up his gun. The Captain twitched his pistol suggestively and put a finger to his lips in silent command to all of them.

Listening, Hal could follow the progress of the truck as it slowed down by Valéry's body at the gate and then accelerated in a roaring circuit through the bomb hole in the wall and into the factory by the same entrance Hal had used for his jeep. Its motor was still reverberating in the main gallery as it met the first burst of automatic fire. Two other bursts smothered that one. The truck motor stopped, and there was a sound of running feet beyond the door and then total silence. The Captain and his men were looking at each other anxiously. Then from beyond the door Hal heard Elsie's voice.

"Hal, are you there?"

He gulped, doubting, sure it was hallucination. The call came again in the same clear words, and the faces of Litard and the Captain showed that they heard it too.

"Yes," he called. "That place *is* Gustel, Elsie."

"Righto; Gustel it is. Are you safe?"

"So far. A Kraut Captain and two privates have us covered. Litard is with me."

"Oh." He could imagine the wrinkling of her forehead from her tone. Then her reply came quickly.

"Tell the Captain his boat guard and the guard out here are both dead. He is surrounded by superior force so" – he hoped the Captain could not read the sarcasm in her tone now – ". . . he may surrender with honor."

Litard was speaking before Hal could phrase a statement. This time Hal could hear through his bold speech the recurrent words: "American soldiers," and then "she merely translates for them." The Captain frowned, silenced Litard with a skeptical hand and indicated that he wanted Hal to speak. Hal repeated in German what Elsie had told him to say, taking pains to let no inflection of sarcasm shadow his mention of honor. The Captain cogitated and frowned unhappily.

"My orders were to capture or kill you both."

Hal repeated this in English through the door to Elsie. There was a perceptible pause and then she spoke clearly in German.

"Captain, if you injure the American Major you are committing suicide. We have flame throwers and grenades out here. The Wehrmacht does not order brave soldiers to commit suicide for political missions. You have no right to your life, Captain. It belongs to the

Reich. Germany has lost this war, as you well know, thanks to the bungling of her politicians. A soldier has an obligation of honor to use his life for his country's greatest need. Your higher duty is now a historical necessity. The Captains of this war will have to live to train your Armies for the next one. You owe your life and your soldiers' lives to the Reich."

She stopped and Hal watched the furrows deepen on the Captain's forehead. His face remained suspicious.

"No one could deny that she speaks the truth. It is certainly honorable to surrender to superior force. Nevertheless, it is well known that women often deceive. How are we to be sure of what she says, Major?"

Litard was silent. Hal called again to Elsie.

"He's biting; he wants to play. But he needs proof of a superior force, for his honor."

"Tell him to get all of you down on the floor, away from the windows and door," she replied.

He translated to the Captain who scowled again and then barked orders to his men. They sat down on the floor with their guns still on Hal and Litard. The Captain crouched beside the desk and with a final gesture waved Hal and Litard to the floor. Outside they could hear feet moving and the muted voices of orders and replies. Elsie called again.

"Down safe, Hal?"

"We're all on the floor."

There was a second more of silence and then a stuttering roar from both the inner gallery of the factory and the yard outside. Glass showered in from the remaining fragments of the windows. The mahogany door erupted a stitching line of splinters and holes along its top. Slugs thudded into the high walls. Abruptly the firing ceased and Elsie called again.

"Tell him to open that door and look out now."

He translated the instruction to the Captain who had begun to nod an approving head at the damage around him. He arose, pistol in hand, took the inner door by the handle and, giving it a gingerly pull, stepped away fast, covering the entrance. Nothing appeared. Nothing happened. The Captain stepped forward for another cautious look. Following his gaze now Hal saw the corpse of a German soldier who had been dragged along the floor and was lying in a pool of blood between the door and the jeep. There was no sign of life in the gallery.

"Captain, you will send Major Brett out, uninjured." Her voice snapped out the German words.

The Captain looked at the corpse again, barked an instruction to his men who lowered their weapons, and then indicated the door to Hal. He arose slowly and with the same deliberation walked to his belt and the automatic where the guard had dropped them on the floor, picked them up and buckled on the belt, making no effort to draw the pistol from the holster.

"Brett coming out," he called.

There was no reply and he walked out the door and into the main gallery of the factory. He had passed the corpse on the floor before a gesture caught his eye. Marcel, from a safe angle of the wall, was covering the door with one of Graves's automatic German rifles. He pointed and, turning, Hal saw that Alphonse, identically armed, was covering from the other side. Beyond him Elsie and Antoine were standing close to the pile of rubble from which the first German had risen. Antoine had another automatic carbine in his single arm. His eyes were glowing as Hal walked up to them.

"You fooled me, Major. You did not fool Mademoiselle."

"You're all right?" she breathed.

"Sure. Where's Graves?"

"I wouldn't know. I left him at Baccarat."

It took him several seconds to get it. He looked again at Marcel and Alphonse.

"This is all?"

"Two more outside; it's quite enough," said Elsie tartly. Then raising her voice, she called again.

"The German Captain will come out with his hands up."

With clicking heels the Captain emerged, hands up, head looking right after he cleared the door. He checked in his tracks for a second of gaping indignation at sight of the solitary Marcel. The mason twitched his gun muzzle and pointed. The Captain turned and saw Alphonse covering him from the far side. His face relaxed: his honor was vindicated. In response to orders from Marcel he walked over to Alphonse, turned his back and lowered his hands behind him. Marcel continued to cover him while Alphonse put down his gun and lashed the Captain's wrists behind him with cord. Then they stood him face to the wall and Elsie called the others.

The enlisted men came out one at a time with exaggerated imitation of the Captain until they too were tied up facing the wall. At a signal of satisfaction from Alphonse, Elsie called once more.

"M. Litard will come out."

There was a second of delay and then Litard walked out the door with his hand in the pocket of his jacket. Like the others he stopped once he was clear of the door to gape in turn at the triangle of armed men covering him. His face went pale.

"Where are the Americans?"

"Gone," said Antoine. "France welcomes you, M. Litard."

He stared dazedly from one to the other of them and then the pistol was out of his pocket, its muzzle lifting toward Antoine. Hal jumped to get in front of Elsie. His ears seemed to split with the deafening muzzle blast from Antoine's automatic carbine. Hal saw Litard stagger and then he saw flame and felt himself lurch with impact on his chest. His knees buckled and he struggled helplessly to stiffen them as balance left him. Incredibly, Litard's pistol flamed again. Hal saw Antoine pitch forward just as he lost the last of his balance. Beyond him Litard collapsed to the floor in deafening cross fire from Marcel and Alphonse.

He awoke to a throbbing ache in his chest and the acridity of strong disinfectants in his nostrils. He knew what that smell was and could not quite remember. He tried again with deeper intake of breath, and the throbbing ache sharpened. Minimal breathing eased it. He opened his eyes to cream colored walls, white ceiling and the upper part of a wide, curtained window.

He lay still a minute, gathering strength, and then tried to turn his head. Instantly a hand on his forehead stopped the motion. Elsie's face appeared between his and the ceiling, looking down. It was lined with fatigue and strain. The eyes were trying to smile.

"Lie still; you've given us enough trouble."

"Where am I?"

"Hospital in Strasbourg."

"No invasion yet?"

"There won't be any. A new American division is here. Their C.O. signaled London for me about Gustel.

Your Colonel Collet has confirmed and said we'd hear more about it soon."

"When was all this?"

"Yesterday, after we brought you here."

"Graves never did come back then?"

"No. I told you: I gave him the slip at Baccarat. The Daivrens hid me till he had to go on, and then lent me a bike."

Someday he would have to think of her crossing the Vosges alone through a midwinter night by bicycle. He didn't have to do it now. She was right there where he could see her.

"What about Antoine?"

"He'd sworn he would kill Litard," she gulped, "and he did."

"I bungled it, Elsie."

"You did not," she flared. "You did perfectly, right up to the end. Then you did get blood all over those proofs, but the surgeon said they saved you."

He lay very still. The pounding in his chest hurt again and it was enough to look at her. She looked back at him, not speaking either, and he watched the lines in her face and forehead smooth out and the muscle knot at the end of her jaw disappear. Then he saw her head lift ever so slightly at the sound of a faint humming far away, rising slowly in approach. She turned an ear toward the window and her face lit up.

"Don't move. Don't even turn your head. I'll tell you."

Her face vanished. Her footsteps went to the window. There was a flutter of the shade and the room became lighter.

"It's Fortresses, hundreds of them very high and far off. They're in boxes, or whatever you call it, all silvery in the sun and going east. That's what he meant about our hearing; that's the course for Gustel. Oh! I do wish you could see them!"

"I don't need to," he said. "Come back here where I can see you."

Glossary

Ack-ack	Slang (British) for anti-aircraft artillery
D Day	Allied invasion of France, June 6, 1944
Dekko	British slang for scrutiny
Etousa	European Theater of Operations, United States Army
Fifi	Forces Francaises Intérieures, or, generically, any unified Resistance Group
Forward	Subdivision of any Main headquarters
G–2	Army Intelligence
Gen	British slang for information
Hole	Underground Headquarters or Staff offices
M–1	American Army rifle
P.O.W.	Prisoner of war
Pukka	British slang for authentic or right
PX	Post Exchange: U.S. Army personal supply store
R.A.F.	Royal Air Force
Shaef	Supreme Headquarters Allied Expeditionary Forces
Sitrep	Situation report
WAAF	(British) Women's Auxiliary Air Force